Nicholas had learned to be wary of his tendency to make snap judgments, but there was something eerie about Father Kane. His control was so vehement it seemed maintained by raw will. Looked at closely, for all its martial surface, it seemed fragile, this calm worn like armor. Used to the bluff, hard-drinking Jesuit cronies of his father and his own expansive, jocular teachers—not to mention the mannered and unpredictable Father Lyon—Nicholas was puzzled, and a little unsettled, by this correct, contained man who for the next two years would be the sole authority to whom he was answerable.

Robert Benard, a graduate of Yale University, lives in New York City.

ALSO AVAILABLE IN LAUREL-LEAF BOOKS:

A CATHOLIC EDUCATION

A NOVEL BY

Robert Benard

LAUREL-LEAF BOOKS bring together under a single imprint outstanding works of fiction and nonfiction particularly suitable for young adult readers, both in and out of the classroom. Charles F. Reasoner, Professor Emeritus of Children's Literature and Reading, New York University, is consultant to this series.

Published by
Dell Publishing Co., Inc.
1 Dag Hammarskjold Plaza
New York, New York 10017

Laurel-Leaf Library ® TM 766734, Dell Publishing Co., Inc.

ISBN: 0-440-91124-9

RL: 8.4

Reprinted by arrangement with Henry Holt and Company, Inc.

Printed in the United States of America

February 1987

10 9 8 7 6 5 4 3 2 1

WFH

To Gregg Mitchell
and in loving memory of
L. Arnold Weissberger.

31. **Q.** What is a mystery?

A. A mystery is a truth which we cannot fully understand.

The Baltimore Catechism

Part One

GOD'S WILL

1

"Is it *always* a mortal sin to eat meat on Friday?" demanded Father Francis X. Lyon, S.J., from his high perch atop the platformed desk. The entire ninth-grade Religion class, eyes transfixed, followed the movement of his wooden pointer as he passed it over them like a dowser trying to divine hidden springs.

Nicholas Manion chuckled silently—another four-star performance from Father Lyon. The priest's eyes had snapped shut, and he tap-tapped with tantalizing slowness across a field of cringing fourteen-year-olds, stretching what Nicholas judged was for most of his fellow students, given their fidgeting and forehead-wiping, no less agonizing than a medieval trial by water.

Lyon moved with the brisk authority of the old Boston money his Jesuit vows had rendered obsolete and with the bombs-away insouciance of the bomber pilot he had by school legend in fact been, among the first to zoom in over

Normandy on D-Day. Come late to the Society of Jesus, from an Anglo-Irish family that could trace its American ancestors back three generations, he exuded worldliness, a panache that made his class the highlight of the week.

He was without unction, Nicholas reflected—a rare treat for boys long since reconciled to a steady diet of piosity.

"Mr. Murphy," Lyon intoned with relish, having opened his eyes only when his pointer had come to a precarious halt on the bony, lank-haired head of Timothy Murphy.

Easing to his feet under the pointer, Timothy responded in a wavering voice:

"Yes, Father. Except in wartime, or while traveling, if there's nothing else available."

Lyon pulled back, his pointer now a lance that jousted with the afternoon's long shadows.

"Those are the sole exceptions?" he demanded. His eagle glare circled the room, quizzical, intimidating; his blue eyes seemed translucent in the waning sun.

"And when you're sick," Timothy mumbled.

"Which you, mister, show every sign of becoming," Lyon parried. "Do resume your place."

The pointer now was a pool cue. Lyon tested shots through the practiced O formed by his rounded thumb and forefinger. Nicholas noticed the serpentine black hairs that crosshatched the top of both his hands.

"Only then? Gentlemen?" he exhorted with ill-disguised exasperation. "No one?" His eyebrows rose.

Lyon ran class with the drive of an impresario. Whatever the topic, he was ready for it, pursuing sudden, surprising twists.

"Very well, since you won't lead, I'll have to. Mr. Blackford, steak tartare?" he prompted.

Jimmy Blackford lumbered to his feet.

"What? Sorry, Father. I don't get it," he replied, staring into the barrel of the pointer-rifle.

"How foolish of me, mister. *De gustibus*, after all.

Perhaps I should have said," he went on acidly, "a cheeseburger. With ketchup. On Friday." He waited, as though his train of thought were as plain as day. "A mortal sin?"

"Of course, Father," Jimmy replied, preening with self-assurance.

" 'Of course, Father,' " Lyon mimicked. He wheeled toward the other side of the room. "A double order of bacon, Mr. O'Connell?"

"Yes, Father. Same thing."

Nicholas read Lyon's mocking eyes: here comes the killer.

"A *rasher* of bacon? Mr. Harris?" he continued, barely emphasizing "rasher." His pointer flycast lackadaisically.

"Yes, Father," Tom replied, as frustrated as the rest of the class, swapping pained glances.

Lyon pulled in his pointer, raised it in both hands over his head, and shifted back and forth on the balls of his feet, as though preparing to jump up and chin himself.

"Anyone disagree?"

A wave of puzzled shrugging broke as he let the pointer drop and clutched the butt end in his right hand, the tip extending at a forty-five-degree angle, his left hand raised behind him like that of a coiled fencer.

"*En garde!*" he challenged. "*Wrong*. You're all, every last man jack of you is annoyingly, but not surprisingly, dead wrong." He slammed the desktop, and the pointer snapped in two with an ugly *thwap*. He flipped the half he still held into the wastebasket behind the desk. As the wood struck metal, the class cheered. "Two points," Tom Harris said, winning a bow from Lyon.

"All right, gang, listen hard," Lyon resumed, shooting his French cuffs and righting the cincture that hung from his snug, tailored cassock. Nicholas saw the thin gold bands of his links glinting and recognized the Jerusalem Cross.

He's forgotten where he's standing, Nicholas realized as,

at the same moment, his mouth opening to speak, Father Lyon tripped off the platform and onto the floor, catching himself on Jimmy Blackford's shoulder.

"Let that be a lesson to you, gentlemen. Even Homer nods." He climbed back up and resumed command from the top of the desk. "I must say, though, in nearly a decade of inculcating"—he made the familiar term sound like brain surgery—"wisdom into the pates of boobies, that is the first time I have descended to the level of my audience."

There were several snorted laughs, a few timid raspberries.

"Enough. *Dictum sapienti sat est.* Now hear this. Mortal sin, a turning away from God and thus a negation of self so total that Lonergan, our leading Jesuit theologian, for those of you born yesterday, calls it a 'metaphysical surd.' A mortal sin, which denies us God's infinite grace as well as Heaven itself and debauches all our acts, however moral in themselves, is transparently . . . pretty serious business." His eyes raked the room. "Now, you all remember the Baltimore Catechism?" The groans told him they did, all too well. "Fine. I'm sure the good sisters did their usual superb job of drilling it all into you." He saw hearty, thank-God-those-days-are-gone nods of agreement.

"O.K. What conditions are necessary to commit a mortal sin? Mr. Manion?"

Nicholas, ready as always, sprang to his feet. A tangle of cowlicky blond hair tumbled across his sharp forehead. His blue eyes were alert and bluntly appraising. They gave him an air of intensity that accounted, at least in part, for his strong sense of apartness from his fellows. He was among them, but not one of them.

"It must be something serious, you must know that it's serious, and you must give full consent—in other words, do it anyway," he recited with assurance.

Nicholas knew that to most of the class he reeked of

seriousness, a paragon of preparation and, what was even worse, a good athlete as well. Sometimes, trying to be one of the guys, his lips would explode into a smile so brilliant it seemed to grab you by the shoulders and shake you heartily—whether you liked it or not. His intensity scared people.

Standing just under six feet, with a lean, taut-muscled physique, Nicholas was a formidable changeling with a hard, daunting grace. At rest he stood, coiled like a linebacker, planted pigeon-toed but nimble, shooting off sparks of nervous energy. In motion he had an easy, loose-jointed stride, almost a strut, but always with something held in reserve, primed yet guarded. Even serving Mass or toiling at his desk he bristled, ever ready to spring, perpetually on the verge of action.

"Good, good," Lyon said with a satisfied smile. "A mortal sin must be a flagrant, deliberate, serious thing. Now back to the bacon, if you please."

Suddenly he had an idea, and decided why not take a shot.

"If I follow you, a strip or rasher of bacon could be eaten on Friday because . . . it's not a serious matter." He regarded the priest with an even, level gaze.

"Exactly," Lyon declared.

Hands shot up all over the room.

"He's wrong," someone muttered. "Isn't he?"

"It can't be!" someone else cried.

The *why*s and *how*s were deafening. Lyon might as well have denied the Holy Trinity.

"Use your noodles," he urged his charges.

Jimmy Blackford gained the floor. "But Father," he began in his whiny voice, "Sister told us—didn't she, guys?"—to a chorus of sure-she-did nods—"any meat at all on Friday, why, it was like we'd choke on it, or something."

"And go straight down the primrose path to perdition, no doubt. Sorry, gang, no soap. These are the bigs, you've left the sandlot now. Less than one ounce of meat does not constitute grave matter and hence cannot be mortal sin. QED."

Nicholas had to give Jimmy credit. For a goody-two-shoes he didn't fold easily.

"But Father," he persisted, "that's not what the Church teaches."

" 'Philosophy is the handmaiden of theology.' Aquinas," Lyon intoned obscurely. "Oh, never mind. O.K. Hypothetically granting your point, which I do not, and which we *will* get back to, do we ever doubt what we believe the Church teaches?"

The noes had it, unanimously.

"But gentlemen," Lyon grinned, breezing onto another tack, "if we don't doubt, what is faith for?"

Nicholas, sensing where Lyon was taking them, let his mind wander. The night before, in the library with his father watching Bob Cousy mesmerizing the New York Knicks, even startling his Celtics teammates at times, as he whirled behind-the-back passes or long, floating ones, tossed in sweet anticipation that the receiver would arrive just in the nick of time to grab them, Nicholas had dreamed of someday having such prowess himself. If not in basketball, in something. He was, as his father put it, a pretty fair country player already. But more from intelligence and ceaseless practice than from God-given natural ability. Cousy made basketball a different game; he competed not so much against the opposition as against his own mental image of perfection.

"Mr. Manion? If you don't mind." Lyon's voice was sharp, irritated. Startled from his reverie, Nicholas jerked his eyes into focus and fixed them on Lyon. Now he was in for it.

"Well?" Lyon hectored.

"I beg your pardon, Father?"

"Daydreaming, mister?"

Nicholas heard his classmates titter, enjoying his unprecedented discomfort. "I guess so, Father," he confessed sheepishly. He could kick himself.

"Guess?" Lyon mimicked. "Can't you be a wee bit more precise?" He wouldn't quit, the ham was baiting him. He was always on the attack, his jocularity never quite hiding his true purpose: to drill into them, over and over, the recognition that Satan, lord of this world as the Bible said, had to be guarded against every moment of life. His pomps were seductive, his lying lures sweet. "We're all born moral cripples," Lyon liked to say. "Concupiscence is our Achilles' heel." Nicholas believed it, all right—too many nights spent obeying his tensed right fist were the bitter sign of Satan's thrall—but sometimes Lyon overdid it. A few weeks ago in class, when Nicholas had persistently questioned the justice of a rape victim's being denied an abortion, Lyon had snapped back at him, "Keep on asking why like that, mister, and you'll wind up in Hell." Nicholas was not cowed by such scare tactics.

Eyebrows raised, Lyon was waiting for his answer.

"Yes, Father. I was . . . daydreaming. I'm sorry." There, that should satisfy him. *Mea maxima culpa!*

No such luck.

"Might the rest of us share whatever subject was so . . . scintillating you deemed it more significant than our ongoing, not to say eternal, quest for truth?" He loves all this, Nicholas decided.

He might as well just blurt it out and get the comic inquisition over with. "I was thinking about Bob Cousy."

Lyon feigned astonishment. "Oh, I see. Hoops, is it? Could you enlighten us as to what Bob Cousy has to do with the subject of miracles, to which the rest of us were sedulously, if inchoately, addressing ourselves?"

From mortal sin to miracles, in two minutes. Only with Lyon.

"Nothing, Father," Nicholas conceded, ready to crawl

under his desk, trying to shake the sound of boy-is-he-dumb out of his ears. Enjoy it while you can, guys, Nicholas thought grimly. Then, unable to let well enough alone, tongue outracing head, inspiration came. "Although the way he plays could certainly be called a miracle."

Lyon, whom Nicholas knew to be no slouch of a Celtics fan, was mirthful despite the impertinence.

"*Touché*, mister . . . but this is neither the time nor the place to plumb that particular manifestation of God's glory. After all, you can't dribble your way to Heaven. Though, from your showing this season, you'll no doubt give it a valiant try." He seemed satisfied, finished. Then, as though glimpsing an immanent, useful connection, he added,

"But it's an intriguing notion. Let's see. Could magical ability, in a secular sense, constitute what we mean by a miracle? Aside from the indisputable proof of God's wisdom in creating Bob Cousy an Irish Catholic and in His mysterious way shepherding him to Boston, his wonders to perform, does Cousy's play hold up as the latter-day equivalent of, say, the Wedding Feast at Cana? Anyone?"

Jimmy Blackford was game for more.

"No, Father. A miracle is by definition something beyond man's power, the direct intervention of God in human history." He sat down looking very pleased with himself.

"Mr. Manion?" Lyon invited.

"He's right, technically. If a man can do it on his own, whatever it is, it's not miraculous. God's hand makes the crucial difference. But, in a subtle way, isn't the hand of God behind the exceptional, the extraordinary—"

"Mr. Blackford?"

"It reflects God's glory," Jimmy argued, echoing Lyon who, *en passant*, had made the key distinction, Nicholas knew, "but it's no miracle."

"Mr. Manion? It would appear Mr. Blackford doesn't know from subtle." Always joking.

"Well," Nicholas continued, "in a way anything in the world that reflects God's glory is kind of miraculous."

"Very good, very good," Lyon chimed, the clerical referee blowing his whistle to declare a standoff. "Now, before we succumb to philosophical Saint Vitus' Dance, our time is almost up." Heads craned to see the clock against the back wall. Four twenty-five. Finally.

"Perhaps in future I'll get more out of you if I resort to more plebeian examples. We'll see. But in view of this lively disputation, for next time . . . you will compose a three-page theme on the subject of God's glory as it is manifested in today's world."

A groan escaped from someone to Nicholas's left. Several fellows whispered in irritation. Themes were for English Comp, not Religion. Where did Lyon get off, saddling them with extra duty! The Catholic schoolboy has no more mortal enemy than the surprise assignment, nor is anything so shrewdly calculated to bond all in a fast case of *miserere nobis*.

"Let this be my contribution to the adumbration of the concept of the exceptional in your daily lives."

The bell rang. All eyes were on Lyon.

"Class dismissed."

Muttering *sotto voce*, Nicholas's classmates shot him annoyed, accusatory glances as they filed out into the corridor.

"Thanks a lot, Manion." Harris.

"Yeah, way to go buddy." O'Connell.

"You gonna write ours for us, genius?" Timmy Murphy, half kidding. He was straight-A all the way.

They taunted him, but not too much, Nicholas reflected. They held their fire. He cringed at the thought of what they'd all have done, himself included, if the culprit had been poor Jimmy Blackford. Nicholas had gotten off easy. Just a few perfunctory salvoes. They'd have mowed down Jimmy with a fusillade. A bombardment.

As the mournful procession wended its grumbling way

outdoors, Nicholas ducked into the bathroom. He relieved his aching kidneys, scrubbed his hands, and stared at himself in the mirror.

Mr. Outside, he thought. That's why the embarrassment of this afternoon was really a blessing in disguise. Screwing up made you one of the boys.

Still, it was the face, unsummed by simple addition, that confounded the others and stamped him an enigma—a face whose parts did not quite fit together, were somehow at odds with one another. Hands off, it said. *Noli me tangere.* What could he do about it?

He smiled, and saw a tyrant of charm. Grimace! Owlish gravity, a tad holier-than-thou. Now, scowl: impenetrable eyes all at once cold and cheerless as the church floor on a December morning.

Guess I'm stuck with it, he told himself. His quicksilver moods, shuffling like slides, were bound to keep others off balance, at a distance.

It bothered him, being set apart, but he didn't know how to prevent it. Maybe steering clear of him was the safest course, for most of them.

So be it.

It was the price he had to pay for his clarity. He knew who he was and where he was headed. Not specifically, of course, but he could tell in his bones he was bound for something exceptional. And he lacked the temperament or the time to pause for explanation. He was too busy hurrying toward his urgent destiny.

With a last wink in the mirror, he ran outside.

On his way to the bus stop, he saw Lyon emerge from the front of the school and turn toward the residence. He was wearing a green and white windbreaker and, as he turned, Nicholas saw, on its back, *Boston Celtics.*

2

A stubby, three-story stucco with argumentative wooden shutters and molding, it was a rambling, no-nonsense pug of a house, but Nicholas never sighted it during his twice-a-day slog along Kingston Crescent without his heart's leaping in pleasure. Fronted by thick hedges and flanked by shoulder-high whitewashed fences, its brusque, weatherbeaten scrapper of a face gazed unimpressed through its ancient seconds of oak and elm, ministering coolly from their posts in the front yard. It never failed to whisper to Nicholas, now in the crisp hush of dusk, in the low, seductive murmur of a fairy tale.

Nicholas knew all too well what a cantankerous host it was. In the violent seasonal shifts of Connecticut, it turned its proud scars of blur and chip and stain defiantly into the air, taking on all comers. Eaves sagging like exhausted sinews, V-shaped roof needing a new undercoat of tarpaper every two years, insulation atrophied after more than one gale too many, the house funneled rather than thwarted the marrow-pulverizing winds that swept down from Canada each winter. The pipes hissed and snorted, stuttered and groaned, doling their small change of warmth, dragged from the coal furnace in the basement.

But to Nicholas the house was really a magic carpet. Of all his blessings, only this muttering, comfortable, gone-to-pot old punchdrunk house was utterly unmixed. (Except that his father refused to finance other than crucial repairs. It was his way of thumbing his nose at the Joneses, of demonstrating that, while he had made his fortune, he was above the panicked dumb show of keeping up with anybody.)

In back, the lawn stretched to the bank of the Farmington River. In front of the two-car garage, his boyhood hideout with its warming jungle of odors, the sharp tang of paint and two-by-fours mingling with the delicious tartness of rubber and gasoline, stood his bent basketball hoop. Down beyond his mother's rosebushes and glowing greenhouse, just where the grass dipped into sandy brush along the riverbank, he knew that the remnants of his old treehouse still clung tenaciously to the stately oak, bending toward the rushing water.

As Nicholas turned off the sidewalk and into the front yard, he was grateful they lived here in Farmington rather than in one of West Hartford's Wasp fiefdoms. This neighborhood was well-to-do, but hardly ritzy. It had none of the Colonial or Greek Revival mansions of that gold coast, with their iron gates and forbidding walls of penal brick, signs of *Trespassers Beware* somehow signaling that guilty secrets cowered within. There were no manicured lawns here, their perfection arranged by permanent but invisible Italian gardeners. No such luck, Nicholas grumbled. As his aching muscles could attest from their Saturday-long stints with his stubborn father's antiquated mower, in this openhanded, unpretentious, and hard-scrambling community, people mowed their own lawns, never thought to warn their children against trespassing, and went to bed peacefully each night behind unlocked doors.

Nicholas yanked the door open and bounded inside. To his left was the creaking staircase that led to his third-floor eyrie. To his right was the living room, its muted elegance swathed in darkness, and just beyond it, winking faintly, the yellow wicker of the sun room. To his immediate left, door closed, was his father's library, his father's retreat. Just before the stairwell, a door led to the formal dining room. To its left, invisible from where he stood doffing his jacket and resting his schoolbooks on the telephone table, was the spacious kitchen that now emitted a noisy ruckus and the aroma of pea soup, his favorite. He could hear Tina, their elderly housekeeper who came five times a week, clattering expertly while she hummed a rollicking mazurka.

He was, he suddenly realized, famished. He swung through the shortcut provided by the dining room and saw Tina drop her thick wooden spoon and turn toward him, wiping her hands on her apron. A bright smile filled her creased-leather cheeks.

"Nicolai!" she trilled, the scapular medal she always wore bobbing against her prodigious bosom in time with her pinned-up, chaste bun of tawny hair.

"How's my girl?" he asked, lifting her off her feet and kissing her. She resisted friskily, blushing, her gnarled fists flailing at his shoulders.

"Nicolai, put me down!" she commanded. "Me an old lady," she added. It was three years since she had escaped from the old country, but coming to America had made no dent in her notions of proper behavior. Though forced by fate to dispense *golabki* to the Manions of Hartford, she clung to her Polish heritage.

"Father be home soon, Mother in her greenhouse," she said. "You have homework?" Incapable of anything but an honest day's work, Tina was often unsettled and confused by the time these strange, subdued people wasted, though she would have taken a commissar's heel before she would have said so.

"Boy, do I," Nicholas replied, thinking of Lyon's sneak assignment and turning to leave. "Guess I'll head upstairs." Impulsively he turned and added, "Tina?"

She glanced around from her gurgling soup pot. Nicholas touched his index finger to his lips and blew her a kiss.

"Save the last polka for me."

"Silly," she clucked. "Naughty boy." But seeing him stay put, like a captain come to court, she released a heavy sigh, plucked the wafting kiss out of the air, and pressed it to her lips.

He whirled and raced upstairs, three steps at a time, determined to show Lyon he was still the class standout.

He'd racked his brain for the last two days and still hadn't found the right approach. He'd made several false starts, fumbling with ideas that petered out into glib obviousness or labored insipidity. Hunched over his desk in front of the bay window, surrounded by crumpled balls of notepaper, Nicholas ransacked his imagination for the perfect strategy, the line of attack he was certain he would recognize, as soon as it nosed into view, as fresh but inevitable.

Downstairs he could hear his parents chatting, savoring their highballs while Tina readied dinner. It was their nightly ritual, this hour and a half of mild banter during which they skated with seeming aplomb over their respective days, steering clear of contentiousness, the currents of unease that roiled just beneath the thin ice of decorum. It was their private, vigilantly polite time together, but Nicholas over the years had glimpsed and overheard enough to know in his bones that their civility, the balancing act of give and take, their quiet, measured voices exchanging inconsequential information, were all signs of the tacit code that seemed to govern their marriage; raised voices were for other people. Peace and quiet were their household gods.

At fifty-nine, Thomas Manion, second-generation descendant of Irish immigrants, had built one of the largest independently owned insurance companies in Hartford. Never once had Nicholas seen his father waver in his steely self-belief. "Second-guessing," he was fond of saying, "is for losers." For him it was blithe to be a believer, bracing to be an American. And why not? He was, as he said, living proof that the dream still breathed, pregnant with promise, for any man with the ginger to clutch it.

He had come a very long way. With the help of the Jesuits who tended his tenement parish, Thomas had managed to support his widowed mother via a host of odd jobs while he slaved through night school to win his college degree.

Early on, he'd taught Nicholas the biblical lesson of the talents. As one had, one owed. Money, position, opportunity were talismans, "basic obligations," but also instruments to propel oneself forward, fleeing the humiliating specter of the past. "I've gone about as far as anyone weaned on Alger stories can," he once confided to Nicholas, "but with your advantages, you can do much better. Anything, really."

A victim of timing denied two great wars, Thomas in his heart yearned to walk with Caesar. He acknowledged that the Greeks had given Catholicism spirit, "but it was the Romans who supplied backbone." To him the Jesuits, upon whom he lavished grateful contributions—"I've got a long memory and I always pay my debts"—were like the Praetorians of old, with their gallant missions and virile, iridescent camaraderie. Did they not exhort their charges to *laborare sicut bonus miles Christi*? He had enrolled Nicholas at St. Paul's a month after his birth.

An avid reader, Thomas enriched his imagination by plunging into the past. The boilerplate of insurance policies, the forced bonhomie of business lunches and early-morning golf games ("Only a damn fool—or a Jebbie—would get up at this ungodly hour!") earned him long nights alone in his wainscotted library, his private universe bounded by sturdy mahogany bookcases, shelf after shelf of richly gleaming volumes, the *Gallic Wars* in hand-tooled emerald green leather, Horace in austere, pebbled black.

Reverence for authority was no sentimental contrivance, mere middle-aged inertia, but a bulwark against chaos, a means of measuring what was in a man's power and what was not. Here in his sanctum, Thomas Manion peopled an ordered world with his true ancestors, men who triumphed and failed on a grand scale, inevitably yanked by the tether of fate, but always daring greatly.

When Nicholas was nine, his father began to invite him into his retreat. "Homework all done? O.K., come ahead."— only to saddle him with special projects: Stoddard's *Lectures* ("the only thing your grandfather left me") and Carlyle's *Heroes*, Gibbon and Tacitus, *The Lives of the Saints*, and Duff Cooper's biography of Napoleon. There were no "guts" in Thomas's cram course in the classics. When one night Nicholas brought home *The Three Musketeers* from the library, his father dismissed it as "anticlerical bushwa, and besides it's on the Index," and forbade Nicholas to read it.

On weekends his father made him pore over the vast *Oxford English Dictionary*, making lists of words in his looseleaf notebook, to be worked in, somehow, to his weekly English Comp themes. "It's what Churchill did as a boy," Thomas explained, mustering what was for him the *ne plus ultra* in contemporary prose. His father's tastes were eclectic, his passions so arbitrary that Nicholas sometimes couldn't keep them straight. But Thomas Manion was protean in his enthusiasm and relentless in recruiting his son into his domain; the boy was powerless to resist. So on special nights he entered a magical world: he trekked with Stoddard, swam the Hellespont with Halliburton, battled the Visigoths, got nightmares from Nero, and stared balefully from Elba at the Continent.

Thomas loved to talk as much as a filibustering senator. No subject was too picayune—or recondite—to escape his curmudgeonly ken. "Spare me the party line," he would begin with glee, as he warred against conventional wisdom, reflex banality, congealed pieties. Speaking *ex cathedra* was a provocative device so long assumed that it had toughened into second nature.

And anchoring him, always, was his granitic faith: "I'm sick and tired of all this nitpicking at the Church. What hooey! They're trying to put Freudian nappies on the cross. *Id, ego, superego.* Just because it's Latin doesn't make it deep. Making the self the be-all and end-all is *the* modern heresy. Why—they even have the effrontery to deny natural law." He made it sound like denying the Immaculate Conception. "Grubbing where they don't belong, sniffing for excuses to explain away moral cowardice. Tommyrot! Let everyone off the hook and there are no values left. It's so bogus—only the Church gives meaning to life. Christ alone is our haven. As mere God He is nothing. But as Man He is magnificent! Without Him, the Frogs are right: have done with yourself. Nick, they've taken sin and slapped a pipsqueak name on it—sickness. Whatever happened to willpower? It's not God who's dead, it's our sense of right and wrong."

Thomas Manion's dreams for his son were so vigilant that by the time Nicholas began high school, he was primed for achievement. All his doubts were trapped in the knot of his inherited will. Quoted high like a stock for so long, even his grammar-school yearbook urged him on. The caption beneath his picture read: "Big things ahead for this boy." His life seemed to stretch out before him in perfect order.

But he was on his own. Thomas made that clear on Nicholas's first day at St. Paul's. "Oh, I'll be around to give you a boot in the fanny if you go cockeyed, but it's time you paid the piper.

At your age I was earning a living *and* supporting a family." The gruff, mock-sarcastic tone his father adopted made Nicholas marvel at his tenderness. "Just remember, whatever scrapes you get into—and you will, if you're any son of mine—come to me. The only thing that cuts any ice with me, as you well know, is plain talk, so give it to me straight, and you can't go far wrong. You've got the best there is right inside you—don't go turning peacock on me, either—so just get on with it."

Is it any wonder Nicholas believed he had a pact with the future and greeted triumph without surprise? He was chosen—the best, the blue chip.

But he still didn't have a glimmer of an idea for Lyon's class. He'd better get a move on. Downstairs, the murmuring voices continued.

Instead, reminiscing about his father, Nicholas automatically drifted toward the subject of his mother.

Breeding.

It was the first word that popped into his mind, his two-syllable summary. She possessed impeccable taste and quiet simplicity. Her sure hand was everywhere evident in this house—from the austerely comfortable antiques in the living room to the Lilliputian-piled Aubusson in the foyer.

Born Diana Forslund, of fifth-generation German-Presbyterian stock, at twenty-two she had scandalized her Philadelphia family by marrying a man twice her age, and a Catholic to boot. But for Thomas Manion, the potato farm still stamped on his face, it was a brilliant match, the quintessential sign that he had made good.

Diana was proud of her forebears and felt keenly the wound of her family's bitter disappointment. But the pressure of inherited sentiment had crumbled before Thomas Manion's mercurial force. Handsome, worldly, and unmistakably on his way, he had almost carelessly bowled her over.

Her armory of decorum had no defense against suddenly quickened desire. As though magnetized by the belated discovery of her original purpose, she yielded to Thomas with an absolute conviction that made her tremble.

She had even given up her music for him. Years ago, exploring the attic, Nicholas had blundered into her cache of mementoes, neatly tucked away in an old steamer trunk. For the better part of an hour he had sifted through age-crisped recital programs that billed her as Miss Diana Forslund. Her certificate from the Curtis Institute was there, and a letter announcing her acceptance as a student with a woman named Boulanger in Paris.

And all that music—Bach, a lot of Mozart sonatas, some Scarlatti and Handel—silent, locked away.

When, later that day, he demanded to know why she never touched the piano that stood mutely in the sun room, she pooh-poohed the whole thing, her voice cavalier, dismissive:

"That was ages ago, dear. I doubt that I could play a note now."

She glanced at her hands skeptically, then fingered the air awkwardly, offering proof.

"Won't you play something for me?" Nicholas kept on. "Please?" He held out Mozart's Piano Sonata Number 12, which he had brought downstairs with him.

She stared at it, her eyes gleaming for a moment, a strange, sad smile straying across her lips. With a small shrug, she took it from him and said, "It's no use. Even in my heyday I could barely struggle through this. Now—impossible."

She lifted the lid of the piano bench and placed it inside.

"But why?" Nicholas asked.

"Out of practice. Permanently out of practice."

The claims of blood and art both shrank before Thomas Manion. She played the hand life dealt her: after a year's instruction she converted to Catholicism; a year after that Nicholas was born.

His first memory of her was hazy. She was there as his father bounced him on his knee, and she was there while his father piggybacked him around the yard. She was present but silent, a shadowy figure, receding into the surroundings, grazing on the fringes of Nicholas's young life, busy but marginal.

Though he strained to see, Nicholas never glimpsed the Diana that Thomas had fallen in love with. Always courteous, husband and wife never seemed close. She seldom interfered; as though by tacit agreement, Nicholas's rearing was preeminently Thomas's preserve. He was in charge of discipline and inspiration. She seemed content, and made no demands.

Instead, she built a world of her own. Come late to faith, the convert making up for lost time, she plunged into devotional waters. She was always off to early Mass, or making novenas, or presiding over the Ladies' Auxiliary. She organized the annual rummage sale in the parish church basement and served as chaperone at the Catholic Youth Organization dances. Her Protestant past balked only at bingo.

At home she tended her flowers, preparing glorious bouquets year-round to adorn the altar at St. Michael's. Muffling all sharpness with self-effacement, she kept moving, puttering in her greenhouse in the backyard or, indoors, redecorating incessantly. The paint was scarcely dry when she began briskly to examine color chips for the next siege of workmen. She switched furniture and shuffled paintings so often that Nicholas always entered the front door braced for surprise. Rushing in at less than mental attention was reckless, a dicey gambit from which he'd acquired sufficient bumps and bruises to discourage him. Memorizing placements was useless. His mother's restlessness never flagged; she kept her family constantly alert.

Clearly, Nicholas reflected, her muse was domestic. And her manners protected her by excluding anything unpleasant. So carefully arranged was her life, so strictly tailored to her measurements, that here, on this genteel stage, Diana Manion finally played the leading part.

But it made Nicholas sad, all the same. She never seemed able to satisfy herself that things were just right. Only Thomas's library was left untouched. She never went there. Nicholas watched her pass through their lives like a lovely but mute witness.

Still, if his spunk was inherited from his father, Nicholas knew that it was to Diana he owed his touch of the Teutonic, his stick-to-itiveness, his bulldog streak. He liked to believe that in him his parents' natures were perfectly blended, Thomas's mercury melding with her iron, producing in Nicholas that rarest alloy, a purposeful romantic.

Suddenly his father's voice boomed from the second-floor stairwell.

"Nick? Soup's on!"

Closing his notebook, Nicholas clambered down the stairs and, at the first landing, took the last floor sliding on the thick oak bannister, slithering free just short of the carved newel post.

"Did you wash up?" his mother asked automatically, as he removed his linen napkin from its silver ring.

"Yes," he lied.

He stared at her. She wore a plain beige dress with a thin band of pearls at her neck, tiny gossamer droplets. Her face was as white as china, and like her finest Dresden, the tension of its exquisiteness discouraged anyone from testing its strength. Titian-haired, with eyes of palest jade, she had a classic oval face, dominated by a confident, aristocratic nose and full, determined lips.

"Your father will be in presently," she informed him.

Nicholas glanced around the luxurious room with impatience. Against the wall that flanked the living room stood the carved mahogany sideboard, its silver trays and platters reflecting light from the crystal chandelier over the dinner table and flinging faint banners against the robin's-egg-blue wallpaper. Next to the pantry door, a stately, glass-doored chiffonier, also mahogany, defended her best china and fine crystal, including the fluted cranberry water glasses, thin as Hosts, which were her prized heirlooms. Masterpieces of delicacy, they had been in her family for generations. Nicholas noticed that facing the window overlooking the backyard, a loveseat covered in a miniature floral pattern against a mauve/yellow background had today replaced a filigreed Victorian settee.

Muttering to himself, Thomas stormed in, natty in his inevitable blue pinstripe, white button-down shirt from Brooks, and regimental striped tie. One of Diana's tiny tea roses served as his trademark boutonniere. Hair brushed straight back, military-style, blue eyes unblinking, he took his seat. Deceptively slight, he radiated command, a ruddy-cheeked gamecock with tiny erectile hairs bristling furiously in his nostrils. High-foreheaded and sharp-nosed, he smelled of talcum and Chesterfields. Nicholas thought, as he often had before, that everyday business clothes were too meager for his father, so martial was his stiff-shouldered bearing.

"Nicholas, will you say grace?" his mother prompted, as Tina swung through the pantry door carrying a steaming porcelain tureen full of her lusty pea soup. She placed it on the trivet in front of his father.

They bowed their heads.

"Bless us, O Lord, and these Thy gifts, which we are about to receive from Thy bounty, through Christ our Lord, Amen," he sprinted through without pausing for breath.

Tina held the tureen as Thomas, with tantalizing slowness, ladled soup into his bowl, careful not to spill a drop onto the lace tablecloth. Next she served Diana, who, lips stretched in a tiny bemused smile, took only a perfunctory half-portion. Finally it was Nicholas's turn. He filled his bowl to the brim.

As Tina returned to the kitchen, he hunched over the thick soup, inhaling its lusty aroma. Then, ignoring his father's table dicta, he seized his spoon and dug in.

"Nick," his father cautioned curtly, halting him. He looked up to watch Thomas, deliberately holding his gaze, pass the shakers of salt and pepper over his bowl with agonizing methodicalness.

"The croutons?" he asked, surveying the table with bafflement.

"I'm afraid they were out of French bread by the time I got to the bakery," his mother explained.

"I see," Thomas replied evenly, dipping the spoon, then raising it to his mouth. He held it briefly before swallowing, like a priest playing the connoisseur with the Communion wine.

"Superb, if peasant, fare," he judged. "But it's not the same without croutons. They supply the *je ne sais quoi*. Don't you agree, my dear?" he added in a mildly chastising tone.

His mother, a glimmer in her hooded eyes, agreed.

"Yes, Thomas."

She never fought back. But then, Nicholas told himself, his father's gruffness was not really bullying. It was just his masculine, old-school, oblique way of asserting his standards.

Nicholas tore into the soup, wishing he could chugalug, but being careful not to slurp. Meanwhile, his parents continued their usual cool, remote conversation.

"I picked up your things at the cleaners this afternoon," she said.

"Thank you," Thomas replied.

"I thought you might want your blazer for tonight."

"Tonight?" He looked bewildered. Then, smiting his

forehead in dismay: "Oh, criminy. How stupid of me. The Hoskins's party, right?"

She nodded.

Nicholas waited with amusement. He knew they were about to worry what was for them a major bone of contention. As much as his mother relished their Thursday dinners out and occasional party invitations, Thomas abominated any intrusion on his time to be alone, those scant hours in his library when, free from business pressure, he could pursue his real interests. Like a miser fondling his treasure, he hoarded his privacy. Business affairs were unavoidable; anything else was a red flag.

"I completely forgot. Tarnation!"

"You will go?" she persisted, the light plea uttered without confidence. "You didn't make other plans?"

Nicholas watched Thomas wrestle with himself. He had, of course, but, biting the bullet gamely, he didn't let on.

"No. Of course we must go. Since you accepted the invitation," thus establishing his noble concession, bowing to her preference. "One more excursion into the inane won't kill me, huh, Nick?"

Nicholas just smiled. This wasn't his quarrel.

"The Hoskinses," Thomas repeated, making it sound like a tropical disease. "Mother of God."

Tina appeared to clear away the soup bowls, then deposited a pork loin before Thomas. While he carved, she brought in a dish of scalloped potatoes and another of broccoli.

"I thought you liked Bill Hoskins," Diana ventured.

"Oh, he's all right," Thomas replied as he filled his plate, "it's the Cook's tour of his trophy room I can't abide." Glancing at Nicholas, he continued, "His rec room, as he calls it. It's just a bloody basement, crammed with wall-to-wall tributes to his hunting prowess. A ghoulish graveyard, if you ask me. Anyway, Bill may be my crack investigator, but in his Mitty-ing heart he's the Great White Hunter. He's got heads galore—ducks, deer, an elk—even a buffalo—all stuffed to the eyeballs, and you have to stroke their clammy pelts admiringly—it's a basement, after all, so damp—and coo into their soulful eyes. It gives me the creeps."

With a tiny grimace, Diana took a single slice of pork.

His father disdained all hunting, including big-game, but Nicholas knew he reserved his most scathing contempt for dime-store Jungle Jims who cheated the odds by only shooting animals from a safe distance.

Nicholas heaped his plate with meat and potatoes. Tina left the room.

"Bill always reminds me of that lovely line of Wilde's about fox hunting: 'the unspeakable in hot pursuit of the uneatable.' He's talking about going on a safari his next vacation. Maybe I should take him a pith helmet and a paperback edition of Hemingway's short stories. Or better yet, set him up in a partnership with Buddy Kohmer," he added cruelly.

Karl Kohmer was Nicholas's best friend. His father, Buddy, had spent his whole life watching his reverse Midas touch shove him deeper into debt. Having rolled snake-eyes with Miracle Floor Wax and Buddy's Frozen Delights (eggs, French toast, and frittatas) he was now Buddy's Imported Exotic Delicacies, trying to intrigue meat-and-potatoes Hartford with filet of kangaroo and Canadian bear *au poivre verte*.

"He's a good worker, isn't he?" Diana asked.

"Buddy? Or Bill?" Receiving no clarification, he tackled both. "Buddy's a sad case, really. Nobody in the world works harder, and there's not an ounce of quitter in him. But he's got a permanent case of pipedreams. A modern-day Micawber, really. As for Bill, he's first-rate. In fact, he scored something of a coup this week. You remember that hardware store that burned down mysteriously, just on the point of bankruptcy?"

"Koenig's," Nicholas piped in, his mouth full.

"The very one," his father answered.

"And Mr. Koenig had transferred title to his wife?" his mother added.

"Right. A standard move. Nothing fishy by itself, but it set off an alarm in my head."

"So?" Nicholas prodded, almost ready for a second helping.

"So I put Bill on it. And he may have found something. It may not have been a convenient act of God after all." He paused, and then added meaningfully, "Jewish lightning."

"Thomas!" his mother said, shocked, placing her fork on her barely touched plate.

Nicholas himself flinched at the term, which, even though new to him, was all too clear.

"Bill's tag, not mine," his father countered.

Nicholas plunged in where his mother wouldn't.

"Father Lyon—in Religion class—says we Catholics have a lot to answer for. *Perfidios Judaeos* in the liturgy, misreading the Gospel—"

"No doubt," his father parried. Then, defensively, "But don't get on your high horse with me, young man. I'm shanty Irish, remember? I know what it's like. Some of us," he went on, taking in both his listeners, "weren't born with silver spoons in our mouths."

Nicholas instantly regretted jumping to conclusions. He knew very well what Thomas had been through, his own proud father having turned on the gas one night as forced idleness drove a healthy man to choose death over shame. Sometimes, with pained inarticulateness, Thomas would describe his enraged impotence at seeing the beauty stolen from his mother's face before she was thirty.

"Just don't forget, stereotypes usually start with a grain of truth," Thomas insisted, trying to reclaim his authority.

"They can come just as easily from ignorance," Diana rejoined in a flat voice.

"O.K., O.K. I can tell I'm outnumbered." He beat his

breast grandly. "*Mea culpa*. Nick, you can tell your Father Lyon you gave your father a moral lesson." Then, with a tremor of pleasure he couldn't disguise, he added, "I don't suppose you'd allow me 'where there's smoke, there's fire'?"

Nicholas laughed.

"Thomas, you're incorrigible," his mother said, smiling weakly.

"No, no, I didn't think so." He lifted his arms in surrender.

As Tina served bread pudding and coffee, Thomas began his daily review:

"How is school going?"

"Just fine," Nicholas answered.

"Nothing exciting? Nothing special you're working on?" What he meant was 'that I can help you with?' He always questioned, probed, unwilling to be denied.

Nicholas relayed the Religion-class assignment.

"Very interesting. I'll look forward to seeing what you come up with." Although he lacked the outward piety of his wife, Nicholas knew Thomas considered himself "in my own way a very religious man."

Thomas persisted. "Any bright ideas so far?" He lit a cigarette.

"Nothing definite," Nicholas equivocated, though just moments before, recognizing the bread pudding, a flash of memory had given him the embryo of an idea. He had first eaten bread pudding at his First Communion breakfast. Communion, the reenactment of the Last Supper and literal transformation of bread and wine into Christ's body and blood—what greater, more miraculous expression was there of God's glory? It was, Nicholas believed, a hell of an idea.

"Fair enough," Thomas agreed. "Don't tip your hand. I'd do the same, till I was ready." His father was so old-fashioned in his circumspection that he never revealed more than he absolutely had to, about his finances especially.

Every Monday, like clockwork, Diana got her household allowance and Nicholas his two dollars, and that was that.

As Thomas lifted his cup for a second serving of black coffee, Tina cleared the table.

"Well, pal, you'd better get cracking, don't you think?"

Nicholas led them through thanksgiving and was excused from the table. Grace before and after meals was a strict rule; as the saying went, the family that prays together stays together.

3

First Communion.

"A snap, nothing to it," Nicholas remembered his father telling him that morning seven years ago as he struggled now at his desk to beat the memory of that day into coherent shape.

The nuns had rehearsed them for weeks, putting them through their paces until they should have been able to breeze through the ceremony with their eyes closed.

They were to sit, knees piously together, in their spanking white shirts and red-ribbon ties, and follow the clapper's signal. Then, rising together, they were to proceed in military file toward the Communion rail, pause, genuflect, pause again, then kneel, bowing their heads over the linen-canopied brass balustrade. When the celebrant reached their neighbor, they were to jut their heads forward, angled upward, with mouth open and tongue extended, remembering to nerve themselves for the grazing pressure of the paten couched by the altar boy against their Adam's apples.

Once the Host was deposited on their tongues, they

were to clasp their jaws shut like a safe and be sure not to chew. That was very important. Then, bowing their heads, they were to give thanks for a moment, rise, pause, genuflect, make the sign of the cross, and return to their pew.

Nicholas saw it all again, with indelible vividness. The silly tie making him look like someone's Christmas present. His cowlick that a pint of Wildroot Cream Oil wouldn't make behave, greasing his hands and progressively smearing his shirt and gray flannels as he waited, mortified, to walk forward. His throat was raw, he remembered, and his stomach, denied breakfast, growled for all to hear. He was sure he was going to bite the Host by accident, or get it stuck between his teeth. What would he do then? And what if he couldn't get it down?

As the nuns had drilled into them, this was literally Christ's body he was dealing with. "Don't chew the Baby Jesus," Sister Bridgit had warned repeatedly.

Then it was his turn. Shaking with nerves, begging God to get him through this, he knelt.

Suddenly he felt the cold paten knifing his throat. He fought for control, straining mightily to extend his tongue as far as it would go, at the same time sucking his cheeks for a little saliva. He was bone-dry.

He had to concentrate.

"Corpus Domini nostri Jesu Christi custodiat animam tuam in vitam aeternam. Amen." God had his very own language.

It was on his tongue. It itched! Nicholas quickly retracted it, trying to give thanks. But the itch got worse. Jaws clenched, he felt the Host stick to the roof of his mouth. Grateful, trying to make sure no one saw him, he scratched his tongue. Had he touched it? No, he was sure not.

As he returned to his pew, he realized the Host was glued to the roof of his mouth and it wasn't dissolving. He nudged it with his tongue. Nothing. But he noticed, surprised, it definitely had a taste. Sort of like a comic book cover, waxy.

It *had* to start melting. There was no way he could swallow it whole. He'd upchuck for sure. He tensed his jaw muscles to squeeze out some spit.

Finally, a few drops. He felt it loosen, with terrible suspense, and begin to disintegrate.

Palms filthy, tie askew, nails bitten to the quick, he watched with smug relief as Father O'Mara, their pastor, began the last line. He saw Jimmy Blackford, snot-nosed, whiny little Jimmy, in the middle of the row. O'Mara had reached him, but then Nicholas saw the priest step back. Straining to see, Nicholas put two and two together as O'Mara laid a white cloth over what had to be a dropped Host.

Trust Jimmy. What a baby! Thank God it was him and not me. The Host all finished, Nicholas watched, fascinated, as O'Mara crouched down on the carpet and retrieved the fallen Host. He put it into his mouth, then searched the floor. In case it had broken, Nicholas guessed. Satisfied that he hadn't missed any bits, Father O'Mara returned to the altar. A little later, Nicholas saw him gobble what was left in the ciborium. Could Hosts go bad? Nicholas wondered. Was that why he was finishing off the leftovers? And how come he was allowed to receive more than one?

It was all pretty complicated.

God is inside me, Nicholas mused. For real. It made him swell with pride. Thank you, God, for Your grace, Your love, for saving my soul.

It was thrilling, no doubt about it. God, inside his stomach. But wait a minute. What happens if you get sick? Throw up? No matter how much faith and humility he had, Nicholas didn't think he'd be able to swallow his own vomit.

Anyway, he'd come through with flying colors, which made him feel very grown up. In the vast stillness, his parents behind him, he sensed the personal, simple genius of God's love as reflected in the sacraments. The commanding vestments, the tall candles glowing like torches, the bold tang of incense, the colored light streaming, the music majestic—

he was part of all this. The Mass was now forever changed. Here, with God at the center, all time and space were collected into an eternal now. Every moment of every day, somewhere in the world, Mass was being said—four elevations per second, according to Sister Bridget. And everywhere Nicholas's brothers, his brothers in Christ, were receiving Communion.

It was amazing, if you thought of it like that.

Nicholas put down his pencil and counted five pages of notes. He'd made a good start. The miracle of Communion as *the* exemplar of God's glory. He was sure he was on the right track. And, he observed with satisfaction, a miracle that hinged on a *human* agent, the priest, which would fix Jimmy Blackford.

He leaned back in his chair and stretched. He could hear his parents in their bedrooms below, preparing to go out. A closet door creaked, a bureau slid open, then shut. Water was turned on, the ancient radiators in his room erupting in protest, the staccato bangs sounding like they were fighting tooth and nail against the arduous climb from the basement.

Nicholas surveyed his room contentedly. Aside from the maple-framed bed, the spring-spewing davenport against the far wall, and a bedraggled, elephantine easy chair plumped in front of his clothes cupboard, the room was bare of furniture. His Yankee and Brooklyn Dodgers pennants were on the wall, along with the poster of Frank Gifford, "Pro Hamlet," from *Sports Illustrated*.

His eyes rested on the custom-made plywood storage bins against the left wall. Inside, he knew, were his old toys, his baseball-card collection, a chemistry set, a few vintage Uncle Scrooge comic books, his Apache knife, his extra pair of sneakers, and . . .

He tried to resist the thought.

And? his mind commanded urgently.

His stroke book.

Playboy. June is bustin' out all over. June Wilkinson.

Idle hands—he couldn't say the nuns hadn't warned him.

No temptation was too strong to resist. It was right there in the Baltimore Catechism.

Jesus, Mary, Joseph, not now. Why, why in the name of God did they have to call that prayer an ejaculation?

Go ahead, you've earned it, his hands urged, happy to be the devil's workshop.

Nicholas tried to resist. He knew it was wrong. Every time he did it, he told himself it was the last time. And afterwards, always, he felt sick and repelled by what he had done.

But that didn't help before, not at all.

I'll just look, he told himself, walking over and rescuing the magazine from its hiding place inside his locked grammar-school scrapbook.

As he stared at the cover, he wondered why lately every pore in his body seemed to itch volcanically. Erections would hammer their demands at him at the weirdest moments.

In class there were times he prayed the teacher wouldn't call on him. And he'd learned long ago to stay off the bus unless he had his schoolbooks, or at least his lunchpail. The rhythm of the bus seemed demonically designed to, as Karl said, put lead in his pencil.

Karl. His best friend. He still remembered the first time he saw him. One day, in the middle of the eighth grade, he just turned up without warning, standing alone against the fence at recess and munching meditatively on his sandwich in the lunchroom. He was a year older than Nicholas, but after several days of noticing him out of the corner of his eye while the rest of the guys played pom-pom-pomeray or kick-the-can, Nicholas couldn't make out whether he was just shy or had a chip on his shoulder.

He had the body of a wrestler and the face of a sprite. Trouble radiated from his stormy brown eyes, which, as

Nicholas had long since discovered, could turn feral in certain lights. His hair was a thatch of angry red, slick as an exotic pelt. There was a tiny comical bump on the bridge of his snub nose, which quivered when he granted a wincing smile, or released his oddly mirthless laugh.

At first, as he stuck to himself, a few of the kids had ridiculed him, for he was clearly poor, a ragamuffin. With his shiny white shirt and spotty tie and patched gray flannels, he sported a blue blazer at least two sizes too big, which had obviously seen better days. Probably, Nicholas guessed, a hand-me-down. But his clothes were clean and always freshly pressed.

Finally, about a week after his arrival, Nicholas, more intrigued by his standoffishness than reacting to the taunts about him heard in the schoolyard, approached him nonchalantly, his hand extended, in the lunchroom. He smelled overpoweringly of Tide.

"I've got meatloaf," Nicholas explained. "You?"

"Baloney and Miracle Whip," Karl replied.

Gritting his teeth, Nicholas asked, "Trade?"

Not surprisingly, Karl was game. His father was a food importer, Nicholas learned, and they were renting the top floor of a two-family house three blocks away from the Manions'. Nicholas knew the house, a clapboard badly in need of a paint job.

"When did you move in?"

"A week and a half ago," Karl told him.

"Think you're gonna like Saint Mike's?" Nicholas went on, trying to draw him out.

"School stinks."

This was like pulling teeth.

"How old are you, anyway?" Nicholas pressed.

"Fourteen . . . going on fifty," Karl replied, with a sly smile.

They became fast friends.

Nicholas loved his unpredictability and the angry way he walked, his right shoulder slung low and his body tilted slightly as though about to ram a barricade. He was defiantly devil-may-care and, at heart, a born loner. It was Nicholas always who had to suggest plans, touch base, keep on Karl's tail. Needing no company, he had no social sense.

His work at home kept him busy and made his grades touch-and-go. "I was kept back in the fourth grade," he confided one afternoon. "Can you beat that? Nobody," he observed with contempt, "fails the fourth grade. It takes a lot of screwing up to do that."

There was some excuse for his barely passing at school. He had the equivalent of a full-time job at home. KP, he called it. He did all the housecleaning and shopping and much of the cooking. His father worked eighteen hours a day and his mother split her time, toiling half-days on an assembly line, stuffing maraschino cherries into their chocolate coats and the rest of the time taking in much of the neighborhood's washing and mending. In addition, Karl got up at the crack of dawn to handle two paper routes to scrape together the tuition for school. "For my pop," he explained. "It's either this or the marines."

As that first year raced on, they stole some time to play. Karl was strong, but had no finesse. Rough was his only style. Touch football, with him bulldozing into ball carriers, became padless tackle. Shrill accusations of "cheap shot" soon poured in.

"Bunch of sissies," he grumbled to Nicholas after one such fiasco as they relaxed in the empty afternoon. Feeling lucky and a little pampered next to him, Nicholas studied his sweat-glazed torso. Karl had a drum-tight belly and excellent muscle definition. You could have played xylophone on his ribs. Nicholas knew he was a demon for calisthenics. He'd seen his homemade weights, a broomstick and cans stuffed with sand, in Karl's bedroom hangout above the detached garage. So long as the activity was solitary, he could pick his spots.

"You're not in such rotten shape," Nicholas told him. "Too bad you're all thumbs."

"Find me some real competition, and I'll show you," Karl shot back. "Dipsy-doodle isn't the whole story, hotshot. Somebody has to work the trenches."

If Karl feared anything, Nicholas had yet to see it. He couldn't resist shinnying up a challenging tree or dancing along a fencetop. Hedges obviously were hurdles to vault and no street was worth crossing unless the light was red. Once, as they wandered past a construction site, he terrified Nicholas by doing a carefree pirouette along a steel girder two stories above the ground, never once glancing down at the machinery-strewn pit that yawned ominously below.

Trouble was his middle name. Because pickup team sports were "for babies," he coaxed Nicholas into fitful spurts of "knockout ginger," transforming the neighborhood at mid-evening into a cacophony of ringing doorbells, angry front-light switching, and furious telephoning. Confused, outraged oaths were their Grail.

Sometimes they swiped crabapples together, or, with Nicholas distracting Mr. Josephs at the drugstore, Karl would stuff his jeans with *Dude* or *Tempo*. Often, in a veiled tribute to his father that Nicholas adamantly refused to explain, they would scrawl "Kilroy was here" on garage doors or along fences.

Karl had a mean streak, too. One night, down by the river, sipping home-brewed sumac juice, after fishing for crayfish with bits of bacon, Nicholas watched, shocked yet morbidly fascinated, as Karl built a small bonfire with twigs and leaves and lowered the squirming creatures into the blaze, leaning back to smoke his driftwood "cigarette" with a contented smile.

When he saw Nicholas's disapproving look, he snapped,

"You eat lobster, don't you? What's the difference? Don't be such a sap."

Sometimes, when they had nothing to do, they'd break out the stroke books and one thing would lead to another. "Our own private circle jerk," Karl called it. Other times they would wrestle furiously in the backyard, with the same jolting result.

Nicholas found it thrilling and frightening at the same time. He let Karl set the ground rules, after pointing out weakly that it was a mortal sin.

"You can believe that eyewash if you want to, but I've never seen any proof that God either knows or cares I'm alive." He then related his first and, he claimed, last experience in the confessional.

"I told him I whacked off, I don't know, maybe six times, let's say, and the old fart screamed, actually screamed, so every kid in line behind me, even the girls, for God's sake, could hear: 'Are you crazy? You want to go to hell!' I'm not kidding, Nick, you'd think he didn't flog his dong once in a while. Screw that."

But didn't he think this was wrong, all those potential babies? Doing it with each other?

"This is just letting off steam, and despite their little rules, it won't drive you blind or put hair on your palms. That's all crap. The body doesn't lie."

Still, two Catholic boys?

"It doesn't mean diddly-squat. I mean, it's not like we're in love with each other or something!"

Nicholas stared at the magazine and realized it wasn't doing him any good. No matter what he thought about, he still wanted . . .

Pushups!

Keep busy, that's what Father Lyon always said.

O.K.

Ten . . . twenty . . . thirty . . . forty . . .

It didn't work.

Why didn't they come up with some bright idea that actually worked?

He opened the magazine, and gasped.

Bustin' out all over was right . . .

It was over in two minutes. He was on a hair trigger. Feeling sheepish and soiled, he leaned over the ancient tub that squatted on clawlike feet in his bathroom and turned on the scalding water. Somehow he had to reconcile the ecstasy of sensation with the abstract evil of mortal sin. He sure didn't know how to. Something so wonderful just had to be forbidden, he guessed. Otherwise, people wouldn't bother with anything else.

Confession again tomorrow, he reflected, as he eased into the tub. Thank God he wasn't serving early Mass. It was so humiliating when the altar boy refused Communion. Everybody there knew exactly what you'd done.

He scoured himself with the brush, the thick bristles leaving red streaks. He had such sensitive skin. Scratch his arm for a minute, and a welt would appear. Sit with his head in his hands, pinky fingers pressed to the bridge of his nose, and he'd look as if he'd broken out in a rash.

"Your stigmata," Maureen had joked. Scratch, and presto! the mottles appeared.

He hadn't thought of Maureen in a long time, he realized guiltily.

In the seventh grade at St. Michael's, he'd fallen operatically in love with her. A buxom strawberry blonde with pixieish brown eyes, Maureen O'Connor made his voice break whenever he came near her. With a button nose and full, ripe lips, she blushed whenever she looked at him, her cheeks brimming, whether with health or mischief he was never sure. Half milkmaid and half siren, she smoldered underneath her ceramic calm, pristine but fiery.

They became inseparable at once, arm in arm at recess and between classes, a couple, a fixture, clinging till the last note from the gramophone died at every vigilantly chaperoned CYO dance.

God bless his mother, he thought. She ferried them to and from their first dance and, pulling up in front of the O'Connors' house, nonchalantly announced, "I've got to get some gas. I'll be back in five minutes."

Those five minutes on her darkened back porch seemed an eternity then.

Maureen loved to dance, her sweet body speaking to him in unsuspected accents, her low-cut pink-and-blue jumpers always maddeningly backed up by a proper, mother-buttoned blouse. Under the jack-o'-lanterns, Nicholas pressed himself fiercely against her, holding her arms behind her back, braiding her fingers with his, only their thrilled sighs separating them.

He lay back, legs bent in the short tub, letting his puckered fingers trail through the soap-filmed water.

In class, he and Maureen had checked each other for re-actions to everything. Silently, with their classmates' complicity, they traded *billets-doux*, often scrawling in borrowed wooing "their" song lyrics. Bobby Helms's recording of "My Special Angel" vied with Sinatra's risqué "All the Way" for the status of favorite.

At night, just before bed, Nicholas performed a private rite: he would gaze longingly at her picture, snapped in the bus-station booth and mounted solemnly in a Holy Picture mica-covered frame, kiss it with an innocent rapture that reckoned no experience that could taint it, then swiftly snap off his bedside lamp, whispering holily, "I love you."

Lying in bed, he often lulled himself to sleep with a deliciously teasing trial: if everyone he loved faced a Communist firing squad, and he could save only one, who would he choose? He imagined his father and mother standing there and, a little to the side, Mo. "Who do you choose!" the commandant bellowed.

She won surprisingly often.

The funny thing was, he'd been able to keep control of himself all the time they'd been together, even with a permanent case of blue balls. Temptation didn't seem so irresistible when he had to be apart from her. Somehow the thought of defiling their pure love was strong enough to keep him in a state of grace.

Jerking off after being with her would be a sacrilege.

On Saturday afternoons they had haunted the local movie house, their tireless mouths locked, their trembling hands exploring with an exquisite mixture of desire and trepidation. By mutual consent, their fevered gropings stayed obediently outside their clothes, avoiding what the nuns branded "venereal pleasure."

Nicholas remembered with sweet chagrin spending one whole double feature with his arm slung proudly around Mo's shoulder, debonairly kneading what he discovered, too late, was her ribcage.

She never touched him *there*.

His fingers stole only once inside her blouse, the tip of his finger grazing, for one scalding second, the *sublime*.

"Promise you'll never marry anyone but me," she whispered hoarsely as they sat through their third consecutive showing of *April Love*.

"I promise," he vowed, sealing their pact with a tongueless kiss.

On winter mornings in the subzero dark he would take the bus across frozen, deserted streets to attend six o'clock Mass, snuggling with Mo, their hot, pressuring hands joined beneath their overcoats, yielding themselves, in the portentous calm, to the Mass's ache for immortality.

Often they sat through the next Mass as well, at first winning a reputation for unusual piety, then eventually causing concerned whispers among the nuns. Sister Superior had ordered them—"for the good of your souls"—never to be alone together. And Thomas, maddeningly, had backed her up. With ingenuity they managed to steal a precious few disobedient minutes away from school.

Then, during Easter vacation, he remembered grimly, it happened. Her father was transferred to Chicago. Devastated, afraid, defiant—what could they do? Promising to write each other daily, they swore to meet as soon as possible next summer.

Thomas was sympathetic, but aloof.

"If it's the real thing, it'll survive this interruption," he explained suavely. "Besides, you're too young to get in over your head."

Nicholas flinched at this chiding charge. His face must have shown it, for Thomas quickly added, "Oh, you didn't think I'd noticed you mooning about? Rushing off to Mass in the middle of the night? There is a happy medium, you know. Or are you really that pious?"

For one terrible moment, Nicholas suspected that his father had had a hand in sending Mo away. But that was crazy.

At first, their correspondence was avid. Then distance and the press of activity reduced it to a plaintive trickle, an obligation. His father wouldn't hear of "a twelve-year-old boy hightailing it to Chicago on his own! *Out* of the question."

Finally, a little aghast at himself, Nicholas stopped writing.

"Puppy love after all," Thomas remarked callously one night the next fall.

Was it, Nicholas wondered now, climbing out of the tub, sliding into his bathrobe. Then why did he get a pang of longing every time he heard "Two Different Worlds" on the jukebox at Keane's?

"You'll find someone else, dear," his mother had soothed him.

Staring at himself in the mirror, Nicholas said, "When?" He dropped his voice to a whisper: "Come on, Lord, I'm ready."

Karl didn't seem to have any trouble finding dates, but then, with his self-styled democratic eye, he wasn't hard to please. Nicholas was. Remembering Maureen, he automatically consigned whatever new girl he met to the reject pile. No matter how hard he tried to force his mind open, it was never the same.

Besides, Karl never permitted himself to get, as he described it, "all mushy." Let a girl mention the words "going steady," and he'd cut her dead. "I travel solo," he explained.

That was fine for Karl. But Nicholas wanted to be in love. Since Maureen, it had been slim pickings.

Thank God he hadn't known Karl then. If he'd been around during the big romance, he'd have razzed him royally.

As he slipped back into the bedroom, Nicholas understood the Jesuits' strategy at school. Their motto was "Work hard, play hard, pray hard," and they weren't kidding. In the hyperactive, all-male atmosphere, they kept you running until you dropped.

He returned June Wilkinson to her hiding place in the storage bin, careful that the magazine was completely concealed by the covers of the scrapbook. Strange, he reflected, how afterwards I can't even bear to look at the pictures.

He knelt down beside his bed and bent his head onto his folded hands, slowly reciting the words of the Act of Contrition. He couldn't go to sleep in a state of mortal sin. All it took, he knew, was a firm intention to sin no more, and he had that. It wasn't difficult, not afterwards.

He climbed into bed and flicked off the lights. Pulling the

covers over him, his naked body tingling between the clean sheets, he trailed his fingers across his chest.

"Your body is a temple of the Holy Ghost," he heard Father Lyon insist.

"Some temple," he grumbled, suddenly drowsy, rolling over.

He must have dropped off right after his bath. Now, still half asleep, through the opened window he heard his parents outside the house, on their way to the party.

"Thomas, please, we're late as it is," he heard his mother say.

"I'll just tuck Nick in."

"He's probably asleep already," she persisted. "Let's get going."

"I'll just be a moment."

Nicholas could hear his father's footsteps on the stairs as, outside, his mother drummed her high heels against the sidewalk.

His father had been doing this ever since Nicholas could remember. Sometimes he would feign sleep; others he would reach up for a powerful hug and be rewarded with a merry "Sleep tight, don't let the bedbugs bite."

Nicholas saw the light from the hallway as his door inched open. His father tiptoed in, picking up the bathrobe Nicholas had idly tossed onto the floor.

He pretended to sleep.

"Good night, son," Thomas whispered as he lifted the covers up over Nicholas's shoulders. Then he closed the window an inch or two, and walked out.

4

"—Diana, for God's sake—"

"—just go to bed, I don't want to discuss it—"

Nicholas, startled awake, fumbled for his wristwatch. Jesus, it must be the middle of the night. Pitch black outside. He heard them, in dim, snarling fragments:

"—wake Nick—"

"—a man of your intelligence—"

"—fine thing when—"

The next few words were garbled, then:

"—in his own home—"

They must just have gotten back. One thirty, the dial on his watch said. It must have been some party . . .

Their voices hissed in cutting half-whispers.

It scared him.

He tried to will the sounds away.

The bloody pipes were like microphones. They picked up every noise and magnified it.

"Stop, please," he thought angrily.

He was being silly. Other parents fought. Whose didn't?

Still, it tore him up inside. These were *his* parents, who never fought, who avoided strife like the plague.

Something was very wrong.

"—only when you're drunk as a loon—"

"—now I'm drunk, am I?—"

Shut up, shut up, Nicholas pleaded, clamping his pillow over his head.

"—be ashamed of yourself—"

"—increases—" he heard his father say, then Nicholas missed several words, until "—ruins the performance—" with a high giggle.

God, no!

"—that years ago, Thomas—" she shot back.

He mustn't listen.

Suddenly he heard his father's vibrant tenor.

"—A fine romance, with no kisses—"

"Shush, shush, you'll wake him. I'm warning you."

"Good old Nick."

Then he lost a few words. "—wouldn't want—give me the bum's rush—"

"—just go sleep it off, I've never—"

"—for crying out loud!—"

Had they stopped? No, he could still hear, words unintelligible, the sibilant sounds.

He heard his father in the hallway. Good God, was he coming up here?

"Let him be!" his mother said sharply.

And let *him* be, Nicholas added, in silent anger. Both of you, just go to bed. He could endure forever their strained, civil armistice, but not this open warfare. It would drive him nuts.

"—your precious dreamboat—"

Who was she talking about? Nicholas flared. Leave me out of it.

"—spoiled, no normal father—"

"—now I'm not normal—" Then: "—lovely, just lovely—" and "—this normal enough for you?—"

"—hands off me—" very loud, "—sick and tired . . . for early Mass."

"Yes, yes," his father scoffed, "mustn't disappoint the good Sisters. Should've been one, by God. Flog yourself with a piece of the True Cross."

I'll be good, I promise I'll be good, Nicholas prayed. I'll do anything, just make them stop. He'd serve Mass twice a day, say his rosary till it crumbled in his grip. I'll give myself to You completely, I swear, he promised, feeling the tears brim in his eyes.

Obscurely, but passionately, he felt it must be his fault. He'd heard his name mentioned. Had his sinfulness brought this on? God was merciful, but first He was *just*.

Nicholas heard something thud to the floor downstairs. Should he get up, make some noise, go to the bathroom? If they heard him, maybe they'd stop.

No, that was no good. If they heard him, they'd feel obliged to explain.

He jumped out of bed and crept to the landing. In the mirror halfway down, he could catch any movement in the dimly lighted hallway. He heard a door slam.

"—don't you dare—" Her voice, shrill, alarmed.

"—last time, Diana—"

"—fine, just go to bed—"

Lord, I promise to do Your will, Nicholas prayed.

"—ashamed of yourself, won't remember a thing in the morning—"

"—things don't forget—can't!—"

Nicholas heard his mother's lock click shut like a confessional latch. He stared, full of terrible curiosity, as his father passed by the mirror, lurching toward the bathroom.

Nicholas shrank from his lookout. Repeating Hail Marys inwardly, he went back to bed. Moments later the springs sagged on his father's bed, right underneath Nicholas's.

Please, dear God, don't let them start again, he implored. Make them be quiet. He lay back in bed, wide awake, bathed in sweat, alert to the slightest noise, willing them into quick, erasing sleep.

In time he heard his father's steady, honking snores.

Thank you, dear Lord. He would remember his promise.

He would do anything to make them happy, even if it took a miracle.

On his way downstairs the next morning, Nicholas could hear his father still sawing noisily away. But there were no sounds coming from the kitchen. Saturday. Tina's day off. Damn! he'd have to fix his own breakfast. Basketball practice was at eleven sharp.

At least he wouldn't have to face *them*.

Let them patch things up without his getting caught in the middle.

He heard a low murmur from his mother's room. Creeping to the door, which she'd evidently opened during the night, he peeked between it and the jamb.

She was kneeling at the far end of the room, in the tiny alcove whose bay window overlooked the front yard. Her head was bowed and, her rosary clutched in her hands, she moved her lips silently.

In the alcove, votive candles in red cut-glass containers cast their flickering crimson light on a statue of Mary, carved in marble. With her arms raised in submission, the Mother of God was caught in a moment of triumphant ecstasy, being assumed into Heaven.

Her shrine, Thomas called it. "It takes a convert to show the rest of us what real piety is," was one of his favorite cracks. "With all the novenas and nine First Fridays, she's saved her soul as many times over as our bombs can wipe out Russia."

She had special devotion to the Blessed Virgin. The nuns

at church who helped her with the altar flowers were particularly delighted about that.

Nicholas watched his mother, unaware of his presence, holding herself in a cocoon of prayer.

Feeling guilty, he stayed put.

At last she unbent from her devotions, crossed herself, and then leaned forward to rest her lips for a moment on the Virgin's cool, naked feet.

He turned away quickly and forced himself to creep downstairs.

She had "put on her face," as she liked to call it, by the time she came into the kitchen. Her mask of tense, composed beauty had reasserted itself.

"Good morning, Nicholas."

"Good morning, Mother." He could sense her searching his face for a sign that he had overheard their cryptic donnybrook. But he didn't let on.

At the counter in the breakfast nook, he watched as she broke eggs into a bowl, added milk and a few sprinkles of cinnamon, then beat the mixture with a wooden spatula. Done, she poured the rest of the milk into a saucepan and set it over a low flame, next to the seeping coffee.

"Fresh grapefruit juice, dear?"

"O.K., Mother, sure."

"Sleep well?" she asked, fetching three plump fruit from the bowl by the window.

"Like a log."

"Practice this morning?" she continued, no hint in her voice that this day was different from any other.

"Sure." During the season he put in at least an hour a day.

"Going to church?" he asked automatically.

"Of course. I have to see to the flowers." Since the altar was kept bare for Lent, her offerings were entrusted for its duration to the parish nuns to dispense at St. Francis Hospital. With a rueful smile she added, "I seem to have missed Mass. I guess I just overslept."

She ladled the batter into the electric frying pan. It sizzled instantly. French pancakes, his all-time favorite.

"You'd better call your father."

"O.K. He was still out like a light when I came down." Rounding the corner, he added, "Must have been some party."

"Oh no. Just the usual. He's tired, that's all. You know how hard he works."

Typical of her, Nicholas thought, starting up the stairs. Not only wouldn't she let on to him one bit, she sprang immediately to the defense of her slugabed husband.

"Dad? Breakfast!" he yelled.

He heard his father's just-awake, racking coughs, then a queasily hearty, "Sure thing, pal, be down in a jiffy. No need to wake the dead."

Nicholas returned to the kitchen to find a plateful of thin, crisp pancakes and a steaming mug of cocoa. Reaching for the pitcher of maple syrup, he wondered what his mother thought she was up to. He hadn't drunk cocoa for years. She knew that.

She was at the counter finishing the juice, working the hand-operated squeezer like an outdoor pump. Nicholas swirled gobs of butter into the syrup.

"What a glorious day," his father boomed as he waltzed in. He pecked Diana on the cheek, which she offered to him placidly. "Good morning, my dear," he said. He slid into the chair opposite Nicholas.

His hair was slick, brushed straight back, and there were tiny red lines in his eyes.

Serves you right, Nicholas thought.

Even in his burgundy silk bathrobe, Thomas looked as spiffy as a colonel on parade.

"Quite a spread," he ventured, eyeing Nicholas's plate.

"Same for you?" Diana inquired.

"Just coffee—black and boiling."

"Me too," Nicholas put in without thinking.

"Don't you want your cocoa?"

"I'd rather have coffee."

"But, dear, you always loved cocoa," she persisted.

"I'll bet he'll stick to a man's drink even if it kills him—right, Nick?" Thomas butted in, the clumsy mediator.

Nicholas said nothing, but nodded.

"He's even got a beard going. Look at that fuzz." As his father reached toward his cheek, Nicholas pulled back instinctively. "Come to think of it, I've got something for you. In the library. I was saving it for a special occasion, but . . . Later. O.K.?"

"Sure, Dad. Great."

Diana filled two mugs of coffee. With one in each hand, she wedged the tall glass of juice between them and approached the breakfast counter. Thomas sprang up to help her. At the same moment she flinched, sending the glass crashing to the floor, where it broke into sticky fragments.

"See what you've made me do!" she snapped. She stared in disbelief at the floor, her expression betraying her surprise that she should be involved in such a mishap.

"Jaysus, I'm sorry, dear. Here, let me clean up," Thomas apologized. He always brogued it up when he felt guilty.

"It's all over everything!" she said.

His father eyed him meaningfully. "Nick?"

Nicholas went to the broom closet and fetched a mop and a bucket.

"He'll take care of it, dear. Just sit down and relax," Thomas said.

"How could I be so clumsy," she said, sitting down in Nicholas's place. "Hell, damn, spit!" These were the only oaths she allowed herself.

Nicholas swept the shattered glass into a pile and shoveled it into the garbage can. Then, shaking some Ajax into the bucket, he filled it with water and began to mop up the juice.

"Your pancakes are getting cold," she told him.

His father reached across the table and grabbed Nicholas's plate. "I'll tackle these," he said. "You grab the next batch. O.K., Nick?" He took a hearty mouthful. Still chewing, he exclaimed, "My dear Diana, you've outdone yourself. They're absolutely epicurean. Aren't you having any?"

A wry brief smile. "You know very well I gave up breakfast for Lent."

"Be that as it may, I think a dish like this deserves a special dispensation."

"There!" he said, finished. He rinsed out the bucket, then returned it and the mop to the closet.

"Thank you, dear."

She stood up and, checking to make sure Nicholas had cleaned the floor thoroughly, returned to the stove. As she started another batch, Nicholas resumed his place. Thomas, merry now, continued to munch.

"You don't know what you're missing," he said to her, between bites.

Sure she does, Nicholas thought, feeling strangely close to her all of a sudden. But she'll never admit it.

While his mother readied herself for church, Nicholas did the dishes, then went into the library.

His father, dressed in slacks and sports jacket, both battleship gray, was already reading at his polished walnut desk. On the corner of the desk stood Nicholas's surprise.

Looking up, Thomas waved him in.

"Go on! Open it," he urged.

As Nicholas grabbed the wrapped package off the desk

and gave it a weighing shake at his ear, Thomas placed his book, open-faced, down on the blotter.

Nicholas ripped off the paper, revealing a black box, of calf's leather, he guessed, rich and smooth to the touch like his baseball mitt. He reckoned it was about a foot square and six inches deep. His initials were embossed in gold on the flap: *N.W.M.* Winston was his middle name, his father's Churchillian call to arms.

Nicholas pushed the clasp, and the lid sprang open. A silver toilet kit! He looked up at Thomas in amazement.

"No gentleman should be without his kit." His father's blue eyes danced; his tone was confidential.

The kit contained two military-style hairbrushes; a comb; scissors—cuticle and mustache; a nail buffer; a small lathering bowl with matching brush; a straight razor; and something else he couldn't identify. It looked like a question mark.

"What's this?"

"A button opener. Not much call for those anymore. Like it?"

"Wow, do I ever! Thank you, Dad. It's great!" For a moment Nicholas wondered whether this was his father's way of making up for last night and this morning. No, that was stupid. He'd have had to order it from New York weeks ago.

"I was saving it for a special occasion, but you got a little ahead of my timetable with that fuzz of yours."

As though embarrassed by Nicholas's excitement, Thomas turned typically gruff.

"You'd better start cracking if you're going to get to basketball practice on time."

"Sure, Dad. O.K." Then, with emphasis, so there could be no question of his being blasé, he added, "Thanks a million!"

"You deserve it. You're getting to be quite the young man." His eyes shifted to the window. He was obviously ill at ease, mistrustful of emotion. "Your mother and I are very proud of you, you know."

Nicholas didn't know what to say.

"First in your class at midterms. *And* MVP in freshman ball, no doubt."

Maybe, Nicholas thought. He *was* high-scorer.

"And never any problem," Thomas continued, his recital almost trancelike. Suddenly his eyes swept back and held Nicholas's. "Everything O.K. at school?"

"Sure, Dad."

"Fine. 'Cause I'm always here if you need me, you know that."

"I know."

"So . . . " Thomas sighed as though relieved to be on safer footing, "did you make any headway on your Religion assignment?"

Nicholas told him what he'd decided—and wondered what he'd say if he knew about June Wilkinson. Despite his savoir-faire, where women were concerned Thomas was quite a prude. And a Catholic. No matter how much he ranted and raved, Nicholas knew that, deep down, Thomas believed it *all*. His mother's faith burned more brightly because it caught her unawares. Filling empty space, it glowed for others to see. But his father's pulsed in the blood, as basic and invisible as the wind that moved the world.

As though reading his mind, Thomas made comment:

"Good idea. First Communion." Then, to himself, it seemed, "Keep the faith. It's the only thing that will never let you down. Still going to Mass every day?"

"Not quite," Nicholas answered. But he would, starting Monday. He'd given his word. "But often."

"Fine. Well, you probably know more about your subject than I do. I was never one for traipsing off to church at the drop of a hat. That's more your mother's line. But I've never doubted the faith, not for one second."

"I know." Nicholas was becoming uncomfortable.

"Luther—that Hun heretic—knew what he was talking about: a mighty fortress."

"Yes." Thomas was talking to himself, Nicholas was certain.

"It's an inner music, a quickening coherence that—apart from the faith—has never existed. And in my own way, I think I'm just as religious as your mother is." He paused. "So, what else? Any girlfriends on the horizon?"

"Not since Mo," Nicholas replied immediately; then, aware that it was a sore spot between them, he added, "but with school and all, where would I get the time?"

"There'll be *plenty* of time for all that, you'll see." Jovial once more, in command.

God, he's not easing himself into the birds and the bees, is he?

"And how's Karl?"

No! Decorum wins again. Good.

"He's fine."

"Still, squeaking by, is he?"

"I guess so. He just about kills himself scrounging up the tuition."

Suddenly Nicholas had an idea. It was no joke; Karl was in constant danger of flunking out.

"Dad—it's just a thought, but—I don't suppose you'd be able to help him out? A kind of *scholarship*?"

"A scholarship, is it! Do you think money grows on trees? I'm in no position to start endowing chairs, you know."

Nicholas could see he was intrigued. He just wanted to be coaxed.

"No, of course not, Dad. But just for a year, two years? I've got almost two hundred dollars saved up," he offered. Thomas looked impressed. Go all the way, he told himself. "I guess I could chip in part of my allowance too."

Nicholas could tell it flattered his father's seigneurial

sense of himself, but he clearly enjoyed being, for a change, the recipient of a sales pitch.

"I don't think that'll be necessary, Nick," he replied, then smilingly added, "The allowance part, at any rate. The arrangements *could* be made."

"But . . . anonymously, Dad? So he'd never know where it came from? So it wouldn't be charity?"

That clinched it. "If he thought it was a handout, he'd throw it back in our faces—right?" Thomas asked.

Nicholas nodded.

"I wouldn't expect anything less," Thomas concurred, sounding as though the respect he had for Karl hinged on that very certainty. "So, a scholarship it is, then," he continued, musing. "Does he still have that miserable excuse for a bugle?"

His bugle. Of course. It was Karl's prize. It was really a trumpet, but there was no telling him. He had found it in a trashcan, battered and bent, and nursed it lovingly into a deep, burnished glow. In his room over the garage, Karl could often be heard tooting through "Good Night, Sweet Blues," "Pack Up Your Troubles," or some other tune culled from hours spent listening to Bix and Dizzy and Satchmo. He played with a zip that still managed to sound plaintive. Nicholas would stay at the door at the top of the stairs and watch as, his brows knit in furious concentration, the sickle-shaped scar along his right cheek blazing, Karl pumped his cheeks like a bellows.

As soon as he spied Nicholas watching, he would stop.

"I play for myself," he announced, outlawing all requests.

"Of course," Nicholas answered his father. "That bugle's just about the only thing Karl cares about." More than me, even, he felt like adding, angry at Karl's self-imposed ban on playing, as he put it, "in public."

"I'll have to work out the details—it might just do the trick."

"That would be incredible," Nicholas said.

"Well, I'll take care of it. For the fall term. Keep your two hundred dollars. This, at least," he added in a voice full of dark meaning, "is something I can *handle*. So, scoot."

"Thanks, Dad, for everything."

"No problem. But don't get the idea I'm made of money. And you might give your mother a hand with her flowers."

"Sure." Nicholas watched as he picked up his book off the blotter. It was *The Diary of Anne Frank*. He could see Thomas squinting, trying not to smile. He'd planned this, of that Nicholas had no doubt.

Fair enough.

"Dad? Having second thoughts?"

Thomas clucked combatively. "Actually, I intended to reread this soon, anyway," biting hard on the *re*. "Lest we forget . . ."

Nicholas couldn't help laughing. Thomas was always full of tricks. Had he repented his crude gibes at the dinner table last night? With him, you never knew for sure. He could argue like a Jesuit on either side of a question. And he was often deliberately outrageous, just to provoke counterpunching. Maybe—probably—he'd repeated Mr. Hoskins's slur to see what Nicholas was made of.

In fact, now that he thought about it, Nicholas was sure. Having come up the hard way himself, as Thomas relentlessly reminded anyone who would listen, he was not likely to cast a cruel eye on any victim, whatever the "old wives' tales," as he termed them, might be.

Look what he was going to do for Karl.

He *always* backed the underdog.

Nicholas raced up the stairs, chock-full of anticipatory cheer and welling gratitude. He reminded himself not to breathe a word to Karl about the scholarship. As for last night, terrible as it had been, maybe it was a freak thing. He would try to put it out of his mind.

But he would keep his promise.

Holding the white gloves she was never without when she ventured into the world, his mother stood by the screen door leading from the kitchen to the back porch. She was wearing a deep tan skirt and a blouse the color of butterscotch, topped by a brown and beige houndstooth jacket. Girding her russet hair was a scarf of ethereal blue.

She was a knockout.

"Can I help you load the car?" Nicholas asked, putting down his gym bag. It was stuffed with clean sweatsocks, his jockstrap, and Dr. Scholl's powder, and his red satin trunks with white piping.

She looked surprised. He usually took no interest in her flowers.

"That would be very nice of you, dear."

He followed her along the outdoor beds, cradling his arms as she stacked daffodils and white lilies. Then, heading for the greenhouse, she paused as though trying to decide, then added several crimson tulips to his pile. In the sick rooms, they would look like flames climbing toward Heaven.

She fussed briefly at her row of rosebushes, lugubrious below the white trellis. She bent to test the soil and pulled lightly on one bush to assure herself the roots were nourished and growing.

"Not long till June," she murmured.

He followed her into the greenhouse, cool and moist in contrast to the rising heat outside. Roses everywhere, their sweet perfume overpowering, almost cloying. Nicholas breathed through his mouth.

Delighted by his company, she conducted a tour: "These are old-fashioned, standard roses. They go back five thousand years." He nodded. "These, with smaller flowers, see, are floribunda. This particular type is called cathedral." Moving on . . . "These, of course you know, are teas, your father's favorite. Their true name is La France. They're hybrids too, first grown in France a century ago." She knew her stuff, he had to hand it to her.

Her flowers gave her a lot of pride and, he supposed, consolation. But he was champing at the bit to get to practice. She noticed his brusque, hurry-up nods.

"I've saved the best for last." She smiled. "This"—stopping before a huge, startlingly beautiful bush—"is a real showpiece. Grandiflora."

"Spectacular," Nicholas admitted.

She turned to leave, and he trailed behind her, trying to keep the load of flowers level. He should try to take more of an interest. She'd certainly knocked herself out for him this morning, getting breakfast when she'd probably have preferred to stay locked up in her room.

Sometimes he felt awfully selfish.

"It must be the dickens taking care of so many different kinds," he volunteered.

"No, not really," she responded, unable to disguise her pleasure. "Roses especially are very reliable. Just make sure they get enough sunshine, good, moist soil, and, most important, room for their roots to run free, to find their own way. And keep watch for fungus. Simple, really."

He deposited the flowers in the back seat of her car.

It didn't look simple.

"Well, that's that. Thank you, dear."

"Sure, Mother. See you later."

He watched her drive off to church, loaded with a seatful of brilliant, gay life. Then he picked up his bag, grabbed his bike from the garage, and headed for practice.

5

Lyon gave him an A-minus on his First Communion paper and made him read it to the class.

Nicholas was particularly proud of the ending. After describing that memorable day, he concluded by saying:

"All the seven sacraments display God's glory, but Holy Communion, being celebrated daily—a global, eternal present—is God's masterpiece. Who, graced with Faith, would not kneel in awe and thanksgiving before such a gift, God's supreme gift, Himself?

"And who is more blessed than his human servant, the priest, his sacramental colleague whose transcendent vocation it is to witness and effectuate and bestow his redemptive Presence on all souls fortunate to possess the one true Faith?

"God's glory in the modern world? If you seek his monument, look around. There it is, in the celebrant distributing Communion. There it is, in you all."

When he saw Lyon's grade, Nicholas was put out. He deserved at least an A, if not an A-plus.

He didn't have time before reading it aloud to check Lyon's comments on the back, but afterwards, at his desk, he discovered why he'd been docked.

"Really and truly, very fine," Lyon had scrawled. "The minus is for the purple patches and the crib from Christopher Wren. (Did you *really* think you could get that by me?) Otherwise, your approach is original, your argument sound, and your style vivid. God seems, in His inscrutable wisdom, to have blessed you very liberally, so acute is your grasp of the miraculous reach of His love. You have much to give, and He may ask for it. Are you listening?"

Just reading the last lines made Nicholas tremble.

A priest? Him?

What if it was true?

"He bloody well thinks you've got a vocation," his father boomed in amazement when Nicholas interrupted their cocktail hour to show them his paper.

His mother reacted with mild shock.

"No, he's much too young to think of that."

"My eye! I'm telling you, Diana, the implication is clear." He recited the last few lines, giving them a mock-prophetic cadence.

"He's still a child, only fourteen."

"Mother, please." Nicholas writhed. Did she have to put it like that?

"Nevertheless, the Jebbies like to spot them early, grab them while they're young and impressionable. In my day they recruited them in kneepants. 'Give me a boy for four years, and I'll give you the man.' That's what they say."

"I'm sure you're exaggerating," Diana put in, her voice indicating that she had *no* way of knowing for sure.

"Not a bit. Think of the nuns—your nuns, my dear—and how they swarm all over a boy if he serves Mass a couple of times, crossing themselves and cooing all over him with a little breathless catch in their voices, full to bursting with one word in their throats: 'Father!' Why, they'd groom them from the crib if we'd let them. Practically do, anyhow." He stopped as though searching his memory. "Let's see if I've got it right, the catechism. The difference between marriage and the religious life—see the way they insinuate the notion of superiority there, as though married life were irreligious—is not, *deo gratias*, the difference between good and evil, but between good and better. Right, Nick pal?"

He was really wound up tonight.

"That's what it says, Dad."

"Now, Nicholas," his mother interrupted, concerned, "surely you haven't taken it in your mind that you're to be a priest?"

He hadn't given it enough thought to know one way or the other, but decided to bait them:

"Would that be so disappointing?"

"Oh, my God!" Thomas expostulated.

"Of course not, dear," Diana said, "if it's truly God's will, but you're much too young to know . . ."

There she goes again, Nicholas thought.

"Just a stage they all go through," his father groused.

"Dear, I'm sure Father—what's his name?—Lyon means it as a compliment, but isn't it just a little premature?"

"Maybe," Nicholas replied, conceding nothing, reveling in their comic distress.

"Premature or prophetic," his father snapped. "At any rate, if I may be permitted seer-time, you may have other worlds to conquer, profane though they be. Just remember: faith is a wonderful thing, but doubt is what gets you an education."

Nicholas chuckled as he imagined his father's dynastic visions. Papa Joe Kennedy wasn't the only Irish dreamer on the block.

"There is a happy medium, you know. For the time

being," Thomas went on, summing up, "suppose you just remember—if I've got it straight—the drill is: God calls you; you don't call Him!"

"Thomas, don't joke about it," Diana chided.

"All right, all right," he yielded. "When the time comes"—looking Nicholas in the eye—"it's up to you, of course."

"Right." Nicholas grinned.

"Maybe we should have this Father Lyon over for dinner some evening," his mother suggested, with an abstracted voice that suggested she was already considering tactics for an alien battleground.

"Just one thing," Nicholas declared. "I was—sort of—kidding."

"Go on with you, you fuzz-faced boob, you confounded angel-eyed scamp of a kidder. Out, get out!" Thomas roared as he chased Nicholas threateningly from the room. "Can't we have some peace and quiet around here?"

"Does that mean you don't want Lyon to come for dinner?" he called over his shoulder.

"Begone," his father ordered. "Banished till dinner." Nicholas turned—and saw that he was smiling.

That damned A-minus still rankled as he climbed the stairs to his room.

His folks were right about one thing, anyway. Time would tell.

He *had* been kidding.

However, Nicholas told himself as he let out a loud whistle, who knows?

6

Nicholas watched the high-arcing shot plump softly through the cords.

No rim at all, he noticed, satisfied.

Again, starting at midcourt, a purposeful, whirling dribble, feint once, twice; then, from his patented spot at the top of the key, fake, then up, up, up, the ball flat and warm against his right palm, glued till the last possible suspended second against the back of his head, then uncork like a lithe, fluid catapult, the ball twisting through the cascading sunlight in the deserted school gym as, his follow-through invisibly steering it, grape-sized now and descending slowly, it plops into the hoop.

He never quit till he'd made ten in a row.

Retracing his steps, wiping his sweat-drenched hair with the slick back of his wrist, he went for number eight.

He was determined to make basketball pay off even bigger than football had last term. He'd started the season as a varsity benchwarmer, but by being a good soldier and with his father egging him on from the sidelines, by midseason he'd made starting safety. Cursed with slow feet—size elevens, for God's sake!—he compensated by sharpening his anticipation, by studying patterns and reading infinitesimal giveaway signs at the line. Intelligence, more than raw natural talent, made him sneaky-fast. And he could tackle like Chuck Bednarik. He loved the bone-crunching contact, the leather-popping abandon, the sheer, reckless physicality.

There! Number nine. Come on, train. Swish.

He had a couple of regrets about football, though. The 4-8 year was a disappointment. And he barely got his elbows dirty as a third-string halfback. Offense was the glamour squad. He wouldn't mind hearing the cheerleaders from St. Mary's Academy, pompoms and batons twirling, yelling:

"Two, four, six, eight! Who do we appreciate! Manion!"

In time, he thought. In God's good time.

He tried Nicholas Manion: "St. Paul's Hamlet!" on for size.

Now for ten, and out.

Even Karl, with his "miraculous" tuition-covering scholarship, had made the Crusaders team. Coach Kap Kowalsi, an ex-Marine Corps DI, recognizing a fellow Leatherneck, in spirit if not intention, rewarded his spunk with the last sub slot.

"I must live right," Karl announced, shaking his head in grateful wonder. "Some rich old geezer, whacked out on weren't-those-the-golden-days b.s., decided to pick up the tab, out of the blue, for some lucky stiff who happened to play his old instrument. No strings, either, no Fourth of July picnics or any of that crap. All I've got to do is keep playing. What a deal! I'd do that anyway."

Thomas was a man of his word.

Nicholas watched the ball spinning around the rim, like a top. It curled out, hanging over the side for an agonizing second, then shot home.

Done.

Now for a few hook shots.

Basketball was the thing now. Making the team would be a snap. He wouldn't start, not at first. There was no way he could dislodge either of the starting guards, both seniors. But he'd be a vital sixth man, a gunner off the bench when flashy Patey, the team star, suddenly went cold or got into foul trouble.

The books were no sweat.

Halfway through sophomore year, he was still first in his class. As long as he paid attention and kept up with the endless reading, he managed to breeze through tests. His secret was simple: a near-photographic memory and an inborn drive to give them back what they dished out, with something extra added. Teachers loved to reward what they called originality, as long as you got your facts straight. But to Nicholas it was just a natural contrariness, a stubborn, probably arrogant need to give everything he did a personal stamp, a special, surprising twist, a signature of style. Like Whitey Ford, he thought. If he was a pitcher he'd leave the heat to the morons, the beef. He would motion them silly, outsmart them, curve-and-sinker them out of their jockstraps. Even spit, when it was hardball, was a kind of signature.

Thank God his folks trusted him to know what he was doing. They didn't hang over him like schoolmarms, checking every piddling piece of homework, or ride him for spending too much time practicing.

They respected his independence and let him set his own priorities.

Things were peaceful on the home front, too. Just like the old days.

Satisfied now, Nicholas squatted on the wooden bench just off-court and peeled off his dripping T-shirt.

He loved all this, he realized. The empty gym, stinking of sweat and rubber and ageless dreams. Pressure, *self-*

pressure, was an elixir: intoxicating, one-hundred-proof, brewed-from-God's-private-stock adrenaline.

He was on air.

He heard the outer door, just beyond the gym, bang open and saw Lyon stalk by, shoulders and elbows free-swinging like an antsy streetfighter. He walked at ramming speed.

Stuffing his shirt into his bag, Nicholas headed for his locker.

Lyon poked his nose around the door.

"Well, if it isn't our very own sad excuse of a Bob Cousy," he said. "Don't you ever let up? This is supposed to be Christmas *break*, you know, time to replenish your spiritual resources—or whatever," he added sarcastically.

"Just working on my jump shot," Nicholas explained.

"*Sine dubio*," Lyon tossed back smartly. "As long as you're here, how about a little chin-wag in my office?"

"Sure." What did he have up his sleeve? Nicholas wondered. "What's that book you're carrying?"

"Just my breviary."

Of course—they had to read it every day. "My wife," Father O'Mara called it.

"Oh, yeah. Is it . . . interesting?"

"If you like Latin," Lyon replied, leading Nicholas up the stairs.

As they approached his office, he added, "It's not what I'd term my favorite pastime, but it comes with the territory."

Nicholas stayed standing, in front of the desk.

"Cool your heels, mister," Lyon ordered, pointing to the captain's chair in front of the paper-filled credenza along the left wall.

It was the standard, prosaic cubbyhole: metal desk; phone; typewriter—a battered Underwood, Nicholas noticed, humungous compared to his own nifty Royal portable; cork bulletin board; green file cabinet; and, back behind the swivel chair, a wooden prie-dieu.

Nicholas had caught the standard-issue office before, but only on the wing. To many of his classmates it was the St. Paul's torture chamber. The vice-principal was in charge of discipline, the keeper of the strap.

As one who played his cards too craftily ever to warrant a strapping, Nicholas tried to imagine what the ordeal might be like: *whack, whack, whack,* and then "Thank you, Father."

Behind the door, Nicholas noticed a personal touch: on the iron clothes tree hung Lyon's Celtics jacket. Just to its left was a framed black-and-white picture of a group of men, arm in arm, in front of an airplane.

Nicholas got up and walked over to study it more closely. One of the men, the collar of his flak jacket turned up at a rakish angle, was hoisting a bottle of champagne, his face afire with a swashbuckler's grin. The pilot—Nicholas recognized the wings—had a pert, silent-movie-rogue mustache and a full mane of thick black hair.

Holy Semole, it was Lyon! Nicholas let out an impressed whistle.

"This is you, right?" he asked.

"Yes, mister, for my sins. Even *I* once had hair."

Nicholas returned to his chair.

"That your squadron?" he asked, dying to hear the whole story.

"Crew, mister. If you're going to be nosy, get your nomenclature right."

"Sorry."

"Anyhow," Lyon went on, foreclosing any follow-up, "that's ancient history." Then, in a dark voice whose poignancy his vacant eyes only deepened, he added, " 'But that was in another country, and besides the wench is dead.' "

Nicholas didn't have the vaguest idea what he was talking about.

"I'm sorry?"

Lyon's steel-bore glare returned to focus.

"And just so you won't accuse me of stealing one of your tricks, that was *Jew of Malta*, Christopher Marlowe, not me."

"O.K."

"In case you thought I'd forgotten about Christopher *Wren*."

"Give me a break, Father," Nicholas whined. "All I did was ask a question." This guy never lets up, Nicholas reminded himself.

Lyon raised his right hand.

"*Pax*. That's enough Mademoiselle-from-Armentières for today. Ask no questions, et cetera . . ." He refused ever to discuss his pre-Jesuit life, Nicholas knew that.

"O.K., geez!"

"Mister!" he bellowed.

"Sorry, sor-*reee*!"

"All right," Lyon commenced, satisfied, tossing a letter from his in-box onto the dull gray desktop in front of Nicholas. "Take a gander at this," he urged.

It was an invitation from the Optimist Club Oratorical Society announcing their annual nationwide competition. The subject this year was "Optimism—Ingredient for True Leadership."

"So?" Nicholas asked ingenuously. Did he want suggestions for candidates?

"It occurred to me that the young world-beater who astonishes us all on the gridiron, and thinks he's the second coming of Bob Cousy, is also the author of 'My First Communion.' "

"Uh-huh," Nicholas replied warily, beginning to catch his drift.

"It's only an idea, but I suspected this little epistle might pique your interest, excite your unique combo of—what?— bulldog and blarney."

That wasn't bad, Nicholas decided. Not bad at all.

"I'm no orator," he insisted, making it sound like an

epicene affliction, imagining himself drying up in front of a vast, dressed-to-the-nines, jeering audience.

"Words are just another weapon, mister. Or, if you prefer, game."

"I know, but it takes loads of practice, and with everything else I've got going, where would I get the time? I mean, basketball's starting, and . . ." Nicholas trailed off, stammering.

"I noticed," Lyon replied tartly.

"Besides, what would I say?" Nicholas sputtered. "I don't know beans about leadership."

"Oh, no?" Lyon pounced intently. "Where did I get the idea you went to noon Mass every day?" The VP missed nothing.

It was true, he did. Ever since that awful night. He'd kept his part of the bargain. But what did that have to do with orating? With leadership?

"Yes, but what—?"

"And," Lyon drilled, brooking no interference, "aren't you the chap who's first in his class?"

"Right, but I don't see—"

"What's more, wasn't that you I just caught sweating buckets in the gym during vacation?" He made it sound like the Ninth Wonder of the World.

"So what?" Nicholas asked, thoroughly confused.

"So what?" Lyon mimicked grandiloquently. "Example. Standards. Values. Excellence." He spit the words out like bullets. "How would you define leadership?" he challenged victoriously.

"I see," Nicholas surrendered. "But, Father, what would I write?"

"All I ask is that you give it some thought. I'm sure your father would have some . . . pregnant ideas, too."

For sure, Nicholas reflected, Thomas would revel in the chance to send his homemade David into battle against the smug, I-Like-Ike, organization-man Philistines. He could hear his father smacking his lips and ransacking his books for balls-out, antediluvian citations. The Optimists? Thomas would eat them alive.

"And," Lyon continued, "you could always come to me if you paint yourself into a corner."

"I don't know," Nicholas equivocated, hooked. "When would I have to do it?"

"The first round is a month from now."

Time enough.

"You'd really help me—with the writing and gestures and all that?"

"You bet. I'll whip you into shape, have no fear."

Nicholas nodded assent.

"So—I can submit your name?"

Feeling more flattered than imposed upon, Nicholas agreed.

"Why not?"

"Indeed," Lyon replied, smiling.

7

"Try it again," Father Lyon instructed from somewhere in the darkened auditorium.

Once more, Nicholas launched shakily into his introduction:

"Our age is a risky one. Under the fearful shadow of the Nuclear Cross we cower, paralyzed by the specter of our civilization consumed in a global conflagration."

"O.K., stop!" Lyon ordered, visible now as he came down the center aisle to the stage.

Nicholas had spent nine hours memorizing the speech, and already Lyon was making changes.

"Cross is the wrong image, and it's a little confusing." He gave Nicholas a rewrite.

"Ours is an awful age," Nicholas began. " 'Beneath the mushroom cloud we cower, fearful that civilization itself will be consumed in the witch-fire of nuclear war.' "

"Better?" Lyon interrupted.

"Better," Nicholas yielded.

"Go on."

"A conflagration of our own making, because we are truly heretics inviting the global pyre, when, in our Iron Curtain of the soul, we turn with impunity from the faith of our fathers, the Declaration of Independence."

"Never mind 'with impunity,' and start with 'A deliberate suicide.' " He worked over the rest as well. "Go ahead."

"A deliberate suicide, for we are heretics indeed if we, in our Iron Curtain of the soul, shrink from the faith of our Founding Fathers."

"Good," Lyon applauded. "Smoother and shorter. Keep going."

"Aristotle defined man as a rational animal, but God created man a free being. We ignore our birthright, moral even more than national, at our own peril."

Lyon stopped him again. At this rate, Nicholas groused to himself, they'd be here forever.

Lyon made corrections and Nicholas plunged in once more.

"Aristotle's rational animal is God's creature—"

"Hit the 'God,' " Lyon urged. "Make it stand out."

Sighing loudly to signal his frustration, Nicholas continued.

"Aristotle's rational animal is *God's* masterpiece," he chanted—two could play at Lyon's fussing game—"created in His own likeness—free. To turn away from that liberating truth is both moral and political madness."

Nicholas paused to see whether Lyon would object again, then pressed on.

"Descartes wrote: *cogito, ergo sum*: I think, therefore I am. But the man who cannot think freely is nothing but a slave."

Outlining the fear of freedom inherent in Communism, Nicholas tackled the nature of leadership and ticked off his examples: Washington, Lincoln, FDR. Lyon didn't interrupt.

"Will we be slaves or free men?" Nicholas asked, commencing his peroration.

" 'Better red than dead' is a kind of slavery."

His voice retreated into a whisper:

"But wait a moment. Are we really threatened? Don't I exaggerate?"

Nicholas feigned jauntiness.

"After all, we are the richest, most powerful, most blessed people on earth. What do we have to fear?"

His voice assumed a weary, philosophical tone.

"The Communists? Not really. They are only as powerful—or as impotent—as *we allow* them to be . . ."

He paused, then his voice rang out like a rifle shot.

". . . ourselves!" Now, conversationally, sadly: "Only ourselves. The enemy within. Our own tragic pessimism."

He paced back and forth briefly, as though puzzling out his next thought. "And what must we do?" He answered himself: "Discover anew the original optimism, that irrepressible faith that galvanized our Founding Fathers and armed our proud march into the Promised Land that, once and forever, is America."

"Applause, applause, applause," Lyon said. "O.K., mister, that should do it for now."

He ambled toward the stage, checking the stopwatch he wore safety-pinned to his cassock.

"Six-twelve," he informed Nicholas. "We still have to cut a minute and a half."

"O.K. Was it all right?" Nicholas asked, needing reassurance.

"Not bad at all," Lyon allowed, stingy with praise as always. "Buy you a Coke?"

"You read my mind," Nicholas smiled.

"We'll have to keep you away from the ward heelers," Lyon remarked as they descended the stairs into the basement canteen. "They might spot a comer."

"No way."

"You've got the makings. Blarney and bulldog," he quoted himself tauntingly. "A Janus of a gift."

"Not me," Nicholas insisted, pausing to open his locker and fetch his towel. Even under the single light, he had sweated like a horse.

Lyon pushed coins into the slot, and a frosty Coke clattered into view behind the plastic door. He repeated the process, then uncapped both on the built-in bottle opener.

Nicholas drained half the king-size soda in one long, parched draught.

"Seriously," Lyon began with deceptive casualness, leaning against one of the rickety lunch tables, "what are you after? There's not much you couldn't do, if you reach for it." He sipped his Coke.

"I don't know," Nicholas muttered, not ready to broach the subject that, like a persistent, unreachable itch inside his ear, had been agitating him for some time. He drained the last cool drops.

As much as he loved being a world-beater, there was always the sense of something missing. Triumph, however heady, lacked dimension somehow, and weight. The stakes were never high enough. Victory was never sweet enough. And it didn't last. That was the worst part. No matter how thunderous and enveloping it was, applause always died.

There were moments when the sense of puniness and transience and futility almost overwhelmed him. Like the poem they had been forced to memorize in English Lit. "Ozymandias." What did anything prove?

Work, strive, achieve. My very own trinity, he reflected sardonically. But for what? For his parents, for his teachers? For St. Paul's? No, not really. For himself. For his own precious, preening, vainglorious, ego-rotten self.

Only by dedicating himself to God, he was beginning to accept, did his talents make sense, have lasting value. Think of Ignatius. In the world, but not *of* the world. That was the hard, liberating key. The *why* of things, not the *what*.

And hadn't he dedicated himself to God, unofficially? Yes, and God had heard his prayer. It was a pact they'd made that frightening night in his room. A pact that he now felt inchoately, but with fierce certitude, portended more than he had bargained for. Infinitely more.

Lyon plucked his cigarettes from the folds of his cassock, flicked his familiar Dunhill once, and smoked contentedly, ignoring him.

That was what had always been behind his strange sense of apartness. He *was* singled out, but not because of the other boys' jealousy. "You can do anything." That's what his father said. The prophecy had been both rich bequest and stern injunction. It emboldened Nicholas to take huge, premature risks, hardening his stomach early for battle on the toughest, most exacting scale.

But, equally, he now realized, it leashed his emotions, locking him in and keeping him on track.

He thought of the other kids. Even Karl. Nicholas did not share their foibles, their vagaries. He exempted himself from their feisty chameleonizing, their graceful burlesques. All of them seemed to juggle identities like quick-change artists, to audition possible futures with wanton delight.

But Nicholas was different. He reeked of seriousness, as though prodded by an implacable inner beat that was his alone. He took nothing easy.

His father and his teachers never quarreled with his self-possessed nature. But it made his peers pull back. Except for Karl, who found it obscurely amusing. None of the others would have misrepresented him as easygoing, or fun to be with, or a lot of laughs. He didn't pal around or play practical jokes, or get sent to Lyon's office for a strapping.

He was mercurial, but reserved. Single-minded, driven.

But driven by whom, and toward what?

He was beginning to see.

If his hunch was right, his father was going to be in for a big surprise.

"Come on, mister, spill. Use your noggin. What's perking in there?"

"Nothing," Nicholas insisted. Not yet.

"Oh, no? I can see your top three inches hopping a mile a minute," he said in a kidding tone, poking Nicholas in the shoulder, setting his empty bottle on the table.

"Well, my dad would never say so, but I'm sure he expects me to join up with him," Nicholas equivocated.

"Carry on the line, huh? Does that appeal to you?"

"Not really," Nicholas admitted. "I mean, it's great for him, and you can make a lot of money, but . . ."

"But?" Lyon pressed.

"If I'm going to sell something, it sure won't be insurance. There are better things to gamble on than when you're going to die. Or a different sort of death to deal with."

"Gotcha. *What*, then?"

"I don't know," Nicholas retreated. It was hard. Lyon might laugh in his face, accuse him of impertinence, presumption.

"Come on, what's itching you?"

"I'm just not sure," Nicholas said stubbornly. Lyon had already accused him of having a superiority complex. Why give him more ammo?

"All right," Lyon breezed, seeming to quit. "But there's something going on inside all that gray matter."

"Myself," Nicholas whispered.

"Come again?" Lyon asked.

"Myself," Nicholas repeated, more firmly now. "Except 'sell' is the wrong word. More like 'offer.' "

"But not politics?" Lyon harped, playing dumb. He wasn't going to help, Nicholas could see that.

"Why settle for that?"

"Something else, then," Lyon mused aloud, "something—what? Higher?"

"Yes!" Nicholas declared. "I know it sounds arrogant, but, damn it, yes!"

Lyon's coldly serious eyes bored into him. "It doesn't sound arrogant, mister," he said in a sharp voice. "Humility-with-a-hook, there you go again. Nothing but reverse snobbery. Deny a compliment to win a second."

"All right," Nicholas went on uneasily, unsure. "Well, for about a year now, I've been wondering . . ."

"Yes?" Lyon hooked.

". . . wondering if maybe . . ."

"Yes?" Lyon prompted again, jerking up now.

"It's just an idea, but maybe . . ."

"Yes? Yes!" Reeling, impatient.

" . . . I have a vocation." There, he'd said it. Landed.

Lyon stood up, brushed off his cassock, fastened his collar, smoothed his hair, and turned his intense, challenging eyes on Nicholas.

"Could be," he said softly. "Could very well be."

"I've thought about it a lot, prayed for guidance," Nicholas burbled. "I feel it, but . . . I mean, how do you know if it's genuine, if it's really a call, or if you're willing it?"

"You may not, at least at first," Lyon answered him soberly. "But in time it becomes clear. *Nemo dat quod non habet.*"

"Sorry?"

"You speak the language," Lyon teased.

"O.K.," Nicholas yielded with an exaggerated sigh. "Let's see. Nobody gives, no, nobody *can give* what he hasn't got."

"Rather idiomatic, but . . ." Then, with a grin: "See how easy it is when you use the talent God gave you?"

"So I should just wait?" Nicholas asked.

Lyon nodded.

"Just sit tight. Hold your horses. Pray. Many people flirt with the notion, but it usually peters out pretty quick."

"I hate this not knowing, not feeling sure."

"Let it simmer. There's plenty of time. No need to rush off half-cocked."

Nicholas saw pride mingled with concern in Lyon's swarthy face.

"Aren't there signs, or something?"

"Sure," Lyon replied easily, "and you know them as well as I do. It's all in the catechism. Suitability—physical, mental, and moral. No problem there. No impediments. Your parents hardly need *you* to support them. And the right intention."

"Which is?" Nicholas had to know, exactly.

"The desire to please God, of course," as though amazed that Nicholas had to ask.

Nicholas wanted that more than anything else. Everything good he had came from God. He'd do anything to pay him back. He had no doubts on that score.

"But it's a call, remember," Lyon explained. "It's not what *you* would prefer to be, but what *He* prefers."

"So what should I do, Father?" Nicholas wanted specifics, a plan.

"What you are doing. Pray, keep in a state of grace, go to Communion, say your beads. And beware of selfishness."

"I haven't told anyone about this," Nicholas confided, concerned that Lyon might tell his parents or one of his other teachers.

"My lips are sealed," Lyon offered suavely.

"You're not even surprised, are you?" Nicholas demanded, a little affronted.

"I wouldn't say so." Lyon seemed amused.

"You've been onto me since that bloody essay in class, haven't you?"

Lyon guffawed, the big-game fisherman exposed—posing.

"I see it's no use trying to con you."

Nicholas, qualms all gone, felt playful, curious.

"How do you spot it? Intuition?"

Lyon chuckled, wrinkling his brow quizzically.

"Something like that, I guess. Nick, we see so many

gifted, square-shooting, hell-raising, honest-to-God good boys—who, by the way, never seem to age—that you never know which one is going to pop into your office, panting for breath, to announce he's got a vocation. One never knows, not at first. A few do, most don't. Some you send off to the seminary full of hope, gleaming with your imprimatur, sure they'll make it, and then, after years sometimes, even some of *them*, for reasons that are no one's fault, fall by the wayside. Over the years you develop an eye, a sixth sense about these things. But it's still one of God's trickier mysteries."

"And me," Nicholas insisted, "where do I fit in?"

Lyon fixed him with a level, affectionate stare.

"You've got a lot going for you, more than most. Work on intention. But you've got the stuff to go far."

"But in which direction, right?"

"Precisely! You're a lucky stiff. God has blessed you tremendously. But, looked at another way, it's a heavy cross to shoulder. You not only can tell right from wrong, you can communicate it and, even more important, by example, embody and thus further it. It all depends on how you use it. It's a great gift." With a sly wink, he added, "Miraculous, even."

Nicholas laughed in recognition.

"You make me sound like Typhoid Mary," he joked, a bit embarrassed.

"Gospel means *good* news," Lyon rejoined merrily. "You can't hide your light under a bushel—or a basketball. Remember the parable of the talents. But work on intention, be sure your motives are pure. *Mutatis mutandi*, you'll know. Time will tell. Now you better hop home and get cracking on those revisions. Can't leave the fate of the Western World hanging."

Nicholas bowed from the waist.

"Yes, *Father!*" he replied smartly.

He hurried home, his heart pounding.

8

A fanfare, close by, urgent, trumpet blaring.

I must still be dreaming, Nicholas thought, though he could feel that his eyes were open, blinking into the stinging sunlight that bounded through his open window. He could see motes of dust capering like confetti in the brilliant chill of morning.

There it was again: insistent, strangely familiar. A call to arms? Cavalry. Cavalry?

Were there aural mirages? More annoyed than curious, shivering in the icy gust that nipped at his exposed neck, he wormed under the comforter, determined to get back to sleep.

Now boots stomped as the clarion continued. Right outside his door, on the landing, unless he was hallucinating. Some poor madmen, he knew, heard voices. But brass bands?

Exasperated, he threw off the covers and padded across the frigid wooden floor, flinging the door open.

Karl, in tan Hush Puppies, filthy, grass-stained chinos, chocolate-brown sports shirt, and football helmet, was stationed in front of the bathroom door, tooting away.

"What the hell?" Nicholas sputtered. "Who let you in?"

Karl ended his flourish, then dropped his horn in the best bugler tradition, grinning maniacally. "Your dad. I thought reveille was a better idea than taps."

This is the first time, Nicholas realized, he's played that damn thing for anyone.

"You crazy?"

"Though I see you didn't need this to bring you to attention," Karl sassed, pointing his horn to below Nicholas's belly. Nicholas looked down. Waking up was just another bus ride. "Who're you gonna please with that?"

"Wouldn't you like to know," Nicholas answered, wriggling into his shorts. He'd gotten rid of the stroke books just about a year ago now, tossing them into the furnace. He had had to do it. If ever there was an occasion of sin . . . and he had promised. Still, it hurt, seeing the flames lick the glossy paper. He felt he was watching his youth go up in smoke.

It hadn't eliminated temptation altogether. There were times when, no matter how hard he prayed, he still "fell." But they were few and far between—rare, really. He kept busy, and the Jebbies kept him tired. It grated on him to have to kneel in the confessional and, knowing that the priest recognized him, hear the disappointed "Remember who you are. You have to set an example for the other boys."

Karl's eyes were feral, the tiny scar on his freckled cheek glowing red. "Nick, I swear, going to Mass all the time is turning you into a goody-goody."

"Bullshit."

"Oh, yeah? You already act like a bloody priest. Now you're beginning to sound like one, too. Pretty soon you'll decide you want to *be* one." He looked furious, thwarted.

Nicholas said nothing, and Karl, with his usual, one-second span of attention, moved on. "You want to have a go?" he offered, extending his bugle.

"Really?" Nicholas asked.

"Sure, try it," Karl insisted.

Nicholas grasped the cold horn in his left hand, puckered his lips to limber them up, and fingered the stops for a few moments.

"Who're you supposed to be—Ed Norton?"

All right!

Nicholas blew for all he was worth. The insulated sound was somewhere between a Whoopee Cushion and an alley cat assaulting the moon. He tried again, his cheeks aching. A banshee shriek.

"Nick, old buddy," Karl said, with a seraphic smile, "you play like a dog screwing a ruptured football." He was delighted.

"Thanks a lot," Nicholas muttered, handing his horn back.

"You may be a whiz at school and sports, even at orating, but in my department you're strictly a palooka."

"Karl, give me a break."

"Strictly amateur night."

"Karl!"

"Least there's one thing you can't do . . ."

Nicholas slipped on sweatpants and noticed—finally!—that he was half-mast.

"What time is it, anyway?"

"After ten," Karl said.

The final run-through with Lyon was scheduled for two o'clock. The next leg of the contest was tomorrow night. He hoped it would bring him luck.

"Karl, what in hell are you doing here, anyway?"

"Well, lazybones, *I've* been up since dawn delivering the

daily blatz. My musical genius won me a scholarship, not a free ride, not like *some* people . . ."

"Tough," Nicholas snapped. "Well, as long as you're here, how about some breakfast?"

"Thank God!" Karl replied with exaggerated relief. "I was afraid, this kick you're on, you'd taken up *fasting*."

"Then," Nicholas continued, eyeing him like a school-master, "you can help me mow the lawn."

"Oh, go on."

"Karl?" He waited until their eyes met.

"All right," Karl surrendered, "but only for a while. I've got a hot date tonight—gotta get my rest."

"Good for you," Nicholas said, not wanting to give him the satisfaction of showing curiosity.

"Yeah, well—I figured one member of this team should keep his oar in, sort of give sex equal time, you know?"

Nicholas grabbed a sweater and shoved Karl into the hallway.

"Aren't you the romantic!" Nicholas said.

"I don't know," Karl replied, "but *I'm* not taking any vow of chastity."

9

SUNDAY, MARCH 20, 1960

Under the high arc of sweltering lights on the dais in the ballroom of the Heublein Hotel, Nicholas fidgeted with his starched collar, squinting into the boisterous audience of parents and Optimists, chomping their lusty way through heaping platefuls of gelatinous-looking *Poulet au Roi*.

The Regional Finals.

Next stop: St. Louis.

The first two rounds had been a breeze. He had won easily, both at the community-level preliminary and the Connecticut Finals in New Haven.

Tonight was for the whole New England area.

The ballroom was jammed to the rafters. The antique acoustics, accustomed to minor-key tea dances, now recoiled from the strident medley of positive-thinking boosterism. The nursery-tinted room seemed to flinch like a dowager blundering into a sock hop.

Nicholas spied his parents at one of the front tables, just

to his left. Their first time to hear him, adding to his nervousness. Lyon had forbidden their presence at the first two rounds. He needed time to break in the routine. His father had squawked but, after the promise of private, polishing run-throughs, had permitted his authority to be overruled.

Karl was there as well, and Uncle Bob. Bob Toppings was Thomas's best friend, and no relation. His bridge partner at the club and family doctor—he had presided over Nicholas's difficult birth—Toppings was an honorary uncle.

Peering through the bank of spotlights and tugging futilely on his collar, Nicholas saw his mother chatting demurely with Karl, who looked absurdly swank in his father's shiny, cut-down Sunday blue suit. His nervous, raking, huge eyes telegraphed his discomfort.

His father, Nicholas saw, huddled cozily with Uncle Bob, tic-like smiles straying with strained debonairness across his taut face. Every few moments Thomas eyed his watch. He had only picked at his entree. Inclining his head to listen, he reached for his drink, gulped it eagerly, then hoisted his glass for a refill.

By comparison, Diana was quite composed. Nicholas wished she hadn't used her connections to publicize his wins, though. Seeing "FIRST PAROCHIAL SCHOOL STUDENT REACHES OPTIMIST REGIONALS" blaring from the *Courant* was bad enough. He also had to endure the embarrassment of hearing about himself on WTIC News. "It's just that I'm so proud of you, dear," his mother had explained. Reflected glory was her daily bread. She looked for nothing more.

Nicholas stared down at his own untouched meal. He'd just about choked on the breadstick! This was worse, far worse, than the cartwheeling butterflies before a game. He almost welcomed those nowadays, since—the season almost over—the Crusaders team was, like Nicholas, a winner. He searched for a comparison to this feeling: the three-hour fast before his daily noon Communion, rough as it was, had nothing on this. Tonight his belly was raising holy hell.

It was all worsened by his bum luck in the draw. Nicholas was to be lead-off man. He reminded himself to be extra sharp. Going first, he *had* to be.

Pushing the nauseating banquet dish away from him, Nicholas looked up to see Lyon standing at the rear of the ballroom. "I'm too nervous to sit," Lyon had explained beforehand, but Nicholas believed his coach simply had chosen not to crash Thomas Manion's party. "Besides . . . I'll hear better how well you project. St. Louis'll be a much bigger room, you know."

The last couple of months had been a marathon of preparation. At home Nicholas had blessed the mood of peace and quiet, keeping his sense of his vocation to himself.

Nicholas now looked again at their table. His mother and Karl had barely touched their dinners, Karl being miffed, probably, that *his* father—Hartford's only exotic-food importer—hadn't been asked to supply the main course. In the Manion party alone, there was enough chicken à la king to feed a horde of starving Chinese babies.

In an alcove to the right of the dais, a trio droned perfunctorily through "My Blue Heaven."

Directly in front of the head table sat the judges, their pencils and notepads at the ready. The prim lady to the left was Miss Gertrude Peters, dramaturge at the Hartford Little Theatre. A pill, Nicholas decided, but she'd go by the book. The florid fellow with brilliantined hair, at the opposite end of the rectangular table, was a familiar sight from Thomas's club, Harold Patter. No crony by any means, he was an Aetna branch manager with too much of the revivalist about him to suit Nicholas's father. He was famous locally for his well-oiled spiel, haranguing prospective clients on the rubber-chicken circuit, "Invest in your future—and America's!" "Nothing but a pipsqueak Joe McCarthy!" Thomas had remarked acidly once after Patter had fawned over him with glaze-eyed insincerity.

Both Miss Peters and Patter had been introduced before-hand, along with the flibbertigibbet who now sat between them, his upper body gallivanting. Dr. Ebeneezer Cheviot, Professor (Emeritus) of Elocution at Trinity College, had a crest of orangey hair. His fine-boned hands, fingers like ta-pers, fluttered before his pince-nez, then flew to the martini glass that he cradled protectively, like a chalice. Nicholas had heard him order several refills already, in a prissy litany: "Tanqueray martini, straight up, no fruit."

The waiters were clearing off the dinner plates and dis-tributing coffee and dessert.

Almost time.

The other contestants kept to themselves at the head of the table, all five, he guessed, probably running through their lines. Nicholas didn't know any of them. They too had poked queasily at their food. Three Nicholas dismissed out of hand as no competition. The only ones who troubled him were the bullet-faced blond, who seemed to stiffen to keep from dis-membering himself atom by atom, and the preening, pom-padoured matinee idol seated next to him, who shot his cuffs and patted his patent-leather hair incessantly. Control and ego—he knew both well enough to give them their due.

Dr. Cheviot lifted his tall, bony frame and turned to the audience. He clutched his glass and raised it to his beak for one last swallow. Then, his mere presence having failed to mute the din, he snatched a knife from the table and clicked it fastidiously against his glass. He peered over his pince-nez, his nose pink.

"Ladies and gentlemen," he trilled, "now that this Lu-cullan repast has refreshed our bodies, let us compose our-selves for more cerebral nourishment. Our first Ciceronian is"—and here he paused, staring down at his list—"Nicholas Manion, representing"—his filament-thin eyebrow rising—"St. Paul's *Catholic* High School." He began to sit, then added, "No doubt the good Jesuit fathers will refine our understanding of the gentle art of persuasion. Mr. Manion?"

Applause.

Here goes nothing, Nicholas told himself, taking a deep breath as he did before every foul shot and mentally making the sign of the cross. He strode to the lectern and shunted it to the side. Notes were of no use to him now. "Get them early," Lyon had drilled him. "If you lose them, they'll never come back."

Nicholas let his steady gaze sweep the room slowly, collecting their attention. The silence was funereal, two hundred pairs of eyes trained right on him, as though on a preacher in the pulpit.

God, Nicholas prayed, don't desert me now.

Squaring his shoulders, he cleared his throat once, and began.

Applause.

All for him.

He'd done it!

Rising, stretching, climbing, gorgeous applause.

A few even stood up.

He had felt the audience floating to him, hanging on every twist and turn of his speech. The feeling of power was intoxicating. No wonder priests loved to talk. Did anyone have a more captive and enthralled audience than they did?

"Festina lente, mister," Lyon had urged.

He hadn't rushed, not at all, but he was pretty sure he'd come in safely under the five-minute wire.

As he made his way to his parents' table, he was certain he'd come through with flying colors. He saw Lyon, still in back, fists raised in gung-ho joy, the right brandishing a V-sign. Then he bent down and held aloft a piece of cardboard: 4:56, said the numbers scrawled on it.

Thank God.

"You were wonderful, dear," his mother whispered as he slid into a chair, the applause still ringing in his ears.

"A-one, Nick, pal, A-one," his father said as Uncle Bob

pumped his right arm. "Great, absolutely great, kiddo." His father, Nicholas noted, seemed oddly subdued.

Karl, feigning boredom, swirled his spoon idly in the dregs of his dessert.

Nicholas remembered he'd felt a surge of adrenaline as he sailed through the speech, but now it was a complete blank. He couldn't remember doing it. He was exhilarated and exhausted at the same time.

He felt a viselike grip on his knee, under the table where no one could see. "Not bad, hotshot," Karl growled, his face inching into a proud grin. He whispered in Nicholas's ear: "But this orating business has nothing on bugling!"

The final roars muffled into an urgent hum, Nicholas watched confidently as the judges conferred. Miss Peters, her finger jabbing Patter's chest, seemed to be in a snit. As she spoke, Cheviot shook his head emphatically, pecking at air, his long-nailed hands tracing awkward arabesques between them.

What did they have to debate? Nicholas wondered. He was in like Flynn.

As he'd guessed, three of his rivals were no competition. The blond bullet had caved in halfway through, flubbing his lines. The greaseball, Nicholas had to admit, had made a strong impression. His speech was slyly reassuring, a shrewd, oblique appeal to the smugness of the audience. He had honed in on the self-congratulatory streak that plainly linked the members of the resolutely bourgeois club. Nicholas had concentrated on leadership. Pretty Boy, cannily, had hit Optimism: "You are the true leaders of America, you Optimists who symbolize the American dream," ran the gist of his smoothly applied, liquid-voiced message.

Nicholas had to admit that while it was snake oil, it was prime snake oil.

Still, he wasn't worried.

On to St. Louis!

The crowd retreated into a suspenseful hush as Dr. Cheviot, folding his notes and tapping his stopwatch with finality, turned from Miss Peters. Lifting his hands palms out toward his shoulders, he began to speak:

"Ladies and gentlemen, and noble contestants: I'm sure the judgment is unanimous that we have been given tonight a trial that is knotty indeed—Gordian, one might say." A few nervous titters greeted this *bon mot*. "And I am equally certain you will all concur when I say that every one of our orators merits our respect and warm applause."

There was a brief spurt of impatient clapping.

"He's really dragging it out," Nicholas carped to Karl. "He loves it, the old humbug."

"It is indeed unfortunate that but one of our contenders can win. *Optimus ex optimi*, shall we say? The best *of* the best. At any rate," he sped up, noticing the coughs among his listeners, "after sober reflection, scrupulous scoring and"— now glancing at Miss Peters—"some rather spirited *ad hoc* debate, we have a winner."

Come on, come on, Nicholas urged silently.

"And he is Mr. Anthony Zalant." The gasps were immediately overwhelmed by accelerating gasps and cheers.

Hit by a sucker punch, below the belt. Nicholas felt pain slice through his gut. He bent forward, breathing hard, kneed in the balls.

The smoothie, the wavy-haired hunk of beefcake!

Everyone at his table was frozen, too stunned to speak.

"Sweet, crucified Jesus," Nicholas swore.

The breadstick, rebelling inside him, was now a spear, skewering his gorge.

He gulped water.

"I don't understand," he heard his mother say.

Uncle Bob was patting his arm consolingly.

"Should have been you, kiddo," he whispered.

Karl grasped his hand, squeezing it without mercy.

"You were robbed," he hissed. "The creeps. The phony creeps."

He was dizzy.

Just breathe. Breathe deep.

He was no loser.

There had to be a mistake. Had he run over? Maybe Lyon's stopwatch was on the fritz.

Nicholas eyed his father. Thomas sat stock-still. He seemed to be meditating. Watch out, world, Nicholas warned. As long as he's bloviating, he's a pussycat. When he clams up, beware!

His father caught Nicholas's expectant stare. With a swift grimace, he snapped his fingers like a visiting field marshal at the passing waiter.

"Sir?"

"Champagne. Dom Perignon, if you have it."

"Yes, sir! Right away."

Thomas turned toward his son.

"Nick, pal, why don't you ask Father Lyon to join our celebration." His face was full of strangled rage.

Tiny tears spurted from Nicholas's eyes. Why didn't he say something?

"You should have won," Thomas said quietly, full of worldly authority. "On *merit*," he added, spitting Steele's word, "and, before God, you did. Nothing can alter that. Now scoot. And hold your head high."

In a fog, Nicholas jostled his way through the crowd, warding off Optimists singing out "Way to go!" and "You were just as good."

Just as good, baloney! Nicholas spat under his breath. Their sympathy was intolerable.

Lyon was slumped dejectedly against the wall just outside the ballroom. Faintly, Nicholas could hear the trio slogging through a foxtrot.

Spotting Nicholas, Lyon snapped out of his daze, sprang

to attention, and with a solemn, hailing spark in his eye, he saluted.

Letting him down is the worst part, Nicholas thought. That, and sitting there like a dolt with spit slithering down my cheek.

He fought for control as he searched Lyon's face for an explanation.

"I'm sorry, Father," he choked, fighting the tears.

Lyon held his face somberly in his hands, then shook his shoulders.

"Don't talk rot. You were terrific!"

"Not terrific enough," Nicholas croaked, his voice raw.

"Bull*shit*!" Lyon cried, biting down on the second syllable. "You were letter perfect. It went just the way we planned. Without a hitch."

"The time?"

"Four-fifty-six." He fumbled for the stopwatch and hung it in front of Nicholas's nose. "See?"

"Oh, God, Father," Nicholas moaned, his nose streaming, his legs buckling.

Lyon put his arm around Nicholas.

"Go ahead, let it out."

Ashamed, Nicholas pulled back, shuddering.

"Dad ordered champagne," he announced with a giggle.

"Fine."

"He wants you to join us."

"Love to."

His sobs having subsided, Nicholas struggled to cobble over the fissures in his control. He couldn't let the others see him like this, bawling like a two-year-old.

Lyon plucked the handkerchief from his breast pocket and handed it to Nicholas. It was soft and white as an amice.

Furiously he blew his nose; then, with a sheepish look at Lyon, he pocketed the handkerchief.

"Ready, mister?"

"Ready," Nicholas sighed.

Lights dimmed, the trio gone, the waiters hovering impatiently nearby, the room was almost deserted. The last stragglers were calling it a night.

At the Manion table, champagne still flowed.

Tired of the post-mortems and the feeble rationales of Uncle Bob and his mother, Nicholas waited to hear what his father would have to say. Polite but uncommunicative, Thomas was still ominously quiet.

Uncle Bob had queried the judges. Dr. Cheviot claimed Nicholas had run overtime, 5:10 by his count. Miss Peters had disagreed, insisting she saw the dial read 4:55, but Patter sided with Cheviot, who had accidentally pressed the knob, returning the hand to zero, erasing the proof.

Lyon, quietly, was adamant. Four-fifty-six it was.

Uncle Bob repeated Cheviot's apologies. "So very sorry. Such rum luck."

As Thomas sipped his Dom Perignon, Lyon tried to muzzle the well-meant excuses with practiced stoicism. Karl sat rigid.

"Just a bad break," he heard Lyon say for what seemed the tenth time.

Nicholas was never going to put himself in this spot again. It was one thing to lose because your teammates didn't hold up their end. He couldn't do a blessed thing about that. But from now on when he, all by himself, went out on a limb, he would make sure he had his ass covered. Solo, he had an edge.

It was an important lesson. Stick to what you can control. That way you could take your best shot. Keep the odds in your favor. Never again would he let anyone who mattered to him down. Most of all, himself. Not if he could help it.

"Perhaps it's God's will," he heard his mother suggest, unconsciously stitching her sampler of submission.

God, Nicholas thought, had had nothing to do with it. She who was so fond of maxims, hadn't she heard? He helped those who helped themselves. Open yourself up to a sucker punch? Then don't cry if you're decked. That was why

Nicholas always felt stupid praying before a game. What did God care who won? He didn't play favorites, back one team against another team. Even Notre Dame lost once in a while. But with talent, discipline, and judgment, Nicholas just knew you could manage to come up aces.

"The champagne is delicious," Lyon said, lifting his glass in a grateful toast.

"I'm pleased you like it, Father," Thomas replied. "You did an excellent job."

"Nick did all the work."

"Be that as it may, you coached him brilliantly, far better than *I* would have."

What's he driving at? Nicholas wondered. I get my humility-with-a-hook from him. He couldn't be *jealous*, could he?

"I doubt that, but thank you," Lyon countered graciously.

"Too bad," his father went on, "that the deck was stacked."

Nicholas saw Karl nod his head vigorously.

"Now, Thomas," Uncle Bob sputtered, "even if the judges' watch went haywire, that's no reason—"

"The fix was in," his father said softly.

"Damn straight," Karl agreed.

"It's not like you to be a sore loser," Uncle Bob cajoled.

"Didn't you notice how that fruit almost choked on the word 'Catholic'?" His eyes were glistening now, combatively. "No way to prove it, of course, he saw to that." Then, as though making sure, he added, "You must have noticed his snide knock at the Jesuits."

"Oh, dear, really now," his mother cautioned.

Thomas was rolling.

"The Heublein Hotel. Did you know I worked here, must be forty years ago. A busboy I was. And it's still a place you've got to prove you're not the Pope's errand boy."

"Thomas, honestly . . ." Uncle Bob tried to stop him.

"Bob Toppings, do you think I'm deaf? 'St. Paul's *Catholic* High School.' " He mimicked Cheviot maliciously, making *Catholic* sound like something that should be hidden from sight.

"Mr. Manion, even if you're right . . ." Lyon said.

"I've heard that little twist most of my life," his father asserted fiercely, lighting a cigarette.

". . . there's nothing to be done about it."

Nicholas could see from Lyon's face that he bought it.

"You can fight back, by God!" Thomas thundered. He turned to stare straight into Lyon's eyes. "Nick tells me that before you took the cloth you were a bomber, a pilot."

Lyon nodded grimly.

"You don't look like any conscientious objector to me. Fight back! Maybe not here, not now, but wherever, whenever. What's that motto of Jimmy Hoffa's? *Illigitimi non carborundum*, or somesuch?"

Lyon smiled.

"Anyway," Thomas pressed, "what it boils down to is: *don't let the bastards grind you down.*"

"Thomas, really—" his mother flinched in shock.

"The Latin leaves something to be desired, but the sentiments are understandable," Lyon conciliated.

"Or as Kennedy would say: 'Don't get mad, get even.' " As though sensing he'd made a *faux pas* by advocating vengeance in front of a priest, Thomas grudgingly added: "Not very Christlike of me, I suppose."

"Our Lord admonished us to turn the other cheek," Lyon offered suavely. "He did not command it."

Unless Nicholas was crazy, Lyon was doing his damnedest to cede authority to Thomas.

"Thank you," Thomas beamed.

"Still," Lyon interjected, "there's no point in stooping to their level."

God! he agrees with my father, Nicholas realized.

"Do you really think . . . ?" he asked the priest.

"It's the likeliest explanation, mister. You were the best. And my watch isn't fast."

"You're not just saying that?"

"I wouldn't lie to you, Nick."

"Well, unjust or not, what's to be done about it?" Uncle Bob complained. "He still lost."

"But there is a different way to look at it," Lyon continued, ignoring Uncle Bob, gazing hard at Thomas.

"Such as?"

"Offer it up."

Nicholas saw his mother nod, drawing the consolation of faith around her shoulders like a shawl.

"Oh, come on, Father, no son of mine is going to lie down like some namby-pamby," his father flared. "Nick's not one to back off from a fight."

"Not so much back off as enlarge the ring." Lyon was firm.

"I don't get it," Thomas insisted, scrutinizing the others' faces.

"Turn it to advantage," Lyon went on smoothly. "Inside-out. There are times when no matter how badly we want something, no matter how valiantly we pursue it, no matter even how truly we deserve it, it's just not in the cards. Stacked deck or no."

"Grin and bear it?" Thomas asked acidly.

"Triumph through it," Lyon said. "Accept what you can't control. And learn what you can."

"Great jumpin' jehosaphat, I don't believe my ears! Don't fight city hall? Jaysus, we'd all still be pounding the beat or washing fancy people's dirty underwear if we had that mentality."

"That's not what I mean," Lyon murmured.

"He means accept God's will," Diana said. "It's all for a purpose. Yes, Father?"

"The ironies of fate," Thomas mocked. "That's a big help."

"The mystery of Providence," Lyon said quickly.

Exasperated, his father snapped for a waiter, and instantly the check, all ready, appeared.

"Choose your ground carefully," Lyon continued. "Know when to go in, guns blazing, and when to pull a tactical retreat."

What's the opposite of a Pyrrhic victory? Nicholas wondered. A salvific loss?

"Most of all," Lyon finished, "know your enemy."

"And love him, I presume?"

Nicholas suddenly remembered the nuns, in the third grade, sending them home to pray for the repose of the soul of Joseph Stalin.

"Yes, love him, if possible." Lyon didn't flinch. "Not what he does, of course. And even if he turns out to be yourself."

Nicholas watched his father stub out his cigarette and then slap several bills onto the table. "I've got a rough day tomorrow, so . . ." He stood up. "I'm sorry. Maybe it's the champagne, but it's all a bit too casuistic for me. He extended his hand, which Lyon took. "Good night, Father."

"Maybe so," Lyon conceded.

"Karl, dear, we'd better get you home."

Karl slunk off, all but Lyon trailing behind him.

"Nick," Lyon said in a low, insistent voice, as though emphasis would accomplish what his words so far had not. "You deserved to win, and still you lost. You're too big a person to nurse a grudge. Rise above it. It's unfair, a big letdown, tough. But faith makes sense of everything, even the senseless. What matters is what you do with this. You can let it eat away at you like gangrene, or let it get better." He patted Nicholas on the back. "O.K.? Shall we go?"

"Whatever you say," Nicholas replied, still unconvinced. Suddenly he felt bone-tired, past tears and sick of talk.

His mother had gone to bed just after they reached home, telling him he'd feel better tomorrow. Now as he lay in bed, trying to sort out his reaction to the whole absurdly up-and-down evening, he could hear Thomas rattling around downstairs. An ice tray cracked violently open.

It was highway robbery. I deserved to win, Nicholas told himself.

But Lyon was right. There wasn't a bloody thing he could do about it.

Learn from it.

Right.

What he'd like to do was grill that old geezer, Cheviot—force-feed him a dose of truth serum.

But no ump ever reversed his call.

Outside, snow swirled, a few stray flakes skittering across his desktop through the half-open window. There was no moon, but a trio of stars pulsed faintly like golden grottoes.

Grin and bear it was just not his style. *Loaded* for bear was more like it. Learn from it? Cold comfort. A big help.

He should just sleep it off, but the more he buried his face in the pillow, the more he was stark, staring awake and p.o.ed.

There was a creaking sound from the stairwell. He could hear ice cubes tolling against glass. Thomas was coming up.

Play possum, Nicholas told himself.

Spying through slitted eyes, he saw his father peering into the dark room. Nicholas, eyes clamped shut, parceled out his breaths in steady cadence. Thomas's were loud, wheezy. For several moments he stood stock-still, then muttered, "Bastards!"

Please go to bed, Nicholas urged silently. I'm too old for these late-night tuck-ins, he told himself. I'm no baby crying in the dark.

He could take whatever was dished out.

His father was concerned for him, he knew that, so why

did he resent this intrusion? It was pretty awful to think of your own father as invading your privacy.

He just wanted to lick his wounds by himself. There were some things no one could help.

The icy wind whistled, making Nicholas shiver. It slammed the shutters against the side of the house, sounding like the clapper the servers used at High Mass. He heard his father slurp his drink and stumble across to the window. It whined as he lowered it.

Rolling over, Nicholas felt his feet brush the covers, bunched at his ankles. Opening his eyes for a moment, he saw his father staring outside, etched by the thin light that spidered from the hallway.

He kept perfectly still. Thomas crept over and Nicholas felt the comforter being pulled up over him, its familiar, satiny surface smooth and pleasant against his cheek.

His father's hand brushed his hair and patted his forehead lightly, the fingers still cold from the glass and smelling of nicotine.

"Dear old pal," he whispered.

Suddenly Nicholas felt his father's lips graze his cheek roughly, almost catching the corner of his mouth. The smell of brandy was overpowering, sweet as vomit.

"Sleep well," Thomas said. "Tonight was nothing." He sounded as if in a trance, his voice low, robotlike. "There's nothing to be afraid of. You'll go far. There's no limit to what you can be. None." With a deep sigh he pulled himself up and made his unsteady way down the wincing stairs.

No, Nicholas told himself, it was *not* nothing.

Whatever worlds there were to conquer, he knew now with a vengeance: put your trust in what lasts. Maybe fate could never be understood, but it was only heads-up to choose your weapons and your arenas with exquisite care.

There were plenty of things that were within a man's control.

The trick was to home in on them.

Part Two

HIDDEN LIFE

10

It was the driest summer anyone could remember. The farmers mournfully surveyed their seared crops and turned their eyes, in dubious entreaty, toward Washington or Heaven. The brittle bush veining the countryside was a tinderbox: in parks and forests, many closed indefinitely, patrols of rangers were doubled, then redoubled. Birds drooped in flight and grazing cows slumped exhausted beneath patches of shade. The thermometer stuttered in the upper nineties.

But the car was air-conditioned, and Nicholas was grateful for it. He leaned back against the cool leather and closed his eyes and let his mind wander as his father's driver, Gerald, sped the car soundlessly toward the Jesuit seminary in Cornwall.

Everyone should set aside five minutes a day for daydreaming, Nicholas thought. The mind needs time to be aimless, to roam freely. Denied it, he believed, distractions would invade at the most awkward, inconvenient times, destroying concentration.

And he wanted his wits about him today, of all days.

As if to emphasize the momentousness of his undertaking, today was not just a fresh start, but also the Feast Day of Saint Ignatius of Loyola, the founder of the Society of Jesus.

Introibo ad altare Dei, he prayed. I go to the altar of God.

Early last April, Nicholas had received his acceptance to Harvard. His father had beamed with pride, pronouncing the name as though it were a numinous, exotic kingdom.

"If it was good enough for Jack Kennedy, I suppose it'll do," Thomas declared.

But Nicholas had a secret plan. His sense of vocation had grown, nourished by prayer and Father Lyon's artful guidance, until by his junior year it took shape, sharp and commanding and inevitable.

It would be, he knew, a mortal sin to resist a vocation. With all due respect to Harvard, the decision had been an easy one.

Confiding in no one but Father Lyon, Nicholas had plunged voraciously into Jesuit lore, reading for hours in the school library. This "least society," as they ironically called themselves, whether as pioneers or educators, spiritual prodigies or papal commandoes, seemed more and more to Nicholas the shock troops of the one true Faith.

Jesuits excelled as teachers and missionaries, artists and scientists, gray eminences and martyrs. They Christianized continents, and were accused of assassinating popes. They served as confessors to monarchs, and constructed a model community among the Guarani Indians of Paraguay. Father Kino pioneered cattle ranching in California. Father Fritz mapped the Amazon. Father Clavijero compiled a monumental history of Mexico. There was a Jesuit apothecary in Canada, a pawnshop in Naples, tea estates in South America, and a gold brokerage in Nagasaki. Mandarin Jesuits attended the Ming princess while others embraced lepers in Mozambique.

Jesuits invented the box confessional, the magic lantern, and the first encyclopedia. Jesuit schools produced Voltaire and Richelieu, Corneille and Bernini, Lope de Vega and Diderot.

If it was possible, as some attested, that Himmler patterned the SS after the Society, it was true that almost fifty Jesuits died at Dachau. In perverse tribute, enemies saw their hand everywhere: they were blamed for the Great Plague, the Dreyfus affair, and the assassination of Lincoln; a Jesuit was even rumored to have ghost-written *Mein Kampf*.

"Formation" took fifteen years. After the two-year novitiate dedicated to spiritual training, there were two years of classical studies in what was called the juniorate. Three years of philosophy followed, then a like period called regency, during which the majority taught in Jesuit schools. Then came three years of theology, and ordination. After this, there was another year of theology, and finally tertianship, a one-year echo of the novitiate, a reminder that *etiam si sacerdotes sint*— even if they be priests—humble labor and spiritual simplicity were the crucial tools for their worldly toil. Many Jesuits, called "professed," took an additional vow beyond poverty, chastity, and obedience: a vow of obedience to the Pope, a promise to stand ready to do his bidding at any time, anywhere.

Just after Christmas, Nicholas had taken the Society's exhaustive test, and been interviewed by the rector of his school. In late April he learned that he had been accepted.

The religious life, he believed, was not only an opportunity to propitiate God, to requite His bounty and worship Him utterly; it was also a way out of the unwieldy, disappointing secular world. Within the Society's comprehensive system, by means of its strong personal authority, you achieved concrete proof of your success: the love of God and your fellows. In "the Life," as they called it, things behaved, as he had already begun to find they did not "in the world."

At the seminary, through God's grace, he could belong, be in control. He could give the unpredictable the slip. Because the Roman collar not only separated, it liberated: it freed the priest from worldly entanglements so he could serve both God and man better. Purely.

To hear the faithful say "Father" must be tremendous: to celebrate Mass and hear confession, to advise and instruct, to comfort and ennoble. As Christ raised Lazarus from physical death, so His priest administered the cure for the spiritual death of sin.

He believed his call was authentic, but after a point reason was useless in the face of an annunciation so powerfully intuitive that it carried the force of dogma. Just as the Oval Office was now the height of secular hope for any ambitious Catholic boy, for Nicholas and others like him the priesthood represented the zenith of ideals in action.

While he was growing up, Nicholas realized, he had taken the Faith for granted, just another item in the list that constituted who he was: son, Irish, American, Catholic. He carried with him what Karl acerbically labeled "the only *the* Church" automatically, heedlessly. But as he probed and pondered his future, he discovered that his faith was indistinguishable from his very self. It was the total, uncompromising and enduring nature of the Church that beckoned him to Cornwall.

The Ecumenical Council convening now in Rome was determined to foster Christian unity ("That they may be One," Christ had prayed), and to revamp Church ritual so as to bring believers more actively into the Mystical Body of Christ. Pope John XXIII had decreed *Aggiornamento*, opening his Petrine arms to the "separated brethren" and beyond. Certainly some change was needed. Nicholas could see that. But not in fundamentals. The Church was irrefragable, as though blessed with a special dispensation from history. Truth was not relative, it was immutable. And the Society of Jesus clung tenaciously to the eternals. They continued to seize the human will and tame it, hammer it, bend it toward the pursuit of excellence both spiritual and secular.

"I welcome it," Nicholas told himself.

When he told his father, Thomas sat for several minutes in silence. His back poker-straight against his black leather wingback in the library, his whole bearing too imperial for the meager clothes ordinary men wore, Thomas faced his expectant son.

Was he disappointed? Nicholas remembered all too well his father's proprietary scorn years ago when Father Lyon had implied a vocation in his comments at the end of his First Communion essay.

Then Thomas stood, his shoulders held stiffly back like a general on parade, walked past the fireplace, grasped Nicholas's hands, and shook them with such warmth they were both embarrassed. His eyes drilled into Nicholas, as though seeking that certitude, that mastery of self that, if he could not locate it, he would try to transmit to his son by brute force of will. Slipping his hand across Nicholas's wrist, in the clasp of the ancient warriors, he whispered in a hoarse voice, "The Praetorian Guard."

The looming rigors of religious life, even the three solemn vows, did not daunt Nicholas for a moment. Poverty held little terror when all your basic needs were provided for. It connoted a state of mind only, an obliviousness to material things. None of the comfortable Jesuits he knew would recognize actual privation or duress. That seemed reserved today for the Foreign Missions.

As for obedience, Nicholas was an old hand at that.

And chastity, with its accompanying tradition of celibacy, aroused not even a flicker of anxiety. Still—and now forever—a virgin, Nicholas's sexual memory was an ebbing, hazily glimpsed kaleidoscope of fumbling, thwarted half-experiences. Only once, with Maureen, had he given his heart in reckless tenderness. Letting off steam with Karl had been only child's play.

Pledging himself to God completely was not much of a sacrifice, he decided cockily, for here at last was a Person to whom he could bind himself *in toto*: God and Parent, Master and Best Friend. The perfection of Jesus Christ insured that whatever his needs, He would always be there, ready to take Nicholas's hand. In the world things were always going wrong, but when you pledged to God, "I am all Yours," He took care.

The vows were crucial tools, not really a sacrifice at all, he concluded. But the idea of celibacy troubled him for a different reason: his father. He had been afraid that Thomas's dynastic hope would be bittered by his being denied grandchildren. In a halting, clumsy fashion, Nicholas communicated his anxiety.

"Oh, I see," his father said. "Not to worry. I haven't been bamboozled by the conceit that the Manion line would insure my immortality. I've never subscribed to that bit of secular bunk. Besides," he added, "didn't you know? I'd much rather give you to God than to some girl."

He said that in a mordant voice that seemed to Nicholas less a comment on his parents' wintry marriage than something stranger. Thomas's usual capering mock-vanity here had a harder, more defiantly portentous edge. Underneath the joke Nicholas recognized his father's utter candor: only God, Thomas was saying, deserved *his* son.

Secure in his vocation, Nicholas still recoiled slightly. But he was very moved. God's Praetorian. Unbidden and alien, the link thus forged did not dim the luster of his father's pride and hope. Rather, the incongruity added to the brightness. As sure of himself as he was, his father was even surer.

His mother was a different story. She was proud of him, of course, but instead of direct congratulations, she solicited the applause of others to her son's exploits. When he was admitted to Harvard, she immediately telephoned all her friends. But when he announced his intention to enter the

Jesuits, she rather formally congratulated him and then said no more about it. Nicholas believed Thomas was thrilled, but he sensed that his mother had reservations. As so often before, when it came to her husband's prodigious enthusiasm, she seemed in concord, but not in tune.

Her habitual diffidence prevailed until one night when, his father away on business, she insisted on being heard.

"Nicholas, dear, are you certain, in your own mind, that this is the right course?"

"Of course I am, Mother. It's hardly a snap decision."

"No, I'm sure it's not. But have you really asked yourself what is at the bottom of this?"

"I have a vocation. It's that simple."

"But are you certain it's genuine, and not perhaps a response to your father's hopes, and your teachers'?"

Nicholas noticed her rolling and unrolling a slip of paper as she spoke, the strangeness of this moment preventing her from masking her nervousness.

"I believe it is. Of course, it didn't spring up in a vacuum. I've been influenced a great deal. But pretty much to the good, wouldn't you say?"

"Presumably." She continued to fiddle with the paper. "So you are clear in your own mind that this step, now, is right for you. You have so many possibilities, after all."

Nicholas was puzzled. Wasn't the answer obvious? "Of course I am, Mother. You *know* that."

"Then nothing I can say or do will dissuade you." With that, heaving a sigh, she tossed the paper into an ashtray, walked over to him, and kissed him on the forehead. "Bless your heart." Then she walked out of the room.

Nicholas fished the paper out of the ashtray and smoothed it straight. It was a check, made out to him, for ten thousand dollars.

What had she been thinking of! She just didn't understand him at all. Her aborted gesture was so unprecedented, so extreme, he was shocked. How profound her misgivings must be, he thought, to make her spread aside the protective cobwebs of protocol, to step so boldly out of character.

He would never be able to figure her out.

Maybe if she'd had other children, things would have been different. Nicholas had often seen scandal simmering in the eyes of new acquaintances: an only child? In a good Catholic family?

In a way it was his fault that he didn't have brothers or sisters (Karl had five). He had, as Uncle Bob put it, "come out wrong," and "her tubes had to be tied." A hysterectomy.

That explained what she had done, didn't it? It wasn't just her Tory fastidiousness that recoiled at early vocations, as though spying a salesman at the front door. She too, maybe even more than his father, must yearn for grand-children.

Maybe if Thomas had permitted her to work, she would have been happier. They had quarreled about it over the years. But his father had been adamant: "No wife of mine is going to get a job. We're not that newfangled, not by a long shot." That was one place where Thomas should have bent a little.

Gazing out at the hazy landscape, Nicholas jerked his mind back to today.

When Jesus exhorted, "Take up your cross and follow me," Nicholas, well tutored by his father, didn't bat an eye. He would be a Jesuit. He would strive to serve God's will. The years ahead would be devoted to constructing an axis, against devilish odds, between himself and God. Embarking on a re-creation of Christ's hidden life, those long years of quiet preparation in Nazareth before commencing His minis-try, Nicholas felt exultation. He had been called. And he *would* be chosen. The truth of his vocation to the priesthood was the very anchor of his being. The ubiquitous temptations that stalked the path between today and the day of his ordination were not snares, but goads; they would keep him on his toes.

Approaching the seminary, Nicholas considered he had found a secret that was childlike in its simplicity. Christ had said that the man who would find himself must first lose himself. But within that paradox Nicholas sensed a subtler truth: true humility consisted not in thinking little of yourself, but in not thinking of yourself at all. That was the ideal to be attained, to consummate the self by consuming it.

It was romance, of course, to presume you could attain it overnight. That was for firebrands and fools. Or saints. The struggle was constant to put that secret to work, to give it power enough to wrestle pride to—at best—a draw. But God's true servant—the new man reborn through grace— was measured by his success in emptying himself of personal will. Nicholas yearned to be filled with that humility in which humiliation is impossible because the self, banished from care, prostrates itself before the divine and, *mirabile dictu*, penetrates it.

The car drew closer. Despite his determination, Nicholas knew that his decision to change his ways was just that, a decision, a tentative alliance made with his unpredictable and unwieldy nature. Patterns obeyed for so long didn't vanish with a snap of the fingers. So relentless a need to excel would not go gracefully. But, pursuing his vocation, Nicholas was playing for the highest stakes imaginable.

That was the crucial difference. For the first time, he believed, his need to triumph had focused on a worthy target. The prospect of attaining the priesthood made Nicholas's past exploits seem puny. For a long time he had searched for the battleground that would test his mettle to the utmost: now he believed he had found it.

He was startled from his reverie by Gerald's voice: "Nick, we're there." He flicked a switch on the dashboard, and the window to his left smoothly descended. Next to the car stood a sturdy man of sixty or more, with skin like polished walnut and amused brown eyes. Just ahead loomed rusty iron gates.

The old man leaned toward the window and brushed dust from his faded cassock. "Welcome, Brother. *Pax Christi.* I'm the porter. Most of the others are here already. You'll find them waiting for you inside the main building."

He didn't stay to hear Nicholas's murmured "Thank you, Father," but strode athletically toward the gates. Extracting a heavy key chain clamped to the cincture around his waist, he fingered the largest key and inserted it in the lock. The gates creaked open, the porter stepped aside, and the car inched forward up the driveway.

What struck Nicholas at once was the cheesiness. The seminary sat on a poky hill, surrounded by acres of parched, brownish field. To the south stood a large apple orchard, leached of bloom by the merciless sun. To the north slouched a large barn; he could see a horse poking its head through the half-door. The main building, four stories high, painted cheerless institutional white, was a squat, boxy rectangle perched on what would, but for the drought, be a patch of paradise. Nicholas had expected something awesome, a medieval edifice that evoked its past and proclaimed its purpose. But this was banal, as bloodless and prosaic as a public school. Devoid of drama, it gave no clue to the resonant mysteries that waited within.

Nicholas told himself not to let the vapidity of the building daunt him. It was self-indulgent to be fazed by a lack of grandeur. But he felt cheated somehow, he could not deny it. Obviously it was a fault: feeling shortchanged aesthetically was a mark of vanity. After all, he mused, there could be no more mundane a place than a manger in Bethlehem.

The novices shuffled nervously in the parlor, its corduroy sofa, ill-matched chairs, formica-topped tables, and pair of indifferent landscapes another rebuke to Nicholas's sense of theater. Musty from lack of use, the room seemed an after-thought, designed to handle infrequent parental visits. Nothing important happens here, he thought. It was a perfunctory, utilitarian window to the world, ordinarily—and preferably—kept shut.

The door swung open and a trim, immaculately groomed pink-cheeked priest about forty-five years old walked in. His graying blond hair was crewcut, his light blue eyes alert behind yellow-rimmed, dark-tinted glasses. His thin, cautious nose and even, fastidious lips gave him the air of a clerical Woodrow Wilson. Standing beside the door, he held his left hand, palm up, against his stomach, while the right curled on top of it, so that only the fingers touched. His cassock was shiny at the elbows.

"Gentlemen," he began in a precise, reedy voice, signaling an end to the nervous shuffling, "I am Father Edmund Kane, Master of Novices. Welcome to St. Ignatius Novitiate. Let us begin with a prayer."

They knelt.

"In the name of the Father, the Son, and the Holy Ghost, Amen," intoned Father Kane. Nicholas crossed himself gravely, considering, as he had been taught, each Person of the Blessed Trinity. Then the Master recited the Ignatian prayer, Thomas Manion's favorite: "Dear Jesus, my Captain and my King, give me the grace to be generous: to give and not to count the cost, to fight and not to heed the wounds, to labor and not to ask for any reward save knowing that I do Thy holy will. Amen."

Opening his eyes, Nicholas saw a couple of the others glancing sheepishly about. When prayer was finished, this always seemed to happen, as though the presence of his peers made the young man fear his seriousness was suspect. Adolescent piety often had a tinge of artifice. The zealot in a boy would assume a formal pose of devotion, while the scamp, demanding equal time, would knee the fellow alongside. Public prayer was a tribal act and so always prone to self-consciousness. "No boy worth his salt wants to be thought a sissy," Thomas Manion once said. It was important that spiritual ardor be expressed, but it was dangerous to go overboard. Hotdogging in chapel, or campaigning for "brownie points," sparked instant ridicule from the other boys. So, even here at St. Ignatius, Nicholas mused, prayer was less a humble dialogue with God than a straining attempt by each novice to strike a slippery balance between reverence and shamming.

The Master gestured for them to rise and be seated, and then began to speak. *"Pax Christi."* They bowed their heads automatically at the mention of the Lord's name, as they had been taught. "Welcome to the Society of Jesus." They bowed again. "You embark today on a long, arduous journey that will culminate for most of you, indeed I fervently pray for *all* of you, fifteen years hence, at the end of your formation as Jesuits. It is an awesome undertaking, but it should not intimidate you, for Our Lord, in a very real sense, will be with you every step of the way, with you at prayer, with you during your studies—which will make you the equal of any secular scholar—with you on the playing field, with you at your humble, menial labors and with you most of all during the temptations that, considering the grandeur of your vocations, must inevitably come your way." Father Kane bit off his sentences with meticulous precision. This was a speech he had given often. "You have been chosen, by the grace of God, to become instruments of His will." They bowed again. Was he doing it on purpose? Nicholas wondered. "I am here to help you in every way I can. At St. Ignatius we offer you a community in which you can thrive. But the final responsibility resides with you: the duty to respond, with devotion, patience, and courage, to the demands that God will make of you. The journey toward perfection is perilous and fraught with danger on every side, but the end is always in sight, and it is indeed glorious: to become one with Him.

"Observance of the Rule," Father Kane continued, "laid

down for us by Sanctus Pater Noster, will steel you for every trial that Satan sends your way. Your vocation is an affront to him, never forget that. But whatever the temptation, sufficient grace in all its divine amplitude will be there; you have only to pray and cooperate for it to repel the mightiest doubt. As Ignatius says, 'He who wills the end, wills the means.' "

The Master paused and reached inside his cassock, extracting a white file card.

"Our Founder puts it this way in his Fundamental Principle: 'Man has been created to praise, reverence, and serve our Lord God, thereby saving his soul. Everything else on earth has been created for man's sake to help him achieve this purpose.' Later he adds, 'So it follows that man has to use these things as far as they help, and abstain from them when they hinder his purpose.'

"Having been called to a higher way, we are indeed blessed as Jesuits in knowing that God's will for us has been spelled out in the daily schedule, the *Ordo Regularis*. Observance is our path to sanctity. *Ora et labora*. We strive daily to imitate Our Lord's hidden life, which the Gospel describes thus: 'And Jesus increased in wisdom and stature and in favor with God and man.' Obedience is the invincible means to that end: if you obey, no fault is possible. As Saint Jerome says, 'Oh sovereign liberty! Oh holy and blessed security by which one becomes almost impeccable!'

"We are here as a citadel of light, living proof of the enduring majesty of Divine Love. So we cultivate a holy indifference to the things of the world, secure in our faith that we have been called. As Saint Paul says in Ephesians 6:11, 'Put on the whole armor of God, that ye may stand against the wiles of the devil.' " He replaced the card in his pocket.

"It may be helpful to recall the origin of our Founder's vocation. His right leg shattered by cannonshot from French artillery, Ignatius suffered the agony of having his leg broken and reset, twice. A lump of bone had to be sawed off, and a rack used to stretch the leg to normal length. But it wasn't successful. Taking this as a sign that God had a different purpose for him, he prayed ceaselessly and was blessed with a vision of the Virgin and Child. He vowed instantly to love them, loyally and chastely.

"And he did. From that moment on, he tells us in his autobiography, he was free from all temptations of the flesh! As you must be as well, for the very word 'purity' of course derives from *puer*. Boy. Always remember the example of those Jesuit saints, far younger than you: Saint John Berchmans and Saint Aloysius Gonzaga. No matter what the temptation, we are confident, for our Faith teaches us that 'everything is easy for those who love Christ.'

"Like them, like every Jesuit, you have been singled out by the glorious sign of your vocations, to hear one day those tremendous words, *Tu es sacerdos in aeternam*. You are a priest of the order of Melchisedech forever."

Father Kane relaxed visibly, then said, "Now, Brothers—that is now how you are to address, and consider, each other—you have an hour to walk around the grounds and get acquainted. Those of you who smoke may do so outdoors, but I suggest you cease immediately, since novices are not permitted to smoke. All tobacco will be confiscated when you receive your cassocks. As you doubtless know, the Holy Father asked, as a special sacrifice, that members of the Society renounce the habit. All right, you may go now."

Nicholas had learned to be wary of his tendency to make snap judgments, but there was something eerie about Father Kane. His control was so vehement it seemed maintained by raw will. Looked at closely, for all its martial surface, it seemed fragile, this calm worn like armor. Used to the bluff, hard-drinking Jesuit cronies of his father and his own expansive, jocular teachers—not to mention the mannered and unpredictable Father Lyon—Nicholas was puzzled, and a little unsettled, by this correct, contained man who for the next two years would be the sole authority to whom he was answerable.

11

Trailing the other novices out of the main building, Nicholas turned right and strode past two clay tennis courts, chalk lines dimly visible, the nets sagging, deserted in the harsh glare. Just beyond he spied two swiftly shifting shadows reflected on a cement wall at least ten feet high. A pair of second-year men were playing handball. Oblivious to the troupe of wide-eyed neophytes filing past them, they battered the ball with gusto. Farther in the distance stood the orchard; in the lengthening afternoon the trees seemed to flinch under their burden of pale fruit.

Nicholas stopped and studied his new colleagues. Falling naturally together and enthusiastically rehashing the latest baseball game were the exact replicas of the fellows Nicholas had played ball with in high school. He listened to the predictable chatterboxing.

"Did you see that catch Mays made on Aaron?" one said.

"Incredible!" another agreed.

"He's still no Mantle," a third insisted.

"You're nuts! There's no comparison . . ."

"Aw, go on, if Mickey weren't almost . . . paralyzed, he'd even steal more bases than Willie Mays."

"You're full of it!"

"—out of your gourd—"

"—just not dealing from a full deck—"

The jocks: gruff, hearty, stalwart, and uncomplicated, they were a familiar breed, and made Nicholas strangely uneasy.

He had invariably been a star performer, lacking nothing in talent or guts. And he had found football and basketball—indeed, virtually any sport except for golf, which he disdained—plentiful in excitement and reward. He thrived on competition, welcomed practice, and positively reveled in the countless honing and polishing hours of preparation for a game. Most of all, he loved to win; that was what drew him to sports, the lovely simplicity of victory and defeat.

Nicholas believed there was no cleaner, more precise, and more immediate way to test his mettle, but he could never penetrate the sweet mystique of games, that naive, secret world where young men flung themselves recklessly into clear, decisive contest on a battleground that was childish but exalting.

He had always been apart from those he played with, never truly a jock. His teammates respected him for his talent and his discipline, but they kept him at a distance. He was different, and they could tell he did not really belong. In a way that they would have been hard put to explain and would never have admitted, they resented him. Not because of his performance; that was crucial to their success, and they liked being winners. No, they were resentful, Nicholas believed, because they sensed, profoundly but inarticulately, that he was using them in the same way he used the opposition, that for him there wasn't a dime's worth of difference between outshining his teammates and conquering the other team. And they were right, Nicholas had to admit. He had contended for himself, using all others like props, background for his solitary drama. It would be the same here at St. Ignatius. He would play, and play hard, but, looking at the cluster of athletes buzzing animately, he knew he would not be one of them.

Looking around, Nicholas spied a taut, whey-faced young man gazing at him through steel-rimmed glasses. Nicholas smiled in greeting and saw the intense bantam shift quickly away. Undeterred, he walked over and extended his hand.

"Nick Manion," he introduced himself.

"I know," the boy replied curtly, his face a mask of reserve. He responded to Nicholas's proferred handshake with a weak, finger-pressing squeeze. "Pleased to meet you," he said. Clearing his throat, he went on, "I'm Charles Simpson." He made it sound like a very significant announcement.

"Good to meet you, Chuck," Nicholas said breezily.

Simpson's vanilla face suddenly flushed. "It's *Charles*," the boy stated. Nicholas had touched a nerve.

"Whatever you say."

Simpson nodded; then he turned back to the group. Nicholas moved off alone.

As he walked down the cobblestone path, dotted with dandelions poking through the cracks, he saw that the hand-ball game had ended. One of the players was trudging toward the main building. The other toweled himself slowly and squinted at Nicholas.

He was considerably older than the other novices, twenty-one at least, Nicholas guessed. Straight, glinting black hair; a nose that jutted forward; lips that parted in a welcoming smile.

"Hey, Brother," he said, "come on over."

Nicholas walked across the grass to the edge of the cement court and extended his hand. The young man gave it a quick, strong shake and introduced himself:

"I'm Scott Turner."

"Nick Manion."

"When did you get in?" Turner asked.

"A couple of hours ago. You're a second-year man, right?"

"A *secundi*, yes. And you're a *primi*. So don't forget who's boss. Where're you from?"

"Hartford," Nicholas answered, wondering whether it would be all right to sit down. "My dad's in insurance there," he added. "You?"

"Just a farmboy. Fifty acres in Smyrna, Delaware," Turner explained.

Nicholas didn't know whether to leave or stay. This might be Turner's only time to be alone during the day, and he didn't want to intrude. Still, he wanted to talk to someone who was in the know, who'd been through what he and the others were facing.

"The class system here is pretty rigid, I gather," Nicholas tried.

"Huh?" Turner asked, smiling wryly. "Oh—I see what you mean. Yes. Well, during First Probation—that's what the novitiate is called—the first two years, no one is supposed to speak to us except the Master. And, of course, Father McCarthy, the Latin teacher. But twice during the year we have 'reunions' with the Juniors, so there's some contact."

"How long before we get our cassocks?"

"Not long. You'll find out."

"Till then we're not really novices, right? Just candidates?"

Turner smiled. "I see you know your stuff."

"What I wondered," Nicholas continued, "is are there any special customs or rituals during the beginning—?"

"You mean like hazing?"

"Yeah, or initiation—?"

Turner laughed heartily. "No, nothing *that* entertaining. But things can get pretty baroque." He went on, "What do you think of the place so far?"

"Oh, it's great. Well, I admit it's not what I expected—no turrets and moats and stuff. A bit of an anticlimax, really."

"Don't worry, it'll grow on you. It's what's inside that counts. What about Father Kane? Any first impressions?"

"He's certainly different from most of the Jesuits back home," Nicholas blurted. "Very impressive man, of course," he added hastily.

"Father Kane is *sui generis*. Did anyone ever tell you the smoking story?"

"No."

Turner gave Nicholas his full attention.

"It's a corker. A while back the Pope asked members of the Society to give up smoking as a token of obedience. The morning that the papal request reached his desk, Father Kane, who was a confirmed three-packs-of-Camels-a-day man, plucked the cigarette from his mouth, butted it instantly, and hasn't had a drag since. Father McCarthy was there, that's how I know it's not apocryphal. Impressive? He most certainly is."

Nicholas was pleased. As long as this Turner was around, he'd have at least one person to talk to, when permitted.

"Well, I should get myself into the shower. Good to meet you, Brother Manion."

The novices stood in front of the main building. They waited impatiently for the roly-poly figure in front of them to begin speaking. He was short, with thick, beetling brows, pale blue eyes, a crook nose, and thin, severe, unamused lips.

"My name is Brother Mantello," he began, "and I am the Beadle, which is the term here at St. Ignatius for traffic cop, dispatcher, dorm mother, assignment supervisor, ringmaster, and, right now at least, tour director. If you'll follow me, I'll show you around."

As he executed a practiced about-face that would have done a veteran sergeant major proud, the novices followed him inside and up the central staircase, to the third floor. "These are your quarters," the Beadle trumpeted. The *secundi* had the top floor. "Each of you has been assigned his own cell. There's a name tag on each door." Nicholas found his by process of elimination; it was the last cubicle along the right aisle before you got to the bathroom. He opened the curtain and walked inside. It was very small, no more than six by eight feet, with a narrow window overlooking the grounds. The ceiling was quite high, probably ten feet, he guessed, and on either side of the room plasterboard partitions rose perhaps eight feet toward it, so that anything said was likely to be overheard. There was a single metal-framed cot, a small slate-gray metal desk, a sturdy, straight-backed wooden chair, and a capacious clothes cupboard that opened out like an armoire. At the foot of the bed stood a maple prie-dieu. That was it. The room served the necessities neatly but austerely; it suggested nothing, except for the prie-dieu, about Nicholas's purpose here.

Next the Beadle led them down one flight and into the chapel. Each novice dutifully crossed himself as he entered, careful first to graze his right fingers into one of the founts of holy water placed on either side of the entrance. They slid haphazardly into pews and sat. It was a dark oasis of stillness, the heavy air redolent of incense and candle wax. A stark wooden crucifix towered over the limestone altar, bare now but for two guttering candles. Above and behind, a bank of stained-glass windows cast a muted medley of color across the hushed congregation. In the rear right corner were twin confessionals.

Nicholas bent his head in silent prayer. Here the important work ahead would be done. Here the novices would return several times daily, to meditate, hear Mass, confess, be instructed. This was the nerve center of their spiritual life. It was, Nicholas felt, propitious; here at last his sense of theater had no reason to quail. In this calm, ordered sanctuary, alive with timeless ritual and devotion, the history of prayer and forgiveness invigorated the air. It was, Nicholas realized, almost palpable. This was the true heart of his new home.

At the snap of the Beadle's fingers, the novices rose and followed him out, down the hallway, and into the large, airy, sunlit refectory. Six oak tables covered with white oilcloth stood perpendicular to a longer, ornately carved head table that was topped by a white damask tablecloth. The dwindling sun streamed in through floor-to-ceiling leaded windows.

"All right, Brothers, we'll now go to the ascetory—the study hall and my office," the Beadle announced. They trekked obediently behind him out the door and down the corridor to a large, rectangular room containing several desks and a file cabinet. Dominating all was a huge cork bulletin board so crammed with announcements that it seemed delirious, a pushpin chaos.

He spotted Scott Turner leaning against the wall.

"This is my headquarters. For the next two years you'll come here for assignments, for, as Saint Paul says, 'How shall they gain grace lest they be sent?' If you have any questions—about anything at all—come to me." Gesturing at the bulletin board, he added, "Check here every day for changes in schedule, extra work duty, whatever. If you're in doubt as to whether something is allowed, come here for permission."

He sat down at his desk and reached for a manila folder. He opened it and began passing out sheets of paper. "These mimeographed forms will clue you in to the daily schedule, or *ordo*, as we call it. Any deviation from the *ordo* will either be posted here first thing in the morning, or is not allowed. You can always ask for permission, but exceptions to the rule are few and far between. Now examine those forms carefully and memorize them as soon as you can."

Nicholas and the others gazed at the *ordo*:

    5:30 A.M.   Rise
    6:00 A.M.   Meditation
    7:00 A.M.   Holy Mass

7:45 A.M.	Breakfast
8:30 A.M.	Work
9:00 A.M.	Latin Class
9:30 A.M.	Master's Conference
10:30 A.M.	Examination of Conscience
10:45 A.M.	Spiritual Reading
11:15 A.M.	Work
12:00 Noon	Lunch
1:00 P.M.	Work or Recreation
4:00 P.M.	Prayer (Chapel)
4:15 P.M.	Spiritual Reading
5:00 P.M.	Meditation
5:30 P.M.	Free Time
6:00 P.M.	Holy Rosary
6:30 P.M.	Dinner
7:30 P.M.	Work or Recreation
8:00 P.M.	Points
8:30 P.M.	Litany (Chapel)
9:00 P.M.	Examination of Conscience
9:30 P.M.	Retire

"Acclimatize yourselves as quickly as you can," the Beadle cautioned. "I might as well tell you that there are no prima donnas amongst Ours. We're all here for the same purpose, and we're all subject to the Rule." He pointed to a mammoth book on his desk. "This Diary records every order ever given in the Society. Do not improvise or presume." Brother Mantello leaned back in his chair and smiled sardonically. "If you must make a quick decision, a good rule is to go *against* your natural instinct. Practice holy obedience and you can't go wrong.

"Also, don't indulge in 'personalities.' We aspire to a Christlike spirit of fraternal charity in all things, including recreation. We're all in the same boat.

"If you're outdoors, remember *numquam duo*. Obey the rule of threes. Travel in 'bands.'

"Observe the rule of silence. Between lights-out and Mass the next morning, Sacred Silence is in effect. During the day, if you must speak inside, Latin is required. Outside you may speak English.

"Observe the rule of modesty, modesty of the eyes, the tongue, the body. Those of you who've spent your lives in a locker room, be especially vigilant. Keep your voices down, don't rampage through the corridors, and don't wander around—even in the *lavatorium*—without your clothes on.

"Observe the rule of touch. *Tactus*. Respect the sanctity of your body and your fellow's. Avoid profanity.

"All of this is designed to achieve what Saint Ignatius calls 'custody of the senses.' And the method by which that is achieved is holy obedience. He speaks of our obeying *perinde ac cadaver*—like a corpse. Think about it."

The Beadle then introduced his "Sub," the welcome familiar face, Turner. He handed them small, lined notebooks, as Mantello explained they were to be used to collect insights (or "lights") from meditation and to keep track of progress against *culpas* (or "faults"). He also passed out a miniature set of beads, which was to be carried in one's pocket or pinned inside one's cassock, to tick off *culpas* or "faults" as they occurred, for later tabulation in the appropriate book. A Sub, Nicholas realized, was apparently a sort of quartermaster.

"All right, that should do it, Brothers," Mantello concluded. "Let's see—have I omitted anything? Oh, yes—it's absolutely forbidden to enter another novice's cell. And you may write home once a month. Anything you receive or send will be screened by the Master and passed out at his discretion." There were audible gusts of protest. "If that seems harsh, remember why we're here. The less contact with the world, the better.

"Well . . . that's all for now. Dinner will be at six-thirty. Sharp. Afterwards, the Master will address you in the chapel."

12

Father Kane was giving the novices "points" for their morn- ing meditation. Standing directly in front of the altar, his hands clamped in that awkward, almost prissy grip he'd used in his initial, welcoming remarks, the Master outlined his topic.

"You come here from different families to become one family. Your sense of kinship in Christ Our Lord will be keener to the degree you feel One in Him."

They bowed automatically.

"I want you, tomorrow morning, to imagine a dusty, crowded street in a town not then or since a metropolis of the world. I want you to envision a bustling, toil-worn group of people, not then or since much favored among the affairs of men. I want you to conjure a boy, the same age as yourselves, playing with his friends in the street. He's very like you in many ways. A little bumptious, with a headstrong, slightly urgent air about him. He and his friends play hard, sweating and straining and shouting, when from one of the houses emerges a serenely beautiful woman, calling, 'Jesus! Jesus, come home now.' "

The novices bowed their heads in unison.

"It's a tense moment in the game, the result is still in doubt, and the boy desperately wants to keep playing. But with a small sigh, he stops immediately, and waving so long to his friends, he goes to her. She leads him inside, beckoning toward a small table, where lemonade and little cakes await."

Suddenly the Master's calm, uninflected voice rose sharply. "Perfect filial obedience!" he thundered. "Jesus Christ, Our Lord and Savior, whose Life you came here to emulate in the most profound, literal sense, was once just like you. A boy. A boy with a capital *B*, but a boy nonetheless. As you commence religious life, ponder that lesson in perfect goodwill. Plumb its simple secret, and you will be well launched on your glorious journey. Good night."

Before bed, Nicholas unpacked his trunk, stacking the host of black articles, all neatly name-tagged by Tina, in the cupboard: shirts and socks and workpants, two pairs of shoes, and the black wool suit his father had treated him to at Brooks Brothers. Only the T-shirts and shorts, bright, spanking new, broke the monochromatic unity.

He arranged his toilet kit on the desk, remembering the Saturday morning three years ago when his father had given it to him. He opened it and gazed lovingly at the contents.

Three years ago, when his vocation was starting to inch inexorably into focus: the memory of that night still stung.

Well, he'd kept his promise. Here he was.

He took hold of the prie-dieu and placed it in front of his window. With a tiny breeze gliding softly through his hair, he bent to pray. The grounds were deserted. Only the spiky sawing of crickets invaded Sacred Silence.

The seminary was really something, as exotic as the Foreign Legion. All the rules—don't do this, don't do that.

That Diary in the Beadle's office looked as long as *War and Peace*, Nicholas thought. All the Latin phrases and puzzling code words, like "bands," "faults," and "lights," were charged with meaning. It would be quite a trick just remembering them all.

At least at first.

But he'd get the hang of it, he was sure.

The Jesuits had their own lingo, just like God had His.

At least the period of total silence was limited. The Jesuits weren't Carthusians, after all.

Go against your instincts, the Beadle had said. Fair enough. That was one way to bury bad habits. Willy-nilly. Or *nolens volens*.

All at once he remembered Lyon's parting gift. It was still in the bottom of his trunk. He reached in and retrieved it, hurriedly ripping away the wrapping paper.

The *Missale Romanum*.

A real, grown-up missal, not the usual truncated, simplified version found in church pews.

Nicholas opened the cover, and saw that Lyon had scrawled an epigraph:

> Thou shalt weep no more,
> Though the Lord give you the bread of adversity,
> Thine ear shall hear a voice saying,
> This is the way, walk ye in it.
>
> —Isaiah 30:19

What a man! Nicholas thought. Thank you, Father.

He bent again to ponder what lay ahead. The daily *orda* looked grueling, incessant motion punctuated by the sound of the bell. "Tintinnabulations of the bells," his father would no doubt say. Bells galore. Enough to wake the dead.

Which the *old* Nicholas now was. To be reborn, through obedience. Corpselike obedience, he reminded himself, the phrase arousing an inadvertent shudder of repugnance.

So be it.

The rigorous *ordo*, the taste for martial discipline that the Beadle obviously shared with the Master, did not daunt Nicholas for an instant. Mantello might be a little comic in his major domo assertiveness, but—

Watch that! Nicholas chided himself. Fraternal *charity*.

Whatever it takes, Nicholas vowed. That was Ignatius in a nutshell; everything here was a means to the end.

So what if "custody of the senses" had a sinister, thought-police ring to it? Eros had to be curbed. Nothing must come between the novice and God. The message to the world was: Do Not Disturb.

The bell rang, shrill and insistent.

Thank you, Lord, Nicholas prayed quickly, for bringing me here. Bless my parents, the fathers, and all the other novices. Make me a perfect instrument of Thy holy will. Amen.

He glanced at his watch: ten o'clock on the dot.

He rose and undressed. Before switching off the light, he ran his hand over the rich surface of the toilet kit, and fetched the picture of Thomas and Diana from his billfold, wedging it behind the kit.

As he lay in bed, hearing the other novices cough and shuffle, bedsprings creaking as they settled in, Nicholas realized he was already, in a sense, a new man.

The period of candidacy would be over on Habit Day.

He smiled at the thought.

As soon as he got his cassock, he would sign himself Nicholas Manion, N.S.J.

Novice, Society of Jesus.

13

When the bell clanged at five-thirty, it yanked Nicholas from a deep sleep. He'd been a night owl for years, and hadn't fallen asleep the night before until very late, but, brimming with eagerness, he bounded to the bathroom, furiously brushed his teeth, went to the toilet, and hurried back to his cell. Then he knelt at his prie-dieu and began to meditate.

He strained to imagine the scene as the Master had painted it. Images came in flashes, but they wouldn't behave. There was Jesus as a boy, struggling outdoors under the hot sun. Then he disappeared. Again he was evoked, and again he vanished. This was hard work. Mischief crept into Nicholas's thoughts to distract him. The boy—with a capital *B*—is lost in play, then suddenly this full-blooded youth abandons a torrid game of Judean kick-the-can—because his mother called? Nicholas couldn't identify. It didn't jibe, somehow, and besides, his knees were starting to ache. Before him, invitingly, lay his still-unmade bed. His eyes felt weighted, and his stomach was starting to growl. "I'm not built even to be *awake*," he complained inwardly, "let alone probe the mystery of divine obedience." Maybe the dusty, sweat-drenched "boy with a capital *B*" would've run the second his mother beckoned. But, Nicholas groused, at six in the morning, who needs lemonade and cakes?

So it went until the bell rang for Mass, his mind refusing to settle.

After Mass, the novices proceeded to the refectory, where grace, uttered in stentorian Latin, signaled them to sit. Up now for well over two hours, stomachs noisily and, in some cases, grossly demanding their due, they were greeted by platters of runny eggs, stacks of tepid toast, and large vats of bitter, scalding coffee. So *this* was poverty!

The room soon filled with the sound of lips smacking wolfishly, even, he noticed, from the Juniors' table across the room. No one talked, but the din was considerable. The Master presided from the head table with hawk-eyed calm, taking slow, fastidious bites and frequently arching his eyebrows censoriously when the noise became too vehement. He was flanked by the Rector, Superior of the whole seminary, and the Juniorate teachers.

Nicholas pretended: the powdered eggs were really lush omelettes; the burnt toast, piping hot, flaky croissants dripping with butter; the sour coffee, his mother's choicest Colombian. Here, unlike at his prie-dieu, his mind's eye stayed firmly in focus.

At one of the *secundi* tables he spotted Turner. At Mass, although they were seated just across from one another, he hadn't been able to catch Scott's eye. He had seemed lost in prayer, his concentration impregnable. Some farmboy! Nicholas reflected. When he'd told the Beadle last night about their meeting, his comment about "a farmboy from Delaware" had prompted gales of laughter. "Brother Turner," Nicholas was informed, "was graduated *summa cum laude* from Yale and spent his junior year abroad studying literature at the Sorbonne." *That* explained why he looked older than the other novices. It also explained why he seemed more worldly than his fellows, cryptic, wry, and a bit of an iconoclast—like Nicholas's father. What was he all about, anyway?

The *primi* at Nicholas's table were a study in contrasts. Two of them Nicholas had met yesterday: Bennett, from someplace called Lock Haven, in Pennsylvania, who seemed a bit of an oyster, but very eager, and McMurtrey, a freckle-faced towhead with a puzzled, loony grin stamped on his face. The rotund, pug-nosed, pleasant-looking fellow across the table was Bartlett, from Maine. Rounding out the group was that prepossessing personage, Charles Simpson, who sat coiled and vigilant. His hair had the same military cut, his eyes the identical watchful glare: he was a dead ringer for the Master.

14

The week before the two-day retreat that led to Habit Day passed in a whirlwind of activity. The *ordo* governed all, and its inflexible regimen was adhered to militantly. After breakfast each day, the novices dispersed to their various menial jobs. Nicholas was stuck with *mensa sternit*, which meant clearing the tables after the meal just concluded, and setting it for the one to come. Then they filed to Latin class, where, judging by the erratic forms and pronunciations, it became evident that many of the novices would be doomed, indoors at least, to frustrated noncommunication.

After the Master's orientation conference, the group marched to the chapel for *examen*. This twice-daily examination of conscience taxed even the most scrupulous penitent. They had to sleuth for sin. Was transfiguring toast into croissants a fault, Nicholas wondered. Had he snorted immodestly en route to Mass, or offended charity by dispatching a mild raspberry at the botcher of a Latin conjugation?

Next was scheduled a half hour of spiritual reading in the library. Every saint extant, plus a few of dubious authenticity, claimed his (or her) hagiography. Nicholas scanned several volumes of the devotional primer, Saint Dick-and-Jane variety, before delightedly discovering a biography of Father Kane's namesake, Edmund Campion, by Evelyn Waugh, and a remarkably graphic, privately published account of John de Brebeuf's martyrdom.

Because the novices were denied all access to news of the outside world of any kind, the library carried no periodicals other than the Jesuit magazine, *America*, which was, after all, the house journal. Nicholas had become an avid reader of this tough-minded journal during the last year. It was in its pages he had discovered one of his favorite quotations, from André Gide of all people. The passage, which he had copied in the back of his missal, described the "cramp of salvation" that drives souls to ignore the message of Christ and become "adorers of a niggling divinity with whom they bargain craftily." Nicholas found this to be a useful reminder to be suspicious of the nobility of his own judgments, about others and especially about himself. Finding *America* on the shelves was reassuring, like unexpectedly running into an old friend.

Lunch released the novices to three uninterrupted hours of freedom. Swimming, tennis, handball, and horseback riding were available, but most of the jocks opted for football.

At three forty-five the bell tolled, and the novices trekked to their cells to change for chapel. Then, with permission, they could take what the Beadle wryly called a "Mediterranean cruise," but whose actual designation was *quies*. During this forty-five-minute lull in the regimen, the novices were free to snooze. Otherwise: spiritual reading. Later, congregating outside and forming bands, the novices slowly paced the grounds reciting the rosary aloud.

After dinner and another round of *mensa sternit*, Nicholas and the others had a half hour of free time outdoors before the Master's note-giving session in the chapel for the next morning's meditation. Then Litanies, the day's second *examen*, and to bed.

It was a demanding schedule that left Nicholas physically exhausted but mentally restless. Night after night he would lie awake, staring at the ceiling. He tried to will himself into unconsciousness, but to no avail. A dose of two aspirin, then four the next night, brought not relaxation, but harsher nerve-jangling. Eagerness, discipline, and his vast stores of youthful energy whipped him through the hectic days, but night found him enervated, staring wide-eyed into the deepening night. He struggled to accept it, even offered it up, but it was beginning to get to him.

Unfortunately he couldn't even use football to court exhaustion. He knew tackle football would be out of the question here, but he was surprised when the Beadle announced that even ordinary touch football was a no-no. "At St. Ignatius," Brother Mantello intoned in his usual blustery way, "the game is flag football. Each player must maintain a handkerchief in his back pocket. If a defender succeeds in grasping it, forward progress must halt. It may seem odd to you at first, but believe me, it keeps the usual mayhem to a minimum."

It was a shambles. A hard slap on the butt traditionally initiated monumental bickering. But the keen difference between actually grazing the ball-carrier and somehow managing to dislodge a featherweight kerchief while squealing "Gotcha!" taxed Christian charity to the nth degree. Nicholas had played in makeshift games before, where standard rules were bent and new wrinkles introduced, but this was a travesty. What doubtless seemed a superb idea in the Master's office proved a disaster on the field. The trouble was that the better a ball-carrier you were, the more faith you had in your whiz-bang finesse—your ability to throw a hip in your pursuer's direction, making him think he had you, while your feet were simultaneously dancing off in the opposite direction, leaving him with a handful of dusty air while you dipsydoodled off to paydirt. Squabbles were epidemic. Every "Gotcha!" ignited loud laments of injustice: "You never laid a finger on me!" was the constant complaint. Yet there was the brother, superciliously waving your kerchief.

Flag football was a tribulation for modesty of the tongue. A good novice did not use coarse language and never questioned the integrity of his brother. But football players consider it a tribal duty to swear like troopers, and no euphemism will do when a juicy four-letter epithet comes to mind. Semantic crises abounded. You couldn't call the blind spastic who clutched your kerchief a dirty liar, because that was a fault against charity. And if you executed a glorious feint, faked your defender out of his cassock, as it were, and hightailed it into the end zone, only to have some bifocaled, bookkeeperish brother peep, "I had you," and you were boiling to conk him, what was there to deter you except the fierce image of his clerical rectitude? Or a report of your indiscretion to the Master?

Tempers flared, but behavior, through ferocious willpower, stayed pristine; there was murder in the heart but honey on the tongue. If it is hard to swallow the picture of a Kentucky quarter-horse halfback who sees himself as Pegasus reincarnate meekly submitting as his mercurial touchdown gallop is called back by a tubercular Mr. Peepers, with no more protest than a pointed, "Thank you, Brother," then, Nicholas reflected, you just didn't grasp Catholic school traditions. Picture a fiendishly clever master-criminal-in-training, all of thirteen years old, his blazer stuffed with spitballs, who goes shouting his innocence to the principal's office to be strapped. On cue, hands throbbing, he says, "Thank you, Father." When told "This hurts me more than it does you," he responds with genuine guilt for the other's pain. If this is so, *and it is*, then how difficult is it to accept an out-of-breath, winged warrior of the gridiron accepting the cancellation of his heroism with a graceful, "Thank you, Brother"? The fact that he was secretly saying, "Screw you, Brother," was strictly between him and his next *examen*.

At least you didn't have to play flag football in Latin!

Three absurd sessions and Nicholas quit for good. After disgustedly throwing in his kerchief, he ambled into the orchard, intent on cooling off under a tree. The heat raged on. There was no one else around, so he peeled off his T-shirt and lay flat on the ground, feeling irritation seep from him. After several minutes he heard a far-off voice cry, "So how do you like football *à la* Kane?" Bolting upright, Nicholas spied a figure on horseback at least a hundred yards away. It was Scott. Silhouetted against the relentless sun, he looked like a carving on a cave wall.

He was sitting astride a brindle workhorse, riding bareback, maneuvering it effortlessly toward Nicholas. His body seemed fused to the horse, totally harmonized with this lithe, supple machine. Cantering forward, he exuded the contentment Nicholas believed only came from mastery. Some people were only fully alive when playing tennis or bridge or making a cake or money. Not Scott. His home was clearly atop a horse, gliding ruddy under blistering sun, across a deserted field, his left arm resting quietly on the reins, his right caressing the head, his eyes glistening, the corners of his mouth turned down in a wry, private smile. He rode as if in possession of a secret, gentle and strong and resonant, that no one could ever share.

"Hello, Brother," Nicholas greeted him.

"Hello, yourself," Scott said, bringing his mount to a halt and climbing off. "Have a good game?"

"Please," Nicholas said, grimacing. "No hot-stove league. I'll carry the scars to my grave."

"That bad, huh?"

"I can understand *touch*, everybody knows how paranoid the Church gets about modesty. I was even prepared for saltpeter, but flag football is ridiculous."

"Easy, Bro. Ours not to question. 'Pious reasons,' you know."

"Boy, do I know!"

"You'd better stick to handball like I do. Leave the jocks alone. And the mimps."

Mimps? What a perfect description of Charles Simpson and a couple other *primi*. They fell automatically into a little clique, murmuring in hushed tones about their vocations and "secular people" and "the world," congregating at rosary time, sharing a pew in the chapel. Simpson had actually volunteered to serve as laundryman, along with two of his allies. During recreation they wilted fast and offered to keep score or tend to the water bucket. If they could get away gracefully, they would plump themselves down in the gazebo across from the tennis courts and buzz, skittish as debutantes. All their vigor was poured into a finicky watchfulness, alert to any violation of the Rule.

"Great name for them, Scott. One of the mimps in my year reported me yesterday for walking immodestly."

"I always wonder what Father Kane thinks about it. I mean, where's the danger, anyway? You waltzing around like you've always done, or the ones finding fault?"

"The Beadle told me to take smaller, more Chinese steps."

Scott laughed.

"*That*'s a big help. Well, it takes all kinds, I guess. We get all sorts, a real grab bag. Bound to be a few mimps." Suddenly he scowled, as though reprimanding himself. "But I'm no one to criticize. I'm working on charity," he said sheepishly. "In the world, where 'personalities' are fair game, you can pick and choose people. Don't like Rick over there? No problem, just go your own way. But here the idea, the *ideal*, is to love all equally. 'Supernatural affection.' And no one too much. It's hard sometimes, fraternal charity, trying to spot Christ in someone you wouldn't give the time of day to outside, but it's what we're here for."

Nicholas wasn't so sure. Was it really possible to love everyone equally? And no one especially?

Scott stood and stretched, then hoisted himself up onto his toes and plucked two apples from the branch overhead.

"Catch," he said, tossing one to Nicholas. "So, apart from football, how's it going?"

Nicholas bit into the ripe fruit, juice trailing down his chin. "All right. It's hard work, that's for sure, and I have to keep reminding myself that just because some of the rules may seem Mickey Mouse to me doesn't mean they don't have a sound purpose."

"It's all a lesson in obedience. Offer it up. Submission to authority is the point, not the details."

"I know," Nicholas replied.

"Still, it makes you think. Sometimes I think Kane could have made a great cop. If you spend your lifetime in the relentless pursuit of crooks, don't you develop a similar psychology? Don't you have to think like they do?"

"I suppose."

"Well, I'm no one to talk. I've been called on the carpet more times than I can remember."

"I was going to say, you don't seem all that much of a stickler when it comes to the letter of the law."

Scott scowled. "No, I screw up a lot. But I'm not proud of it. I respect the idea of obedience, even if in practice I miss the mark."

"I want to ask you something," Nicholas ventured. "Why did you push the farmboy bit so hard?"

"Sorry?"

"I mean, why didn't you tell me the rest of it, Yale and the Sorbonne?"

He laughed. "Oh, I see. Brother Mantello's been blabbing, has he? No reason, really. That's all ancient history, and to tell you the truth, I rarely give it a thought."

"But you're no hayseed," Nicholas insisted.

"A hayseed with a *certificat* is still a hayseed."

"Did you know you had a vocation while you were at college?" Nicholas asked suddenly.

Scott frowned.

"We're really not supposed to talk about it, but . . . since you're not official yet," he grinned, "I'm not entirely sure I *know*, even now. I *believe*, that's for sure."

"We all believe, or we'd hardly be here," Nicholas put in.

"*Certe*. I think that year in France opened my eyes, made me look beyond where I was headed. I was shooting off in a dozen directions, drinking everything in, letting go completely. My life was a sweet fable until I opened my eyes. And what I saw made me think.

"I believed in the idea of perfection, of holiness. But I knew I was too weak to go it alone. Here, I'm part of something greater than myself. It's all in the Rule—others triumphed before me, others will after me. And they weren't all saints, either." He paused, apparently finished.

Nicholas realized that Scott's facetiousness and aplomb were a nervous pose. Underneath he was deadly earnest and a little frightened of his own desperate intensity.

"To me, the idea of becoming a Jesuit was like the sun up there," he continued, "and I thought, if I keep pointing toward it, only an idiot would bother criticizing my finger."

"Yes, I see."

"I guess I decided that unless I gave myself one hundred percent, I'd end up squandering my talents, chasing false gods, if you will, and wake up some morning to find I'd forgotten what it was all for. What *I* was all for.

"But with perfection as my goal, the simplicity of religious life would save me. The collar would free me to be 'all things to all men' and yet keep my eye on God."

"And keep the world at arm's length," Nicholas volunteered.

"Yes." Soctt nodded somberly. "That too." And he added, "It may sound corny, but to me the Jesuits *are* Christ in history. He lives in us. We fulfill His revelations, embody the message of salvation: His Kingdom has come."

"I think *I* always knew, in a way," Nicholas offered. "It seemed almost inborn. Now that I think back—early on, at school it was not exactly expected, but hoped that I'd be a priest. By the time I was halfway through high school, it was no contest."

"You were groomed? The old-boy network?" Scott asked wryly.

"Sort of, I guess. Not that I needed much prodding."

"No doubts at all? Your parents didn't try to talk you out of it?"

"Not really."

"*My* folks had a conniption when I announced I was coming here. Such carrying on, you'd have thought I was a prince who had abdicated. They've simmered down since, but I think it still galls them."

"What made you finally decide?" Nicholas asked.

"Nothing specific. No light blasted me on the road to Versailles, nothing that dramatic. It was a stimulating year, actually, and I did my share of alleycatting. Somehow, in broadening my perspective, it also narrowed my focus. By showing me all I could have—all I *was*, really—it enabled me to choose and to limit. I was nineteen, and it was time to get going, time to get serious. So here I am."

The bell rang out at that moment, summoning them to supper. Scott rose and leaped onto his horse. "Hang in there, Brother Manion. I'll see you later." He trotted off.

Nicholas put his shirt back on and started trudging back to the seminary.

He thought about Scott. At one moment merciless in his opinions, at the next he became the very model of single-minded piety. At Mass, long after the rest had finished their prayers of thanksgiving, he would still be kneeling, lost in private communion. What an enigmatic person he was. Nicholas didn't think he was a hypocrite, just complex—a veteran who managed to retain his "singularity" while hewing to the Rule. His moods were quicksilver, veering without warning from strict "observance" to playful improvisation. Volatility surrounded him like a magnetic field, and if it was contained, it was never chastened; he bristled with intensity.

The next morning in the rocky course of meditating on the infinite mystery of divine love, Nicholas experienced his first "light." Distractions and irony vanished and, like a runner gasping from strained labor suddenly given wings by his second wind and released into effortless speed, Nicholas jumped onto an unprecedented plane of clarity and insight. He was filled and overwhelmed with the personal specific love of God for him. God, who created the world and sustains it every moment of the day, who fashioned man in His image and watches him all the seconds of his life, loves me—singly, separately, uniquely. You are a Person, Nicholas whispered ecstatically to himself, a Person unlike any other who ever breathed, beyond description or imagining, but a Person all the same, who can yearn and be frustrated, laugh and be driven to tears, hope and suffer and love. Nicholas felt transfused with the grace of God's love. He pictured Him: not the unutterable, angry Yahweh of Israel nor the sentimental, white-bearded, jolly paterfamilias of the storybooks, but a clear-eyed Person who watched eternally, without surprise, but always with hope. Please, Lord, Nicholas prayed, help me to empty myself of all selfishness, to shear off all vanity, to banish all care for my own petty desires. Arm me with Your love. Make me a weapon of Your holy will, a perfect arrow, fired straight, fired true.

Finally he had something to put in his "light" book.

15

During the two-day retreat that led to Habit Day, Father Kane drilled the novices on the purpose of the religious life. He preached on obedience and humility and faith and discipline. He was not Master of Novices for nothing: his sermons were fervent, logical, and vivid, with a shrewd balance between strict homiletics and pointed, homespun anecdotes. He even managed to work in the suicide, earlier that summer, of Marilyn Monroe. "Beautiful, talented, successful, she nevertheless found nothing to live for," Kane analyzed. "It is a sad, pitiable, tragic spectacle. 'For what doth it profit a man,'" he quoted uncompromisingly, "'if he gain the whole world and suffer the loss of his immortal soul?'" He was careful never to hector or trivialize; he neither lectured from Olympus nor stooped to patronizing by trying to talk at their level. Only once during the retreat did he stray from form. Not surprisingly, his topic was purity.

Father Kane stood before them and expiated on self-abuse. He began calmly, mustering medical terms to explain the physical phenomenon of tumescence, carefully exculpating them from blemish if "erection arrived inadvertently," or if the body demanded release "naturally and unsolicited" through nocturnal emission. "What is natural is not culpable," he emphasized evenly. One thing about Father Kane: he was not embarrassed by his subject. Many of Nicholas's teachers had dreaded inquiries about sex and blanched, fleeing into mealymouthed vagueness when confronted in Health or Religion class with innocent curiosity. Often this delicacy boomeranged, serving not to stifle the questioner, but to tantalize him, sending him off in frustration, determined to do a little personal research. But Kane obviously relished his topic, and tackled it with accelerating gusto, his voice rising, his eyes glowing.

He enunciated Church teaching, marshalled the distinction between biological norms and "venereal pleasure," discoursed on the *lacunae* of "consent," and elaborated eloquently on the body's status as temple of the spirit. He itemized the dangers of masturbation, then launched his peroration. "And so, my dear novices, remember always that it was a filthy snake who made our first parents fall from the Garden of Eden. It was that pernicious snake who caused Adam and Eve to be flung from paradise into this vale of tears. Think of that—oh! what a loss was there—*think* of it, I enjoin you, as you lie in bed at night, your minds teeming with the penalty of Original Sin."

My mind, Nicholas joked silently, teems with everything *but*!

"Think of that catastrophic fall as the devil toys with your idleness and your energy and your youthful innocence. Think of the infinite pain we give our Father when we yield to our base animal natures. Are you men? Very well, then, *be* men! Not slaves tyrannized by the snake, as were our first parents.

"And if their terrible suffering does not deter you, if despite your valiant efforts to remain pure in the face of

Satan's attack, if his assaults cannot be rebuffed by prayer or resolve, then picture your dear mother as you contemplate this abomination. Think how she would feel if she could see you.

"And if that fails, think of Mary—Blessed Mary, ever Virgin, that's what we pray—whose entire life was without stain, and how grievously she would mourn your fall.

"And if even that, the image of how profoundly you would grieve her, is insufficient, if the snake refuses to quail and retreat, then . . ." Here a shudder went through his audience. What would he say now? *If thine eye offend thee . . . ?* No, not *that*. "Then take it and wrap a wet towel around it." The novices sat in stunned silence. Saliva flecked the corners of Kane's mouth. His gaze was steely. Nicholas wondered whether he had heard correctly. He knew he had when McMurtrey, sitting next to him, elbowed his ribs and whispered into his ear, "He's got delusions of grandeur. A cold washrag would do fine."

THURSDAY, AUGUST 9, 1962

The novices squirmed nervously in their pews as Father Kane, Mass over, summoned them, one by one, to approach the altar and receive their cassocks. He presented them gravely, two to each, one brand new, the other shiny and tattered. The fresh-from-the-box cassock was for special occasions such as feast days, while the worn hand-me-down that had served God knows how many of their predecessors was for everyday use. Nicholas trembled as the Master handed him his cassocks. Grinning with pride, he returned to his seat. Running his fingers tenderly over the patched and threadbare garment, Nicholas speculated on its history. His pastor, Father O'Mara, might have worn it; or Father Mc-Carthy, their Latin professor; or Father Kane himself, for that matter; or Lyon. He grasped, in a new and intense way, his kinship with his forebears here. Succession was symbolically asserted; he fit into a tradition that stretched back half a millennium. He stood fixed unshakably in an unbroken, rich, and resilient tradition; he was part of a continuous line that spanned the centuries. Caressing the cassock, he wondered what secrets still clung to it, what emotions continued to irradiate? Its mysterious history was mute but almost tangible, and as Nicholas clutched it, uttering a silent prayer for perseverance and shivering with anticipation, he felt nostalgic. The link with the past, this connection, reassured him; it would carry him into the future.

"You may put them on now, Brothers," Father Kane said. "Congratulations." As he eased himself into the everyday cassock, Nicholas looked around as the others did the same, trying to accomplish it with a practiced smoothness, but in some cases hamstrung by nerves and exhilaration. Most, however—veteran altar boys that they were—slipped into their new habits with effortless grace.

Outside they stood preening. Even porky Bartlett and prunish Simpson had suddenly become more authoritative and substantial. The *secundi* arrived en masse, and hailed them heartily. Brother Mantello was formal, extending "felicitations." Pictures were taken, one by one, to be sent home. A couple of others slapped Nicholas on the back, offering boisterous "way to go"s. Turner soberly shook each hand in turn, with a subdued "Congratulations, Brother." Nicholas had hoped to be singled out, but was sorely disappointed; Scott gave no sign of their previous encounters, but merely glanced, then swept by, mumbling his rote recital. What a moody guy, Nicholas thought. But nothing was going to daunt his spirits today.

Tradition fulfilled, the Beadle clapped his hands for silence. "Brothers, in celebration, the *orda* is suspended for the rest of the day. You will be going to our cottage in the woods, known as the villa. There will be swimming, games, birdwatching or hiking if you're so inclined, and a barbecue.'' The novices hoorayed, but Mantello quickly brought them back to earth: "I'll be along as chaperone, as will Brother Turner. After breakfast, just put on some old clothes and congregate here. We'll be taking the pickup.''

During breakfast the novices shifted restlessly in their seats until the Master jiggled the small brass bell in front of him at the head table, and said, *"Deo gratias."*

The other tables erupted into raucous conversation. The *primi*, startled and confused, looked to one another for explanation. "You may talk freely," Father Kane told them. After ten days of silence during meals and the excitement of receiving their cassocks, the novices were ready to burst. They yipped and chortled and hooted as they gave their high spirits free rein. Huzzahs were hurled. Tears of joyful relief were spilled as pent-up energies exploded. Bartlett's pudding jowls shook giddily. Bennett and McMurtrey were clucking in a private joke. Simpson directed his challenging eyes at Nicholas.

"Congratulations, Brother Manion.''

"The same to you, Brother Simpson.''

"I see no one has forgotten how to converse," Simpson observed drily.

"If you can call it that," Nicholas replied as the din increased.

"They had best get it out of their systems now," Simpson continued.

"Sorry?" Nicholas wasn't certain he had heard correctly.

"Brother Mantello says the Master gives very few *Deo gratias.* The rule of silence is strictly adhered to, except on very special occasions.''

"Why is it called that?" *Deo gratias* was a refrain that occurred frequently during the Mass, most poignantly toward the end, when the celebrant turned to face the congregation and said, *"Ite, missa est."* "Go, the Mass is ended." And people replied in unison, *"Deo gratias"*—"Thanks be to God."

"It's a Jesuit tradition." With seeming pique, he added, "I don't know the reason."

Before Nicholas had a chance to tease Simpson about his supercilious "They had best get it out of their systems"— who the hell was he, anyhow?—the bell rang again, and all noise ceased.

One of the *secundi* rose and strode purposefully to the front of the head table. He made the sign of the cross, knelt, and said, "Reverend Father and loving Brothers, by order of holy obedience, I tell my fault—breaking silence yesterday— for which fault holy obedience imposes on me this penance . . . " He then bent over and kissed the floor.

Astonishingly, Nicholas noticed, as the novice stood up and returned to his place, this ceremony hadn't aroused a flicker of interest from the head table or, for that matter, from any of the Junior tables.

The Master rose and led them in saying grace. The *primi* hurried to their rooms to change clothes for the trip to the villa.

Nicholas stopped off in the *lavatorium* on his way to his cell and studied himself in the mirror. The cassock was loose on him, even with the cincture.

Not bad, he congratulated himself. Not bad at all. If Lyon could only see me now! He'd grow into it. No sweat.

The collar made all the difference. Nicholas had worn a cassock hundreds of times while serving Mass. But they didn't have the crisp collar that he now found smooth as mica to his touch. Nor, giving it a twirl, did they sport a cincture.

Now I look official, he mused, turning and hurrying to change clothing.

The blistering heat still had not let up, though clouds had begun to flock overhead. The "villa" turned out to be a barnlike structure plunked down improbably in the middle of thick woods. It had a few sticks of broken-down furniture, a peeling leather sofa, a rickety, ramshackle dining table, and not much else. There was no indoor plumbing, and water for washing dishes had to be fetched from a nearby brook. A large, brick-laden pit outside served as a barbecue, and as soon as they arrived, Scott deployed two aides to produce a multiplication of hot dogs and hamburgers. Jugs of Kool-Aid, dangled in the brook to cool, were passed around.

Afterwards, several novices took off on hikes, while others organized swimming. Nicholas played a desultory game of H.O.R.S.E. with McMurtrey, but the weatherbeaten backboard was so warped that more often than not a perfectly aimed shot would unaccountably wriggle free of the rim. Their hearts weren't really in it, so when McMurtrey announced he was going for a swim, Nicholas found himself walking alone through the woods.

He was annoyed and perplexed. Scott Turner's aloofness that morning had irked him. Couldn't he have given some sign that Nicholas was not simply "just one of the group"? And that ceremony of self-abasement in the refectory—were they all at the mercy of any tattler who decided to pipe up? Were these sessions (called penance, he learned en route to the villa) screened, or was it left up to the individual? What if you were unjustly accused? Could you rebut the canary, proclaim your innocence? Probably not. It left a bad taste in Nicholas's mouth. It was a custom that seemed made for mischief.

As Nicholas walked on through the woods, he entered a small clearing. A pond rippled in the sunlight. Overhead he heard hooting. Suddenly something struck his shoulder. He yelped and looked up. The hooting continued. Then he spotted something high up in a tree. A figure rustled, then emerged to hang from a branch. It was Scott.

"Manion, I presume . . ."

"Hello," Nicholas mumbled sulkily.

Scott let go and landed like a cat. "Congrats, by the way. How's it going?"

"O.K."

"You looked pretty spiffy in your new duds this morning."

"Uh-huh."

Scott slapped Nicholas on the arm. "Come on, Bro, aren't you just a little excited?"

"Sure. It was great." He seemed to think he could turn friendship on and off like a light.

"I thought you looked terrific. I didn't let on, of course. Our friendship is between us—right?"

So that was it. He wasn't being standoffish, just maintaining their privacy. That altered the whole episode.

"Right," Nicholas replied, smiling brightly. Fair enough.

"How was the retreat?"

"Fine."

"We've got to do something to celebrate." Scott reached inside his back pocket and handed Nicholas a small package wrapped in aluminum foil. "Here."

Nicholas was delighted. "What is it?"

"Open it and find out."

Nicholas ripped off the paper and opened the box. Underneath a layer of cotton batting was a tiny gold nugget.

"Like it?"

"Yes, but—"

"No buts. It's yours. My dad gave it to me when I was twelve—it's a good-luck piece."

Nicholas was thrilled. "Thank you. I'm really touched."

"For God's sake don't show it around, just keep it in your pocket. You know what happened to that guy in Rodriguez."

"Huh?"

"Sorry. Of course you haven't started reading Rod yet. That comes later. It's a huge book: *The Practice of Christian Perfection*, by Alphonso Rodriguez, S.J. Crammed with piquant spiritual tidbits, including the story of a pious hermit who gave away all his possessions and dedicated his life to prayer and fasting in the desert. Probably in order to maintain some contact with the real world, he kept one penny. A lousy penny. When he died, and this 'worldliness' was discovered, he was laid to rest on a dungheap. According to Rod. With his penny.''

''Incredible. Tell me more.''

''The choicest morsel Rod attributes to somebody called Saint Pachomas: 'I say to ye verily, unless ye conceive a hatred for your mother and father, your sisters and your brothers, and all the things of your own very flesh,' '' Scott quoted orotundly, '' 'ye cannot be true followers of the Lord.' ''

''You've got to be kidding!''

''Wait!'' Scott laughed. ''There's more. Later on, in the same section, Rod mentions someone writing a letter to his parents, and says to him, 'Ye have no place here. Get ye out from this holy place.' ''

''That reminds me,'' Nicholas laughed, ''I'd better write my folks.''

''Not quite the reaction Rod was trying to inspire.'' The sky was darkening. Scott sprawled on the ground and began pitching pebbles into the pond. ''So how do you like the sem so far?''

''Fine. Oh, the routine gets a little tedious, and I'm having a heck of a time getting to sleep, and there are moments— like at breakfast this morning—when it seems a little weird. But it's O.K. How often do they have those penance sessions, anyway?''

''You'll see.''

''Anyone ever name you?''

''Not lately.''

''I take it that it's another exercise aimed at perfecting obedience?''

''Sure. What you saw this morning was the mildest. If

the fault is more serious, you have to do an *os pedes*, which involves the same rigamarole plus crawling underneath the head table to kiss Kane's feet."

"Go on."

"I swear. Then, sometimes, you kneel throughout the meal with your arms spread out cruciform. That's called *brachialis extendit*."

"So someone accuses you of a fault to Kane, and he dishes out the sentence?"

"Well, it's not always done in the refectory. Later on there'll be 'particular chapter,' or *exercitium modestiae* in the ascetory. Everybody stands in a horseshoe with Kane at the mouth, and each novice in turn gets the benefit of his brothers' criticism." Scott smiled. "Always in the spirit of charity, of course. 'Objectively and without rancor,' according to SPN Ignatius."

"Sounds like fun," Nicholas said. The sky was blackening ominously.

"And then, periodically, each of us makes a private 'manifestation' to the Master to discuss his interior life, his temptations and difficulties."

"That makes more sense than the other routine."

"Don't worry. The sessions with everybody together are really pretty soft. Nobody goes in with guns blazing—on the theory, I guess, that they might get the same treatment. It's usually pretty tame stuff. Something serious, like a PF, gets told privately to the Master." Scott seemed to enjoy showing Nicholas the ropes; he was at once animated and tactful, a friend and a mentor.

"Hold your horses," Nicholas interrupted. "Let me be sure I've got this right. We're *literally* our brother's keepers?"

"Up to a point, yes."

"And what's a PF?"

Scott looked surprised.

"A particular friendship. *Numquam duo*, remember? 'Unwonted' friendship."

"You mean . . . Really? Does that happen often?"

Scott smiled.

"No, of course not. But it has been known. *Nihil humanum alienum a me*. Then," he went on quickly, "there's the 'discipline,' of course."

"What's that?"

"You don't know?" Scott seemed genuinely surprised. "The discipline is a 'flagellant,' a whip made of tightly coiled rope, that we chastise ourselves with twice a week."

Nicholas was shocked. "You're kidding!"

"Nope. On Monday and Wednesday, at five fifteen sharp, a bell rings, and we flail away."

"Why?"

"Mortification of the flesh. Expiation of guilt. Chastening concupiscence. Working off time in Purgatory."

"It sounds like sexual terrorism to me."

"Not really. Not in theory. Then there's the chain. The penitential chain. You wear it around your thigh, again twice a week."

"I can't believe it . . ."

"It digs into the skin a little, but the pain is usually superficial." He looked so serious that Nicholas began to believe he wasn't kidding.

"Are you sure you're not putting me on? What's next—hairshirts?"

"Not at all. The chain is standard issue, just like the discipline. The hairshirt *is* optional." He smiled, indicating that at least the last was a joke.

"It's medieval. You mean all those priests, my teachers at school, our pastor—?"

"Exactly. Theory aside, it's a practical and effective assault on the libido. *De more*, like saltpeter in the grub."

Nicholas found it hard to believe. The Bible was full of

hairshirts, of course, but this was the twentieth century. Surely men today didn't strip and flagellate themselves, seeking to suffer for sin now in order to lessen punishment in Purgatory? It had to be an old wives' tale.

Except it wasn't. Scott was serious. And Nicholas was expected to join in, obediently, willingly. "I find it grotesque." The air suddenly was as cool as liniment.

"It's really no big deal. I probably shouldn't have gone into it now. You'll see. It doesn't hurt *that* much. Just offer it up."

"You do it?"

"Sure. It's just a symbol, Nick. You don't have to be gung-ho about it. Just respect the idea. Tame the beast. It's valid enough. It's been going on for centuries. *Nihil novum sub sole.*"

"That's a big help."

"Keep an open mind."

The woods were eerily, preternaturally still.

"That's one thing I hope they've got on the agenda in Rome," Nicholas declared. "I wouldn't mind if they outlawed that . . . anachronism."

"Don't hold your breath," Scott said.

"We don't matter?"

"Oh, we matter, all right. But the eccentric traditions of the Jesuits are the last thing on their minds right now."

Suddenly they heard a deep, crackling, reverberating roar. Thunder erupted like cannonfire. They craned their heads skyward, and saw bolts of lightning streaking across the opaque horizon. Finally, Nicholas thought, rain! It assaulted them torrentially.

"We'd better hustle back," Scott said, bolting toward the path. Nicholas quickly trailed after him.

The earth was already soft and shifting, the furious downpour carving muddy craters underfoot. Head lifted into the pelting rain, Scott suddenly tripped; he seemed to hang frozen in midair for a second, his half-turned face swept with surprise. Then he toppled down to the ground. Trying to stop, Nicholas slid on the slick surface and tumbled on top of him.

"Watch it," Scott said, laughing, "this isn't a wrestling match!"

Nicholas relaxed for a moment; he could feel Scott's heart thumping underneath him. Then, crying "Oh, no?" he went for a quick pin. Instinctively, Scott tried to wriggle free. Sodden and mud-greased, he quickly slithered out from underneath Nicholas and flipped him. Prone beneath Scott now, Nicholas struggled fiercely, then suddenly wrenched himself away. As abruptly as it had begun, the storm was waning.

It had excited him. Karl suddenly popped into his head. Karl, lying back against the bed in his room. Just an infinitesimal flicker, but there.

He saw Scott looking at him, daubs of mud smearing his face, primed for another round.

I didn't yield to it, it was inadvertent, Nicholas told himself. I didn't consent.

A blur of confused, appalled gentleness swept through him.

He could hear Scott panting.

The rain had slowed to a mournful trickle. Nicholas gazed up at the bruised sky, a fiery purple now.

Scott lifted his hand to be quiet. Evidently he heard something, but Nicholas hadn't noticed anything. A few moments passed, then the spare figure of Simpson inched into view. He seemed taken aback to find them there, but quickly masked his surprise and, with a barely perceptible smirk on his lips, announced, "We're getting ready to go back to the seminary. Brother Mantello asked me to find you. *He* thought maybe you'd gotten lost." He stood expectantly, as though waiting for them to trail back behind him.

Scott took charge. "You go on back, Brother. I'll make sure this joker doesn't get lost again. We'll be there in a jiffy."

"If you say so," Simpson replied, and turned to head back to the villa.

"That's Simpson," Nicholas explained. "He's the one who reported me for my walk."

"Him?"

"He's probably figuring out some way of working this into a fault that he can accuse me of."

"Take it easy. You got lost and I happened to bump into you, that's all."

He brushed his clothes futilely. "Simpson won't see it that way."

16

The next morning, after breakfast, the novices were summoned one by one to the Master's office. Father Kane told Nicholas, in a dry, matter-of-fact voice, that they were expected to practice physical mortification four times a week. He acted as though he were issuing weapons for field exercises.

"It's intended to be symbolic," he explained, "so don't be overzealous. Every Monday and Wednesday, the bell will ring promptly at five-thirty, and you may use the *flagellatio*. On Tuesdays and Thursdays, upon rising and until after breakfast, you will wear the penitential chain." He held them aloft: the tightly braided, waxy-sheened whip and the dull gray chain with its prongs like nails.

"We don't want you to hurt yourself," he announced. "Saint Ignatius advises us to scourge ourselves superficially, to avoid internal damage. But it *is* meant to hurt." His voice took on greater force. Nicholas wished he could see Kane's eyes behind the tinted glasses. "At least a little. To remind us of how much Our Lord suffered for us. Though, of course," he said, his face now seraphic, as though fixed on some distant, delicious vision, "we can only dream of sharing such magnificent pain." The Master leaned back in his chair and gestured at the implements on his desk.

Nicholas grasped them and pulled them apart, running his finger lightly over the prongs. Although flattened to mere nubs, they were still sharp and forbidding. Then, weighing the "discipline" in his left hand, he noticed it had four strands, instead of the standard-issue three.

"Father?" he said, hoisting the flagellant so Kane could see. "Is this some kind of hint?"

Kane smiled weakly. "Perhaps you require a little more than the rest, Brother Manion. *Pax Christi.*"

At five-twenty that afternoon, Nicholas waited in his cell for the signal to begin, still abashed by the prospect of calmly inflicting pain on himself. He'd given his hand a few swipes, and it hurt. The chain looked inconsequential, but its blunt, protruding, quarter-inch-long "nails" would dig into the flesh, especially against the thigh.

Nicholas had read about Saint Benedict's avoiding temptations of the flesh by hurling himself into a bed of nettles. Saint Francis Xavier had burst a blood vessel grappling with concupiscence. Some zealots truly became deranged in their furious pursuit of perfection. One Jesuit had developed knee tumors from constantly kneeling on damp floors. Another had scourged himself bloody in public.

There was even one who would lie for hours in a cold bath in the middle of winter, Nicholas remembered.

Maybe Scott was right. Chastise the flesh. "Tame the beast." It could be just what I need, Nicholas thought, but you don't become holy by regarding your body as evil, do you? Isn't there another name for that—masochism?

No, it was just symbolic, he must remember that.

Still, Nicholas was uncomfortable seeing his body as the

devil's domain, to be watched vigilantly, checked, guarded against.

So much fretting and fussing went on. For years the nuns, and then the priests, had drilled them on purity. Purity in thought, word, and deed. So much time spent trying to stifle natural instincts that even in grammar school Nicholas had bridled.

You'd think the Manicheans had never been condemned as heretics, he thought. Man had been created in God's image, hadn't he? Not the devil's?

It seemed pointless to try to deny what was as automatic as breathing itself. Besides, at school anyway, the tactics boomeranged, drawing attention to the very temptations they were aiming so sedulously to scotch.

Only last night the power of the body had manifested itself. He'd had a wet dream. And enjoyed it.

It wasn't culpable, of course. It wasn't something you could resist or consent to, so it wasn't culpable.

Sex without sin, Nicholas mused.

The bell clanged. Obedience dictated that he give it a go. He unfastened his cassock, tossed it on the bed, and peeled off his T-shirt. Standing in front of his desk, he raised the discipline in his right hand and stared at his pale, unblemished shoulders. In the neighboring cells he could hear the swatting sounds, the noisy medley of cord striking flesh sounding like a siege of cap pistols. Slap, slap, slap. He felt nauseated.

Just *do* it, he ordered himself.

He raised the thing and slammed it down hard. The whip stung his shoulders, making him wince. He gave himself several more smacks before petering out in halfhearted fly-swats.

It *was* medieval, Nicholas believed. In fact, it was a bizarre variant of a circle jerk. He was willing to bet most of the others were just shamming, whipping their palms. He couldn't believe that they were meekly following orders, docilely submitting to this weird ritual. They weren't desert fathers, after all, crazed Coptics fleeing the corruption of Alexandria. This was 1962, for God's sake. What would the Ecumenical Council make of this twisted relic? Reading Rod was one thing, but were they actually supposed to ape his strange crew? Genuflect incessantly like Blessed Macarius? Or spend forty years on top of a pillar like Saint Simon Stylites? When the Master urged them to imitate Saint John Berchmans, the precocious novice saint, did he mean that, like him, they should despise laughter and disdain sleep, so courting an early grave? Were they expected to be new Aloysius Gonzagas, flogging away in an attempt to transform the flesh into "angelic substance"?

It turned his stomach. This abuse was much more unhealthy than the circle jerk, because it was so dishonest. If Karl could see him now, he'd have a field day. Their childish game brought about a normal release of pent-up tension. But this—the "circle whip," Nicholas dubbed it—tried to drive the body's cravings deeper within, to bully them into dormancy, a temporary submission that paradoxically assured they would eventually spring back with escalating virulence. Rather than satisfying or transcending them, it sought to stifle, shoving them toward release in a channel they were not designed to seek.

"It's perverted," Nicholas told himself. Father Kane might dream of magnificent pain, but to Nicholas, as he flung the flagellant to the floor at the sound of the bell, this was the *real* self-abuse.

However. His *lectio spiritualis* of late had focused on Saint Francis Xavier, the Jesuits' incomparable missionary apostle, whose Alexandrine zeal had propelled him through India and Japan, only to fall a mere thirty miles from the gates of China. Named by Pope Pius X the patron of all works for the propagation of the Faith, his response to God's love was to risk his life unstintingly in the world he described as a "seminary of martyrdom." What a lesson in sanctification through suffering he provided! Thriving on adversity, he trekked barefoot through three hundred miles of snow to meet the Mikado, leaping and singing as he went.

To his fellow Jesuit, Simon Rodriguez, Xavier had written: "There is no better rest in this restless world than to face imminent death solely for the love and service of God Our Lord."

And how much more subtle and treacherous is spiritual death than the physical one, Nicholas thought. Sacrifice was the oxygen of faith. Let me in every respect manifest my eternal gratitude for God's love by infusing my life with love of Him, he prayed.

As Christ suffered for all men, Nicholas would try to welcome whatever suffering might come to him. Even the "discipline."

How else, he wondered, could one become truly Christian?

That night, as the Master had instructed, he placed the chain underneath his pillow. He would put it on first thing in the morning. How terrible could it be, he asked himself. But he couldn't bring himself to clutch it while he slept.

SATURDAY, SEPTEMBER 1, 1962

Nicholas sat in his cell composing his first letter home. Bleary-eyed from so many restless nights, he ignored the inviting bed and hunched over his writing-pad.

A.M.D.G., he scrawled automatically at the top. *Ad maiorem dei gloriam*, the Jesuit motto: To the Greater Glory of God. Although, McMurtrey had joked to him one day, sometimes it really signified "for the greater convenience of those in authority." He'd also suggested that the *Te Deum* should, much of the time, be spelled *te-dium*.

The pictures had come back from Habit Day. Nicholas had to admit he looked grand. He hoped his parents would like their copy.

His letter said:

Dear Mother and Father,

My first month here is over. They really keep us busy around here—I've barely had time to catch my breath since I walked in the door. Except at night, unfortunately. Lights-out is at 9:30, and for some reason I toss and turn until one or two. It's probably nothing but overexcitement, but the lack of sleep is beginning to have its effect: the other day in Latin class I completely dried up doing a simple translation, something that hasn't happened in years. Father McCarthy, our teacher, a marvelous old-timer with a tremendous zest for his subject, appeared puzzled, if not a bit shocked. It was no big deal—as Father Lyon always says, Dad, even Homer nods—but it's sure kept me on my mental toes since.

Life here is wonderfully ordered (as the enclosed daily schedule will indicate!) and meticulously designed to minimize distractions and concentrate on the spiritual. Everything is secondary to the annihilation of the self, the erasure of singularity (the term used here), and the immersion of us all in the Life. Every rule—and there are plenty—is a way of inculcating obedience. "Observance" is the whole point. Nobody is supposed to ask why, just docilely follow orders, like, I imagine, the army. Our sergeant, known here as the Beadle, reprimanded me last week for using toothpaste. Apparently Colgate is "worldly," an ostentatious creature comfort. He introduced me to a weird house product (that is *de rigueur*)—a combination of salt and baking soda called Dental Dynamite. Ugh!

But it's wonderful here, beautiful grounds, ample food, and total dedication to prayer and the religious life. It may not be what I expected, but overall it's just what I wanted, if that makes any sense. I miss you!

> All my love,
> Nicholas, N.S.J.
> (Novice, Society of Jesus)

P.S. I've met one real character so far, a second-year man named Scott Turner, a farmboy from Delaware, who went to Yale and the Sorbonne. He's sort of taken me under his wing and is showing me the ropes. You'd like him.

P.P.S. I enclose a shot of my new "look." What do you think?

17

On the following Sunday afternoon, McMurtrey and Bartlett were already splashing in the swimming hole when Nicholas arrived. He moved behind the large outcrop of gray rock that jutted over the water, wriggled out of his clothes, and slipped on his trunks.

Bennett was waiting modestly as Nicholas emerged, clutching a rolled towel.

"O.K., Bro, all yours," Nicholas said.

Nicholas climbed the rock and prepared to dive into the glimmering, translucent water. He gazed in distaste at his own pale legs.

Taking a deep breath, he joined his hands in front of him, tucked his head down, leaning forward into gravity, and, at the last moment, kicked off.

He knifed the water cleanly, hurtling into the chilly depths. His hands quickly grazing the mossy bottom, he propelled himself up, up, with calm, familiar assurance until he reached the surface. Tossing his hair, he settled into a lazy backfloat.

"Hot stuff, Bro," McMurtrey said, lolling nearby.

"A gold for sure," Bennett said, standing atop the rock, his Olympic savvy belied by his knock-kneed, sparrowy frame.

"Beginner's luck," Nicholas joked.

From his perch on the shore, Bartlett spoke:

"Come on, Bro, I'll race you," he said, pointing to a raft about one hundred yards out.

"Later, later," Nicholas countered. He was winded. God, he told himself, I'm really out of shape. He dog-paddled to the shore.

McMurtrey pressed him. "Not afraid you'd lose, are you?"

"No way," Nicholas said.

"O.K., then, let's do it—the three of us."

"Yeah, come on," Bartlett chimed in, rising.

The others, their interest piqued, volunteered their two cents' worth from their lounging-places astride rocks shiny with algae.

"Go on and race, Bro."

"Let's see who's fastest."

"Don't be chicken."

Nicholas realized there was no avoiding it.

"All right," he announced, with what he hoped was noble forbearance tinged with exasperation. "Enough static from the peanut gallery. Let's do it."

"Great," McMurtrey said. Alleluias were shouted from shore. "Come on," he motioned to Bartlett, clambering out of the water, his skin sleek and pink. Climbing the big rock, he declared, "We'll start from here, *quercus*?"

Bartlett hurried to stand beside McMurtrey and Nicholas.

"Ready?" Bennett asked, a born signal-giver.

Nicholas nodded.

"Stop stalling," someone yelled.

Bartlett did a few knee-bends in preparation.

"O.K., Bro, we're all set," McMurtrey said.

"Very well," Bennett spoke methodically. "Ready—"

They stood erect, limbering their arms and legs.

"Set—"

"Go!"

They dived as one, Nicholas reaching the surface only to spot Bartlett slightly ahead, as he swallowed part of his furious-footed wake. Falling into a steady rhythm, he stroked, gradually gaining power, gulping air automatically as his arms carved the water.

Nicholas had no idea Bartlett was so strong. Despite his pudginess, he maintained his lead past the halfway point. McMurtrey lingered in third place, just behind Nicholas.

Suddenly, Nicholas stepped up his tempo and drew even with the leader. Opening his eyes, he saw Bartlett grin. Nicholas took in some water and playfully blew it into his face.

At last he was in the lead, a torpedo gliding inexorably toward paydirt. The rooting from the shore, loud but indistinct, rang in his ears. He was just able to make out the words "Go, McMurtrey, go . . . come on, Bro!"

Sure enough, McMurtrey was gaining. He could feel him right behind. Nicholas turned to check, and in that moment's slowing, McMurtrey zoomed past him. In effect, it was a relay: Bartlett went all out at the start, tiring Nicholas, only to yield to his partner, with plenty still in reserve for the stretch. What an idiot I am, Nicholas accused himself, scrambling to catch up. They suckered me.

Nicholas accelerated fiercely, his arms and legs thrashing, but the new-found urgency ruined his form. McMurtrey won easily. Gasping for breath, Nicholas barely nosed out Bartlett.

"You turkey," he told McMurtrey, who waved his arms in the air, "you sandbagged me."

Nicholas climbed onto the raft and flopped on his belly.

Bartlett hoisted himself out of the water, and clapped the victor on the back. "Way to go."

McMurtrey grinned beatifically.

They lazed on the gently rolling raft. The cheers had finally petered out; the others, even Bennett, were cavorting. Squinting, Nicholas could see one brother dive toward another, disappearing for a moment. Then the second somersaulted into the air, turning several times before he hit the water with a vicious smack. He had played the same game many times as a child.

Losing was no big deal, he reflected, although he preferred never to lose. He had to hand it to McMurtrey; he'd tricked him by playing possum. It was his own complacency that had done him in. As Yogi Berra said, "It isn't over till it's over."

Nicholas yawned, stretching under the sun.

"Will you look at Brother Bennett," McMurtrey said.

Nicholas opened his eyes. Bennett, back on shore, was stalking butterflies. He crept forward on tiptoes toward his prey, then with agonizing slowness closed his hands in a cup, the butterfly easily escaping.

"That will *never* work," Bartlett commented.

Nicholas closed his eyes again.

"He's an oddball," he heard McMurtrey say. "Off in his own world."

"But he's solid," Bartlett said, quick to muzzle unwonted criticism.

"For sure," McMurtrey agreed.

Am *I*? Nicholas asked himself. Didn't *solid* mean you were like a rock, that doubts bounced off you, that observance of the Rule was second nature to you? God, I want to be, Nicholas told himself. But didn't *solid* also imply there was no way to get *in*, either? Nicholas, as so often before, felt cut off, apart. He wanted to open up to someone, to discuss the questions that plagued him. But you couldn't ask your brother if you *were* solid, or how you got to *be* solid, because that delved into the taboo area of one's vocation.

He wanted to confide, to beef, to swap notes, to discover whether anyone else had his difficulty in settling in. But sharing confidences, asking for help, was not done.

Except with the Master, of course, His Spiritual Father. But Kane had forgotten what it was like to be seventeen; he spoke an entirely different language. "Everything is easy for those who love Christ." That was his recipe, his panacea. Father Kane had thought everything through so long ago that the emotions seemed burned out of him. Nicholas wanted to open up to someone like himself.

For all its fabled intellectualism, the Society, here at least, certainly looked down its nose at dialectic.

If only Lyon were around, or his father, they'd help Nicholas sort things out in a jiffy. He couldn't imagine Lyon in this atmosphere. How could his detached, mocking, discriminating—yes, worldly!—mind have crabbed through these two years? It was strange, really. The novitiate seemed to bear no resemblance to their actual future lives as Jesuits. In "the world," Lyon sailed first class; here was Nicholas, stuck in steerage.

What would Lyon say if he could hear Nicholas now? "Offer it up"? *"Quid est ad aeternitatem"*? Probably. Well, what *was* it in the light of eternity, anyway, Nicholas demanded. Small potatoes, no doubt. If Nicholas could just make himself believe it . . .

"Isn't this glorious?" he heard Bartlett say.

"We're sure blessed," McMurtrey agreed, without irony.

Can these two be *that* different from me? Nicholas asked himself. He hated feeling lonely, longed to share their carefree confidence.

"Too bad this isn't *de more*," he tried.

"Then we might get spoiled," Bartlett answered quickly.

"So spoil me!" Nicholas continued, mock-imploring.

He saw McMurtrey eye Bartlett uneasily.

"Back home I used to swim every day during the summer," Nicholas explained.

"*This* is our home now, Bro," Bartlett said solemnly. "The Master knows best."

"Evidently," Nicholas said, irked.

"If you believe he does," McMurtrey continued.

"Sorry?" Nicholas asked.

"I mean he does *because* we believe he does."

"Exactly," Bartlett added.

Either they've both gone crackers all of a sudden, Nicholas thought, or they're making a rather sophisticated point: faith is *ipso facto* its own validation. Nicholas would love to believe it.

The descending sun had left a chill in the air. Time to be getting back.

Nicholas watched Bartlett and McMurtrey dive in and chug toward shore. Maybe the Master had a point; maybe it *was* his "special cross" to feel so excluded.

"Brother Manion," someone called from shore, "come on, we're going back."

He could see they were already dressed. He'd better hurry. As he sat on the edge of the raft, he saw Bartlett disappear behind the big rock, McMurtrey waiting patiently for his turn.

Nicholas slipped into the water and began to swim.

About thirty yards from shore, a cramp spasmed in his left calf. Clutching his leg, Nicholas bucked, plunging beneath the surface. He fought back up, gasping for breath. I can't move, he realized, frightened. His leg felt as if it were caught between garden shears.

"Bro, are you O.K.?" he heard Bennett call.

"What's wrong?" McMurtrey asked.

Rubbing his leg frantically, Nicholas said, "It's nothing." He was damned if he'd cry for help.

"He's got a cramp," he heard someone say.

"Hang on, Bro."

He couldn't rub it away. Swallowing a lot of water now, he bobbed awkwardly, sinking as he grabbed his leg, rising only when he let it go. Either way, he couldn't win.

Suddenly he felt hands on his leg, kneading expertly. A head bobbed to the surface. Bennett!

"Any better?" he asked, his eyes somber with fraternal concern.

"Thank God!" someone said from shore.

"Some," Nicholas said.

"I'll hold you up while you rub," Bennett offered.

"No, let's just get in." It was humiliating.

"Well, hang on to my shoulders, then. I'll guide you in."

"O.K."

Kicking his legs furiously as though that would scuttle the kink, Nicholas let himself be tugged to safety.

The others eyed him with concern and relief. McMurtrey tossed him a towel.

"Nice going, Bro," someone said to Bennett.

"Thank God somebody had their eyes open."

"We'll have to get the Beadle to make a note in the Diary, a new perpetual tradition: Brother Bennett must go along as lifesaver." Nicholas, the pain finally gone from his leg, saw Bennett's pleased smile.

McMurtrey hunkered down beside him. "You all right now?"

Nicholas nodded.

"For a second there I thought we might lose you."

"Oh, don't be crazy," Bartlett snapped, striding off, his trunks slung over his shoulder.

Nicholas stood up. He toweled off, looking at Bennett. Finally he walked over to him.

"Thanks, Bro." He clasped Bennett's wrist.

"You're welcome," he replied, pulling himself free.

"Lucky you weren't here by yourself," someone observed.

"*Deo gratias*," Nicholas said, trudging off to change.

No one laughed.

18

As the days hurtled by, the drama he had expected continued to elude Nicholas. There seemed to be a schism between idea and practice; little of the daily routine touched upon priestly work. The Master regularly referred to their vocations, of course, but clinically, with fanatic calm.

Nicholas started taking long walks alone through the orchard, down to the brook that flowed past its northern corner. He would sit and gaze into it, harried by doubt. At first he had tried not to question his life here too deeply, resolutely tucking the nagging questions away in the back of his mind. He told himself that things had to shape up. Something had to happen.

But when were they going to get on with it? After two months he began to suspect that this might be it, the whole ball game, until the two years of novitiate were over. Ordination loomed, but thirteen years away! This period of spartan routine would end in twenty-two months, but he was no longer sure he could survive it. There was no news, no music except hymns, no team sports except the ludicrous "flag football" brand, and no one to confide in or have fun with, except for Scott, whom he never saw alone. Meditation brought "light" and consolation up to a point, and Mass remained tremendous in its power to soothe and exalt him, but most of the time Nicholas felt he was in basic training instead of in preparation for a life devoted to saving souls. The use of the discipline repelled him, and the public *j'accuse* sessions turned his stomach. And he still wasn't sleeping properly. The showers were ice cold, and his toilet kit had been confiscated as "worldly." Insomnia was not only sapping his vitality, it was throwing him completely off balance. He was becoming cranky and suspicious, a nervous wreck.

The question was, could he survive these two years with anything left to offer? If he submitted now—toed the line and swallowed his misgivings, meekly following the letter of the law without question—what would be left of him when the time was up? You must draw the line somewhere, Nicholas believed. He understood sacrifice, if it had a point. He could even accept a modicum of blind trust in the Rule, since the rules were made by men as fallible, even as arbitrary, as he. But could he, in all honesty, do what was foreign and repugnant to him, to that very self he felt he possessed so securely? Could he perform "internal surgery" on his personality, even violate his conscience—in the name of holy obedience? All his instincts shouted no, he could not do that, he must trust his own sincerity.

But the stakes were enormous. A vocation heard and answered made no provision for ifs or buts or howevers.

And wasn't it possible that he simply resisted being one of the crowd? Nicholas was too truthful not to concede that his anxiety might sprout from egotism, as though the body itself, in denying him sleep, were recoiling from his nondescript role. Perhaps the seminary's ruthless democracy itself was demeaning? Maybe once more he was ranking himself too high and thus missing the essential point of these two years: the substitution of God's will for his own—God's will in this case being Father Kane's. Didn't he lack faith if he set his own judgment against that of the Society? Possibly.

Perhaps he should ignore the sleepless nights and jangly nerves, the increasing doubts and mounting irritations, and accept the identity the seminary was intent on imposing on him. Let those parts of himself that did not fit the mold be tossed aside. But Nicholas didn't know how to do so. How could you let anyone else define what you were? Still, if he couldn't ignore the fact that he had made a false start, he *could* temper his anxiety with patience. Time would tell. Things could change. Maybe the Long Retreat would set him straight.

But he was on warning.

After countless attempts to adjust to the flagellant and the penitential chain, Nicholas asked to see the Master. Kane was distant but understanding, advising him "for the time being, at least, to practice discipline mentally."

He didn't know how the others handled it, but couldn't help noticing that Simpson sported a rather ostentatiously game limp twice a week.

So much of the stoic, against-the-world ethos gave Nicholas a sense of being trapped in a time-warp. Obviously if you were a missionary risking—or was it courting?—martyrdom, certain stringencies were necessary.

Ignatius had been a visionary, but also a daring man of action, and needed to forge his Praetorians in a fiery furnace.

But times had changed. Most of the novices would never even leave the United States. And Kane was no Ignatius.

Was martial obedience necessary for a future French teacher? Or for a parish priest?

Training heroes for God in the sixteenth century was one thing. But the rules handed down from generation to generation now bore little relation to the real future they faced.

The rules seemed petty. Like the Beadle's confiscating his shaving kit, leaving him just the razor and one brush. Of course, giving things up was a sacrifice. But was it necessary in this case, or was it mere rebarbative authority, blinded and musclebound by time, effete?

What kind of God would send that old hermit to Hell for a lousy penny?

He asked Kane whether his problems with the routine constituted a doubt.

Kane said no, he was just "tight" and trying too hard. He quoted Cardinal Newman: "A thousand difficulties do not make a doubt." He said it was just a trial and that Nicholas should pray harder and grace would come. "Grace on nature, Brother. The good get better," he explained. "The devil wants you to leave. Nothing enflames him so much as a vocation. When he attacks, we must detach ourselves, recollect our minds, control our senses, mortify ourselves." Nicholas was not to worry. God's will be done. Strength would come. He quoted Job: "Hidden things He hath brought forth to light." He paused.

"I understand you've been having trouble sleeping."

He'd read the letter! Nicholas flinched as though struck. It was Kane's prerogative, he knew that. Still, it rankled. Snooping was un-American.

"Yes, I've been lying awake most of the night."

Kane told him that people sometimes overestimated how long it took them to get to sleep, and how long they lay awake during the night.

"Satan must fear you very much, he's sending you so many trials," Kane offered. "But what's a Christian without a cross to bear?"

Nicholas, he advised, should not dwell on it. The way to keep strong was to crush questions, evade them, ward them off. "Don't think too much, Brother. Virtue will make him flee."

"Quid faciendum, Pater?" he asked, proud of his Latin. The Master looked surprised, but replied quickly:

"Ora, Frater. Semper ora."

"Bene," Nicholas said, unsurprised. It was always "Pray."

"Optime, Frater."

The next day Simpson saw Nicholas whisper to Scott after Mass and accused him of a fault. Nicholas gamely played out the public breast-beating rigmarole. It was petty and embarrassing and had angered him deeply. Scott watched the whole episode evenly, without a flicker of complicity. Nicholas didn't expect him to rise dramatically and seize a share of the blame, but he felt unjustly singled out, nonetheless. Simpson had obviously had it in for him since that day at the villa when he came upon them in the woods. Nicholas didn't think for a moment Simpson was motivated by "Christian charity." His fuel was cunning spite, a festering resentment at whose origin Nicholas could not guess, but whose vehemence made him wary. He was more complex than the other mimps; his by-the-book, always-play-it-safe behavior masked an inner turmoil that was intense. He was too calm, like Father Kane, his control eerie, as ominous as a stick of dynamite.

Very well, Nicholas decided. If that's how you want to play it, I'll be ready.

19

The Long Retreat was a marathon of meditation. With the Spiritual Exercises of Saint Ignatius as their guide, four times daily for thirty days the novices meditated on the life of Christ. A biblical episode was examined, an hour at a time, using the "tools of sanctity"—the five senses. The Master set the stage, but the use of each retreatant's creative imagination was crucial to the hermeneutic thrust of the exercise: to visualize, concretize, and personalize each lesson. Whatever the cameo, the "powers of the soul"—memory, intellect, and will—were brought to bear. The method was precise, its purpose clear: to observe, judge, act.

In the first week, with windows shrouded, their eyes downcast, avoiding all distraction, a lone candle flickering in the chapel, they grappled with the mystery of salvation. Nicholas forced himself to fast, step up penance, and adopt an uncomfortable posture, even while abed. Consideration of inevitable bodily corruption led to the wages of sin: he "saw" Lucifer plunge from Heaven, "felt" Adam and Eve's exile from Eden, "shared" the torment of millions of souls trapped in eternal fire.

Had he not also sinned, also earned damnation?

The exercise wielded the intellect to move the heart. Confronting his own sin, the sorrowing retreatant purgatively gasped at the love that impelled Christ to become man, requite man's guilt, and thus redeem the world.

If God did that for man, what could Nicholas refuse him?

Simulating Hell, Nicholas saw that the damned soul *lives* in fire. ("Better that he had never been conceived and carried in his mother's womb," the Master observed.) But, though the self be decadent and cretinous, God—astonishingly!— loves man nonetheless.

Prostrate, or standing rigid, or kneeling, clutching the darkness like a cope, eschewing "happy thoughts," Nicholas and the novices stared straight at the vile fruits of sin. They entered Hell: the whirling inferno, the howls of agony, the blaspheming shrieks, the putrid stench, the blistering fire, the gall of despair. It was the pismire of the soul.

This was what Nicholas deserved, but miraculously had been spared by a loving God. Justice demanded reparation; mastery of self must be attained. Emerging from their cataclysmic tour, each novice resolved to do penance, avoid sin, expunge doubt, and amend his life.

Emotion was the key. "Consolation" was a surging burst of Divine Love, a direct transfusion of grace, like Ignatius's "gift of tears." Tears for one's sins and for God's sacrificial suffering worked on nature and enhanced faith. "Desolation," if it came, was Satan's ploy; confusion, doubt, laziness, false priorities, restlessness, all were temptations strewn like nettles by the fiend. Twice-daily *examens*, the *culpa* beads and book, were weapons of resistance against the devil.

During the second week, McMurtrey left. Without a trace of warning, with not a word said, he simply vanished. His place in the pew, that first morning, was glaringly empty;

a wave of the Master's hand and they closed ranks. At table his place was still set when they arrived. In the silence, the emptiness resounded. Forbidden to talk, the *primi* chafed in confusion. It was unnerving, a kind of rebuke. Nicholas liked McMurtrey and missed him, but he struggled to avoid dwelling on it; it was a desertion so swift and unanticipated and poignant he did not know what to make of it.

The second week considered Christ as *Salvator Mundi*. If President Kennedy suddenly appeared on TV to announce that the Russians had invaded Berlin, what loyal citizen would recoil from his country's call? Only a slacker, a coward would refuse to pay the price. Yet Christ was King of the World, and He required recruits against Satan. Could His subjects do less than their extern equivalents?

The Holy Trinity vouchsafed One of Them to become Man to save us, Nicholas realized. He "saw" Christ in Bethlehem. As the Allies had battled the Axis, so must we battle Lucifer. Though he offers power and money, all the world in fact, Jesus offers poverty and the chance to be persecuted. For His sake.

Who but a cretin could fail to respond to Christ's alarum, after what He did for us?

The regimen made some of the novices "tight" and giddy. Nicholas would lie in his cell at night and hear nervous giggles peppering the air. Suddenly, while shaving, a brother might be pelted with a cellophane bag filled with water. Filing down the corridor, horseplay, silent but irrepressible, would erupt. Cabin fever, he decided. Others became rigid with devotion, so "consoled" they seemed catatonic.

Nicholas kept himself remote, sober, placid, welcoming the thirty-day spiritual blitz as armature, a protective shield, a safe passage into the future.

The third week, with gradually increasing light, focused on the Last Supper—through Christ's Passion and Death. Pilate could "find no fault in this man." Of course not—the fault was ours, Nicholas realized. Would we now, like Peter, renounce Him? Could we not wait one hour? One lifetime?

What should we not endure for Him?

Finally came the fourth week, and the joy of Resurrection.

Christ appeared to His Mother and His disciples, His divinity no longer hidden, eager to cheer them. He is among them, among us, still, Nicholas prayed.

Now came the moment of Election: how would each retreatant respond, how would he express his love of God, how opt to serve God's glory?

"Take up your cross and follow Me," He had bade them.

At last, it was over.

Nicholas elected the way of Christ, in gratitude, wonder, and hope. In action, not just words. Like the others, he pledged himself: "Take, O Lord, all my liberty. Receive in their entirety my memory, intellect, and will. And since whatever I have or hold You have given to me, so I give everything back to You to be managed entirely according to Your preference. To me give only Your love and Your grace, and with these I am rich enough and want nothing more."

Thus, in theory if not in practice, was the personality broken down and then re-formed. Much of it was the old catechizing in triple-time, standard homiletics with an ingenious psychological twist. Its purpose only marginally bore on the priesthood at all; its goal was the transformation of the ordinary believer into the paladin *extraordinaire*, aflame with a single-minded zeal. As Cardinal Newman had put it, the Spiritual Exercises at the moment of Election amounted to a clear command from God: "My son, give Me thy heart."

Surely we've already done that, or we wouldn't be here, Nicholas reflected. But the desired emotional sweep eluded him. Although he had strived with all his heart to scale the peak of consolation, that unblinking certitude that he was God's chosen, the retreat had not been Pentecostal.

Fascinating, certainly. Full of insight and wisdom, yes. The quasi-hallucinatory meditations, the hypnotic repetitions, the powerful alteration of light and darkness—all were near masterpieces of spiritual legerdemain.

But he was not changed.

My problem isn't sincerity of purpose, it's authenticity, he told himself. There was a single word that encapsulated all his baffled, querulous, seething, doubt-plagued difficulties here, a terrible word whose nagging refused to abate: fraudulence.

No, it was insupportable. It was the wily devil come round again, nipping at his heels. His vocation wasn't spurious, it was his observance that was faulty.

I'm no quitter, he insisted to himself. I'll just have to try harder.

That morning the Beadle delivered their mail to them in their cells. Nicholas had a letter from his father. He tore it open and saw those familiar, florid strokes on the Manion Organization letterhead. The Master had held it throughout the Long Retreat.

Dear Nick,

Received your good letter. So glad the place agrees with you, though I must admit home seems a little empty without you.

As to the petty rules and such, my advice to you is not to give them a moment's thought. Every outfit has its crotchets, little tests to tease you. Don't sweat the small stuff.

On the other hand, of course, if you think you're right, stick to your guns, come hell or high water. A man finally cares only for his own opinion—and God's. The rest is shadowboxing.

It's up to you to tell the difference. Is it a matter of

principle—or just a trifle? You'll know. Follow your instincts and you'll come out fine.

Remember your Dante?

> "Come what may,
> So that only my conscience gnaw me not,
> Against ill fate I am full fortified."

Your mother sends her love. By the way, Karl is a Leatherneck at last.

Your father

P.S. Enjoyed *your* new "uniform."

They said the Long Retreat made you or broke you, but he did not feel all that different. His grasp on himself remained tenuous, his resolve tentative and fragile. Despite the ordered calm of the last month, he still wasn't sleeping properly. He couldn't keep on like this, cross-examining himself, his will flaccid, careening through the days, reweaving his raveled poise nightly. The strain was bound to catch up with him.

At dinner that night the novices were ebullient. Having kept silent for so long, they burst forth now in joyous gabble, proudly applauding as an array of platters appeared, laden with roast beef, broiled potatoes, green beans, ham, wild rice, corn, and loaves of marvelous, fresh-baked bread. They toasted each other with fresh apple cider, saluted with celery stalks. Even Charles Simpson relaxed, his usual dourness gone as he basked in the glow of shared success.

"Congratulations, Brother Simpson," Nicholas offered.

"Thank you," he replied, a smile crossing his lips. "To you too," he added, raising his glass.

Had Simpson mellowed, Nicholas wondered. There was little evidence of the mimpy Torquemada in him now.

"I hope, Brother Manion," he began tentatively, "that now we can be friends." It was generous of him.

"Fine with me," Nicholas answered, a little disingenuously, still suspicious. "I never understood your enmity, anyway."

"Not enmity," Simpson said. "It was your singularity, your refusal to be like us."

"But I am like you, aren't I?" Nicholas interrupted.

"Ah—I'm not sure. I hope so." He eyed him squarely, a plea in his eyes. "That's our strength. Isn't it?"

"Sure. No harm done. It was probably my fault. Mostly." Simpson smiled. "I'll try to keep a lower profile, O.K.?" As Simpson nodded, Nicholas wondered whether he believed a word that either of them had said.

20

Late November brought more of the *ordo regularis*, and Nicholas's eighteenth birthday. The temperature plunged, and icy winds raged. The novices rarely strayed outdoors, and never without bundling up. Life continued to be both too shallow and overly serious. The letter of the law persisted in triumphing over the spirit.

For his birthday, Thomas sent him a black fisherman's sweater and Diana sent a box of Tina's cookies, those delicious, cakelike delicacies he loved so much. Delightedly he went to Scott's room late one afternoon during *quies* to share his treat as a way of reciprocating for the gift of the lucky nugget on Habit Day.

The *secundi* lived in actual rooms, with floor-to-ceiling walls, and doors that shut firmly. As Nicholas soundlessly inched Scott's door open, he felt no compunction about his disobedience—Thomas's headstrong son winning out over the correct novice.

Scott enthusiastically accepted the cookies but, in pantomime, indicated that Nicholas should not come in. As he walked back to his cell, Nicholas saw Simpson watching him, standing in his half-opened doorway, like a sentinel.

That night, after lights-out, Nicholas sat by his window and studied the moonlit grounds. The luminous sky was profligate with stars. Eighteen years old! If he were still in the world, he would be registering for the draft. And, student deferment or no, induction would be a real possibility. He didn't know the details, but from overheard fragments during kitchen work he learned there had been some sort of crisis recently involving Cuba.

He took a bite of one of the cookies. The taste reminded him of home. No mention had been made by anyone here of his birthday, though surely the Master knew. Remembering the festive air his parents had always created, Nicholas felt forlorn.

He was grateful for the cookies, relishing the thick, sweet chocolate. But he wished he had someone to talk to.

This was the first birthday he had ever spent away from home, the only time he had celebrated—if that was the word—by himself. He understood that Scott didn't want to flout the rules, but couldn't he have asked him in, just for a minute? They hadn't spoken in weeks, not really. Not privately. Was Scott avoiding him? In the chapel or the refectory, whenever Nicholas looked his way, it seemed Scott's thoughts were elsewhere. Deliberately? Was he cutting him, writing him off as trouble?

God, Nicholas asked himself, can't I get anything right! Stop it, he ordered back.

He must not yield to self-pity. What did he have to complain about? Compared to Karl, who was already in the marines, Nicholas had things awfully easy. Here he was, safe, cut off from the tumult of politics, the crazy swaggering of nations. It all seemed unreal from this perspective, a distant madness. The time was drawing close when civilizations might be flung onto the junk heap of history like the skulls of Tamburlaine. And Nicholas wanted to hear "Happy Birthday"?

21

Late Saturday afternoon, Brother Bennett was giving Nicholas a haircut in the equipment room in the basement. He worked smoothly, with the finesse of a pro. Nothing he did would surprise Nicholas anymore.

Bartlett, the next up, was plucking idly on his guitar. Normally it was kept locked away except on feast days; he had it now only because he was supposed to be composing a special song in honor of Saint Francis Xavier's feast day, December third.

"Finished your song yet, Bro?" Nicholas asked Bartlett as Bennett clipped.

"Shoot, no—I've barely made a dent. Just can't seem to catch the melody."

"Well, keep plunking. After all, can't let the team down."

"Right," Bartlett replied, sounding not at all convinced.

"Why don't you play us something now?" Bennett asked.

"Great idea!" Nicholas exclaimed. Anything to break the monotony.

"You really want me to?" Bartlett beamed briefly, then retreated into a skeptical scowl.

"Are you kidding? A private concert by Brother J. J. Bartlett, N.S.J., the balladeer of Bangor, Maine?" Nicholas knew he was dying to perform.

"Aw, give me a break."

"Come on," Nicholas pressed, "don't play hard to get."

"I'm really not sure I can remember anything."

"And spare us your humility-with-a-hook." He fixed his eyes on Bartlett. *"Quercus?"*

"Yes, Brother Bartlett, please do," Bennett put in.

"Very well," Bartlett said in a bored voice, "since you insist. Here goes nothing."

His voice was hard-edged but vibrant, the nasal quality not at all unpleasant. As he relaxed into the song, Nicholas felt Bennett remove his clipper. The song was one of Karl's favorites.

Totally in command now, knowing his audience was hooked, Bartlett gave the tune a big finish:

> *"Pack up your troubles in your old kit bag, and*
> *   smile, boy, smile;*
> *While you've a lucifer to light your fag*
> *Smile, boy, that's the style.*
> *What's the use of worrying? It never is worthwhile,*
> *So pack up your troubles in your old kit bag, and*
> *   smile, smile, smile."*

They gave him a big hand.

"Wonderful!" Bennett said.

"Very apropos," Nicholas allowed.

"Encore, encore!"

Bartlett put the guitar down and folded his arms.

"Not a chance," he said, smiling. "I'm smart enough to quit while I'm still ahead."

At the seminary, *otium* denoted idleness, even though, to be etymologically correct, it meant leisure. Whatever it was called, *otium* for the novice was a rare commodity. Lately Nicholas had seized the few crumbs of free time that fell his way to compile a glossary of novitiate code, that omnipresent *lingua Jesuitica* that controlled every fumbling intramural communiqué and gradually came to govern the inner eye of everyone there.

Under *exercitium modestiae*, Nicholas inscribed the categories:

Repetitio: Particular chapter.

Manifestatio: Novice reporting another's "culpa" to the Master.

Admonitio: Novice-to-novice.

Other terms described parts of the *ordo regularis*:

Scriptio: Sunday-evening penmanship practice.

Lectio: Spiritual reading at table; as in *lectio spiritualis* when alone.

Tones: Sermon practice, twice a month, beginning "Man, having defiled himself by sin, plunged into the abyss . . ."

Tactus: Rule of touch.

Numquam duo: Rule of threes. (To avert *tactus*-breaking.)

Manuductor: Another word for Beadle, signifying "leader of the band" or "by the hand"; hence, *sub*-manuductor.

Ambulatio: The Sunday walk.

Villa: The getaway. (Apparently the original Jesuits fled the Roman summer and took to the hills.)

Coadjutores: Literally "fellow workers," but used to refer to the second-grade religious known as "brothers" who take the three basic vows, but are not ordained.

Mandata: Rotating assignments, e.g., KP.
De Sexto: Re the Sixth Commandment.

On another page Nicholas listed seminary slang, some in fractured Latin, some in English:

Quercus: O.K.
Carne: Meat.
Tight: A failure to "settle in"; the *orda* getting to you.
Solid: Opposite of tight: "in-the-swim."
Vult: The Master requests the pleasure of your company. Often expressed silently, via a Churchillian two-fingered V.

Nicholas wasn't sure whether to add what Bartlett had said last Saturday when their laundry was delivered: *Ubi, ubi sunt mei sububi.* "Where, oh where, are my underwear!" No, better not, unless it became a "perpetual tradition."

He enjoyed making the list. He thought maybe sometime he'd show it to Scott, see whether he had any additions to suggest. It was one way for Nicholas to keep his mind off himself.

Father Edmund Moriarity, according to novitiate legend, was almost one hundred years old. Nicholas verified that he had retired here shortly after World War II, so the century mark was not at all preposterous. Like the sad-eyed priests who occasionally drifted through, some of them obviously drying out or recuperating from breakdowns, Father Moriarity might have outlived his usefulness, but he was still an honored member of the community.

It was one of the best things about the Society of Jesus: they never turned their backs on their own. The imposing iron gates that barred externs might well have borne this sign: *NOSTRIS?* WELCOME HOME.

Nicholas had been assigned to serve the Methuselan priest's Mass this week in one of the side altars in the chapel while the others had their breakfasts. He didn't really mind the extra wait, although Moriarity sometimes tried his patience. If Father O'Mara, back home, raced through in record time (he had timed him once with a stopwatch: twelve minutes flat), Father Moriarity was bucking for the opposite record; yesterday it had taken him an hour and fifteen minutes. He had lost his place three times, and Nicholas, each time, had had to steer him, very deferentially, back on course.

Father Moriarity had huge, rheumy eyes, a forehead peppered with liver spots, and a surprisingly full head of flocculent white hair.

He was a lovely old man, really, for all his pixilation. Two days ago, after Mass, he had reached deep into his cassock pocket and extracted a pitiful-looking piece of chocolate, its surface oxidized almost beyond recognition. "A Frango mint, from Chicago," he had confided.

As he washed his hands in preparation for vesting, Nicholas listened carefully as his high-pitched voice repeated the ancient prayer "that every stain might be wiped away," so as to serve God "without defilement of mind or body."

Nicholas handed him the white amice. He had to watch him like a hawk; his memory faded in and out, and could go haywire at any time. Yesterday he had with absolute conviction mistaken Nicholas for some long-dead colleague. The old man ducked his head through the "helmet of salvation," imploring it to repel "the assaults of the devil." He turned to accept the alb, pristine white also, bidding it to "purify my heart" by bathing "in the Blood of the Lamb."

He motioned impatiently; Nicholas placed the cord, or girdle, in his fluttery hand. Father Moriarity entreated this symbol of priestly chastity to "extinguish in my loins the desire of lust." Next came the maniple, violet for Advent, representing a handkerchief, a reminder that man's lot on earth is "tears and sorrow."

Then he assumed the "stole of immortality," symbolizing man's redemption, "although unworthy," through Christ. Finally, Nicholas eased over his head the emblem of charity, the chasuble, as he prayed, "O Lord, You said: 'My yoke is easy, and My burden is light.' "

That morning, when he had gone to fetch the priest, Nicholas had discovered him lying, with his eyes closed, on top of his bed. Pausing for a moment, Nicholas had seen the old man stir, and shake his gnarled fist in the air. Then, his high voice pinched with distress, he had implored, "O God, why can't I die?"

He turned now, the plea long forgotten, and motioned Nicholas out the door, a priest of God forever.

The next morning, although special detail with Father Moriarity excused him, Nicholas ducked into community Mass to hear what Bartlett had come up with.

Using the Alleluia from James and the Communion from Matthew, Bartlett had fashioned a bold, haunting folk-hymn. "Alleluia," he sang, his voice ringing clear:

> "Blessed is the man that endureth temptation:
> for, when he hath been proved, he shall receive
> the crown of life.
> Blessed is the servant, whom,
> when the Lord shall come,
> He shall find watching:
> Amen I say to you,
> He shall place him over all His goods."

The guitar and the English words seemed propitious, both timely and timeless. Bartlett had done himself, and their year, proud.

Lunch for once, lived up to its "feast day" billing. Brother Cook and his helpers had outdone themselves: the *carne* was steak, an unprecedented treat, done perfectly to a rosy blush, succulent with juice. Along with it came heaping bowls of french fries—another unwonted luxury—and platters brimming with buttered acorn squash.

The *Deo gratias* came early, just after the Martyrology, the room bursting into the usual inconsequential chatter. At Nicholas's table, Bartlett was the center of attention.

For dessert, heaping bowls of fruit were presented, a few pears and bananas mixed in with the apples from the orchard. This was accompanied by a plateful of cheeses: Nicholas recognized cheddar, St. Andre, and Port Salut.

Gazing at the head table, Nicholas noticed Father Kane slicing an apple in half. Cutting out the core, he proceeded first to divide one half, then the other, into neat little pieces. This done, he wiped his hands on his napkin and cut off a carefully measured slab of cheddar. Centering it on his plate, he then cut it into similarly symmetrical pieces.

Nicholas was fascinated. He saw where Kane's logic was taking him. The question was, how would the match come out?

Count to fifty, he told himself. Wait him out, don't gawk.

One thousand one, one thousand two . . .

. . . One thousand fifty.

Finally!

The Master was down to his last two pieces. Two pieces *each*, of apple and cheese.

How in God's name, Nicholas wondered, did he do it? No machine, he would bet, could have managed it.

That afternoon, Nicholas decided to slog through the thick brush next to the orchard. After breakfast, the Beadle had informed him that the Master refused to return the toilet kit. By putting his request through Mantello, Nicholas had hoped not to seem unwontedly eager. Nicholas searched the Beadle's face for explanation; Mantello had said, "Father Master suggested you should ponder Matthew: 'He who loves father or mother more than Me is not worthy of Me.' "

Wending his way desultorily, the cold air sharp and ammoniac, he saw Scott striding toward him.

"Got any more of those cookies?" he asked.

"All gone, I'm afraid."

"Well, happy birthday anyway. Belatedly."

Somehow, Scott had found out. He had his ways, Nicholas certainly knew that.

"Why didn't you tell me, you sap?"

"You didn't give me much of a chance, did you?"

Scott smiled weakly. "No, I guess not. Sorry."

At least he was here now.

"It's O.K."

"Good. Well, now, how're we going to celebrate? You not only made it through the Long Retreat, but turned eighteen! What should we do?"

"I can't imagine," Nicholas answered with a smile.

"Leave it to me, Bro. I'll think of something."

22

In the middle of the night, Nicholas was shaken awake by Father Kane. "Brother Manion, Brother Manion," the priest urged, "you must hurry! There isn't much time." Since this made absolutely no sense to Nicholas, he assumed Kane was terribly upset by something, to the point of being unintelligible.

"What's going on?"

"Your mother just telephoned. Forgive me for alarming you this way, but your father is gravely ill. You must come at once."

"What's wrong with him? Tell me." Kane handed him his cassock; Nicholas hastened into it and trailed behind the priest the length of the hallway and down the stairs. "Your mother will explain. She's waiting to talk to you."

They entered Kane's office, and Nicholas, full of terrible dread, grasped the telephone.

"Hello."

"Nicholas." Even half asleep, he knew that voice. Passionless and precise, it was unmistakable.

"Mother, what—?"

"You must come, now. Your father has had a heart attack."

"Is he—how—?"

"There's a bus at six o'clock. Gerald will be at the station. Go straight to St. Francis. I'll meet you there."

Bleary-eyed, Nicholas fumbled for his watch. The numerals glowed: 5:10.

"Mother?" God, didn't anything faze her, shake her composure? "Can't you at least tell me—?"

"There's nothing to tell. His condition is stable, but there isn't much time."

"Did he ask for me? Is he conscious?"

"He's completely lucid, despite the pain. Of course he refuses to take any medication." Was there a hint of reproach in her tone? It sounded almost like a reprimand. "As for asking for you, it's all he talks about. I'll see you in a few hours, dear."

She sounded so calm, so matter-of-fact . . .

"Mother, just one thing—"

"Yes?"

"Try to . . . restrain your grief."

She paused for a moment.

"Thank you, Nicholas. Yes. I'll try."

The Master drove him to the depot, and once he was settled on the bus, Nicholas, having had time to ponder, regretted the cheapness of his last remark to his mother, its insensitivity. Perhaps she hadn't meant to sound so perfunctory. What right did he have to criticize her? Perhaps her tears were long-since shed; perhaps she had none left and could now—and for him—muster only numb poise.

Nicholas was shaken utterly, shocked clean through. My God, his father was only sixty-two, in the prime of his life, full of vitality, on top of the world. How could he die? He tried to pray, but words wouldn't come—to plead, to bargain with God, to beseech and petition and promise anything if his father could only be allowed to live.

Attacked by his heart. It was a bitter, appropriate irony. No insinuating, implacable cancer for Thomas Manion, no peaceful slipping away in his sleep, no freakish accident on the road; he would require an *attack* when he least expected it, a superior strength vanquishing him suddenly, but not without a fight, game to the last.

As the bus droned forward through the thin light, Nicholas was overwhelmed with memories. Those long, languorous breakfasts at the club after Sunday Mass, just the two of them, coddled and fraternal before the roaring fireplace, when Nicholas could order whatever he wanted, like an adult. Afterwards they would drive to the Heublein Hotel to pick up Nicholas's copy of *The New York Times*, reserved especially for him, his father chuckling at his son's insistence on being "really informed." Then they would take a long, banter-charged drive out into the country. Sunday was their day, and they turned homeward regretfully, rarely before dark.

All those sports events they'd attended together flooded his reverie. The baseball game that introduced him to Roger Maris, whose Ruth-eclipsing sixty-one homers last year Thomas had debunked with caustic gibes about "a much, even suspiciously livelier ball than in my day." He had been a superb sandlot player in his own right, and Nicholas understood that the sarcasm was his father's mock-pompous way of asserting his own credentials. Nicholas recalled the tennis match between Gonzales and Hoad, when his father had arranged for Nicholas to meet them afterwards, to be photographed. He still owned the picture, the two athletes smiling into the camera, himself in profile, rapt as he gazed into Gonzales's face.

Nicholas recalled his father's tough humor, his jeremiads against modern society: "Richard Cory runs this country now. When is the last time we had a politician who even read poetry, let alone wrote it? Even Jack Kennedy reads Ian Fleming! Mere anarchy is the order of the day. Calypso Masses, idiots baring their souls on television. It's a pusillanimous age, Nick."

Upstart religions? "People chase panaceas in the damnedest places. The Second Coming can be anywhere . . . but in *Malibu*?"

The Ecumenical Council? "After the hullabaloo in Rome, the Jebbies may be the only Catholics left."

Unbelievers? "A sophist is a guy who doubts God exists, but hedges his bet. A cynic suspects He does exist, but the irony destroys him. Ha! No matter how you bob and weave, the fiend behaves only as long as our foot's on his head. He never quits and neither must we."

The future? "There *is* no peak in Darien."

And always he knocked Nicholas's tendency to be simplistic, toughening his son with relentless skepticism, firing probing questions, pitting concrete experience against Nicholas's vague fumbling. He had always treated his son with respect, but never spared him the brunt of an iconoclastic life.

And now Thomas was dying. "Please, dear Lord, don't let him die," he prayed.

Nicholas could not bear the thought of losing him. "Live, live!" he pleaded. "Please, God, I beg You: let my father live."

As they approached Hartford, Nicholas gazed out the window, surveying the countryside, glistening blue and amber in the rising sunlight. He tried to compose himself, taking several deep breaths, smoothing his trousers and rubbing his stubbled cheek. The tension within him had not abated. His breath tasted rank. I've got to get a grip on myself quickly, he told himself. This is no time for weakness or, God forbid, panic. He fought for calm, exerting his practiced will against the urge to let go, to cry out. But his body refused to behave, as though on sympathetic strike with his father's. He prayed. Tentatively, shakily, his control reasserted itself. He must be strong. Otherwise he'd be of no use to anyone. The bus hiccoughed to a stop. He grabbed his overnight case from overhead and moved toward the door.

As he stepped off the bus, Nicholas inhaled deeply and felt a punch to his lungs. It was so cold he thought he could grab a piece of the air in his hands and break it. His eyes squinted through the windows of the waiting room, raking it, searching for his mother. But she had said she'd meet him at the hospital, he remembered. As he rushed into the station, he spotted his father's driver.

"Nick," Gerald said, shaking his hand. "Your mother said we should hurry." He handed Nicholas an overcoat. "She thought you might have forgotten to bring yours." And he had, of course.

"How is he, Gerald?" Nicholas asked, full of trepidation.

"Stable, or so Doc Toppings says. Hanging tough. He's quite a fighter, your father."

Yes, I know, Nicholas silently agreed, that he is.

He slipped the coat on as they hurried through the terminal. It was his father's double-breasted camel's-hair. He had worn it as long as Nicholas could remember. Still in perfect condition—Thomas took infinite pains with his things. One night when Nicholas had found him near midnight in his library, diligently spit-polishing his shoes, he'd explained, "If you care for something, you must respect it. Good things are a trust. They're built to last. Longer than us, I'm afraid," he'd chuckled. "All it takes is a little vigilance."

Nicholas slipped into the familiar coat, buttoned it, and turned up the collar. Thomas's smells clung to it eloquently: Chesterfields and talcum. He was grateful his mother had thought to send it, but it made him uneasy to wear it. He felt like an impostor. He followed Gerald into the car, its engine left idling to keep warm. Nicholas felt truth taking shape, and recoiled from acknowledging it. Thomas would no longer require this coat. Now it was his. That's what his mother's thoughtfulness implied. He crouched in the back seat and shivered despite the warmth. Her gesture was too poignant, too resigned, too ominously formal. Couldn't she have waited? Thomas wasn't dead yet, was he? Not by a long shot. And he wouldn't "go peacefully," Nicholas had no doubt on that score. His father would battle to the last; Nicholas was here to help him.

Gerald inched the car forward. As they moved carefully toward St. Francis Hospital, Nicholas saw people chatting happily in cars gliding past him, or striding briskly down the sidewalk on their way to work. Just another day for them. Life was going on. He hated it. The streets were slick, slippery. Time for snow tires and chains. He clutched his coat to him like a blanket, running his hands lovingly over its rich, redolent surface.

They were there. Nicholas jerked open the door and rushed inside. At the desk he asked for his father's room. "Please wait over there," the receptionist said, pointing to a row of chairs.

Nicholas slumped into a chair. It was still difficult to believe. It hadn't sunk in yet. There was an open pack of Chesterfields in the coat pocket. He lit one and drummed his fingers on his knee. He watched the wisps of smoke curling up to graze the ceiling. Outside he saw that a storm was brewing, random flakes of snow powdering the morning's harsh glare. Let it be a blizzard, Nicholas urged. That would appeal to his father's sense of theater. Let the heavens thunder against the sterility of this place. In disgust, he butted the cigarette and threw the pack into a wastebasket.

"Nick, my dear boy," Dr. Toppings greeted him gravely as he approached. He placed his hands squarely on Nicholas's shoulders and averted his eyes. "Thank God you made it."

"How is he, Uncle Bob?"

Toppings shook his head sadly.

"What happened? Mother didn't tell me the details."

"She heard him fall in the library. He was lying by the fireplace, gasping for breath. His head was bleeding. He must have fallen against the andirons. She phoned me immediately, and the ambulance was there in ten minutes. It was a miracle, really, the speed. We've done everything possible."

Uncle Bob looked away, as though confounded.

"But he'll be all right?" Nicholas scrambled for hope, clutching his arm.

The doctor shrank from his touch. "I'm so sorry, Nicholas."

"But other people have heart attacks and recover. Isn't there anything you can do?"

"Come. There isn't much time." There was sadness and defeat in his voice, but anger also. He beckoned for Nicholas to follow, walking ahead with his shoulders slumped. All his knowledge could finally do so little, his melancholy movements said. Delay the inevitable. For a time.

Thomas lay flat against the bed, like a stricken warrior. Father O'Mara, purple stole slung over his cassock, loomed over him, mumbling prayers as he anointed him. Extreme Unction. The Last Sacrament. Church Latin had always soothed Nicholas, the daily ritual prayers giving him, as they gave his father, a sense of connection to the past. The words, martial and majestic, were rich with succoring secrets: *"Domine, non sum dignus ut intres sub tectum meum; sed tantum dic verbo et sanabitur anima mea,"* the priest intoned.

Thomas's eyes were shut, his breath stertorous. "He slips back and forth," Uncle Bob whispered. Nicholas heard his father's effortful wheeze, as if each breath was a rally. "Just sit down, Nick. I'll get your mother."

Nicholas tiptoed toward the bed, trying to rein his growing hysteria. How shocking it was to discover your father's mortality; it beggared hope. He lay there, a broken thing, defenseless before a siege of tubes and bottles that sprung from him like tentacles. I've never seen you at the mercy of anything, he thought bitterly. You always seemed invulnerable. Deathproof.

He grasped his father's hand gently. The touch repelled him. It was a pitiful, sparrowy, shrunken thing. He was shaken anew, more afraid than ever. He could feel his father's life slipping out of him. Nicholas choked back tears. His emotions were in mutiny. I'll do anything, give anything—even myself—for him, he pleaded. Please, merciful Lord, let him live.

The door opened and his mother came in, trailed by a pair of ruddy-cheeked nursing sisters. Diana kissed him, held him to her for a moment, then took up her vigil in a chair by the wall. The nuns bustled crisply in their starched habits, tense in their familiar toil, their eyes lowered. As they ministered to his father, Nicholas heard their shoes squeak on the rust-colored linoleum. Their thick red hands adjusted vials, plumped pillows. They were used to death.

"Nick," his father rasped. Then, stronger, "Nick?"

"I'm here, Dad," he whispered, bending to him. "I just got in."

"Good trip?" Thomas asked, as though the commonplace could deny his bootless state.

"Fine, fine. We even arrived a little early."

"That's good. Glad something runs properly."

Nicholas rested his head on his father's arm.

"Sorry I disrupted things," Thomas said. It was shattering. Even now, here, he seized all responsibility.

"Don't say that, Dad."

Thomas placed his other hand on his son's.

"There . . . don't be afraid."

Nicholas forced his head up. This was unbearable. He thought, Are you still comforting me?

"How do you feel, Dad?"

"How do I feel?" he repeated. "Cold-cocked. Defunct." There was humor in his voice. "Not a pretty sight, am I?"

"You look fine, just like always."

"Don't try to con *me*, son. I'm all caved in, I know it. Well, so be it. Let it be a lesson to you. We all wind up back where we started—helpless and bawling. Surprised I haven't started messing myself."

"Now, Dad . . ."

"So how's the novice? Let me look at you." Then, with an eerie chortle: "Still knocking them dead?"

"Everything's fine." How could he tell him the truth, burden him now with his doubts, his mounting anxiety, his fear that he'd made a mistake? The sudden realization shook him. Was that it? Had he really begun to doubt his vocation? Maybe. He wasn't sure. But this wasn't the time to ponder that. He couldn't turn one last time to his fallen father for strength. Thomas needed it all for himself now, as, adamant in his vision and defiant before this indignity, he kept his moral authority intact.

"I'm glad you're here," Thomas whispered as he squeezed Nicholas's hand with surprising force. It was so unfair. He waited passionately, like Macbeth transfixed by a forest on the march. "I would've preferred something a little more dramatic," he said. "Not just petering out like this."

"Don't say that," Nicholas insisted. "There's plenty of fight left in you."

"Damn straight. They haven't completely drained the spunk out of me. At least I'm no bloody vegetable. Come closer."

Nicholas lowered his ear so that it was only a few inches from his father's mouth.

"They keep trying to give me hypos. 'It'll help you sleep, Mr. Manion,' " he mimicked. " 'It'll ease the pain, Mr. Manion.' Hell, pain's all I've got left. As long as it hurts I know

I'm alive." He raised his head and hissed at the nurses, "I'll be sleeping soon enough, you bovine, mealymouthed—" only to fall back exhausted and lapse into silence.

In the cruel fluorescent light, time's circle was closing. If a man's last passion is his strongest, Nicholas thought, his father's ebullience was still remarkable. What a battler he was! Suddenly he snapped awake. What did he still hunger for, licking his lips so tenaciously? Yellowish stubble glistened on his cheeks. Threads of saliva hung from his cracked lips. His face mapped his long life.

The nurses continued their futile shuffling, their robust bodies bent forward over him. His father cried out in agony, and Nicholas rushed to him.

"Dad, if the pain's too much—"

"I can bear it. I'm not about to drift off in some junk-ridden stupor." He gasped, grimaced with pain, raising his hand as though to ward off help. "I *can* bear it." He paused, then mumbled something unintelligible.

"What? Can I get you something?"

"Communion," Thomas demanded.

Nicholas fetched the pastor from the corridor and led him to the bed. He watched him open the pyx and bestow the viaticum. It seemed to soothe his father. Even here, gaping at eternity, Thomas had twice the faith he had. Could this last Communion, this puny wafer of such old, lavish promise, be as awesome as the first so many years ago? Did the trusted, known, hieratic services console him here and blunt the terrible press of leave-taking? So it appeared. Thank God for that.

Nicholas wished he could do something besides stare as his father's life ebbed. He felt claustrophobic. Incense, pungent and rich, filled the room, overwhelming the fetid odor of disinfectant, that fatuous, hapless feint against decay. Brutal light yellowed the room. The priest, his duty done, retreated to Diana's side. Nicholas studied his mother, poised in her chair, her face glacial, her fingers mechanically crossing her pearl rosary beads. The nuns waited too, quiet but expectant, thrilled piety in their eyes. If his mother seemed unaffected by sacramental solace, the sisters visibly trembled in submission to God's will.

Thomas stirred. Matted from the intensity of his struggle, his hair lay against the pillow like lumps of crepe. Color had fled his face, leaving sallow parchment quilled with savage furrows. As he opened his mouth, his tongue grated against his lips, dry as sandpaper. Nicholas couldn't make out his words. He bent close again. The odor was bitter, rank.

"Get your mother."

"Can *I* do anything?" Nicholas asked, stupidly. The tension in his father's face softened. Mischief peeked from his eyes.

"There's nothing to do. Just wait."

Nicholas walked over and helped Diana to her husband's bedside. He heard his father gasp for breath, sucking the air, thrusting his head forward grotesquely, draining the dregs of his strength. Nicholas moved away.

Diana pressed her hands onto Thomas's, formally, as if now, at the last, meaning would burst forth, some sign, a final revelation. His father spoke and she replied, but Nicholas could not hear their words. As she crouched over his father, Nicholas was torn, resentful. His selfishness appalled him. Was he proprietary even now, claiming Thomas Manion exclusively? How pathetic he was! Despite the schism long life together had precipitated, husband and wife had, still, an intimacy from which the son was barred. Whatever had gone wrong in their marriage, these two beings were still locked together. He crept forward, and heard:

"Diana—" his father said.

"Yes, Thomas."

"We lasted, didn't we?"

"Yes, dear, that we did." She leaned to kiss his lips, then returned to her chair.

"Nick?"

"Yes, Dad."

"Pray with me."

Nick began automatically: "Our Father, Who art in Heaven—"

"No," Thomas interrupted, "you know the one."

Nicholas knew. It was his father's favorite. But it was a request Nicholas did not want to hear. Not now. He shut his eyes, unable to look, but lashed yet to his father's will, he limped through it:

"Dear Jesus, my Captain and my King," they prayed, "give me the grace to be generous, to give and not to count the cost, to fight and not to heed the wounds, to labor and not to ask for any reward save knowing that I do Thy holy will."

"Amen," Thomas ended, then sighed deeply. He stared into his son's eyes.

"Don't worry. You'll be all right," he said. "Just remember who you are. We're so proud of you." Tears poured from Nicholas now. "Be good to your mother. She loves you so."

"Yes, Dad."

"You're the best there is, never forget that."

"I'll remember . . . I'll make it, I promise you . . . I swear it. I'll make you proud. You can count on me, I'll show you."

"No," Thomas said sharply. Nicholas didn't think he had heard right. "You're wrong," his father said. "You don't have to do anything for me. You already have. You're my son, my sweet, strong son. That's everything."

Nicholas clutched his father's hand and pressed it to his lips. "I love you," he sobbed.

"I know."

Suddenly, Thomas's hand tightened in one last spasm. He said, "Remember . . ."

"He's gone," Father O'Mara declared, his hand on Diana's shoulder. She made the sign of the cross.

Nicholas felt ravaged. Nothing lasts, nothing. Now he was truly alone. Who could understand him now? Who would answer his questions, remove his doubts, know his needs? In his heart he felt despair. Thomas was dead. What a world of difference there was between the abstract elegance of God's will and its awful might, its bitter claim. "Goad me fast with grace," Nicholas prayed, "else how shall I come through?" Let no one matter too much, that's what the Bible taught. Put away childish things. They drilled at the seminary: Let go of worldly ties; yes, even family. "Unless ye conceive a hatred for your mother and father . . . ye cannot be true followers of the Lord," the stupefying Rodriguez had proclaimed. But how? They don't tell you how, Nicholas thought. Somebody help me . . . show me how. He felt violated.

He stared at his father. "Remember . . ." he had said. Remember what?

Wait! he wanted to shout. *You haven't finished.*

Something vital to him had been stolen, some inner core of self had been plundered.

His question would not be answered. The dead were terrible. They were no help at all.

Nicholas took his father's hands and crossed them upon his chest, then gently closed his eyes. Someone else would have to pull up the sheet. He couldn't endure that.

Thomas's face was relaxed now, shriven of strain.

"Remember . . ." What? Him? Nicholas was his father's testament. He couldn't forget that. He would always be his son.

Nicholas stared as the body was wrapped in a sheet. He loved his father unreservedly. But he could not be like him, could not match his faith. If he'd ever really possessed it at all, and himself through it, it was gone now, a chameleon melting into the landscape. As much as he admired Thomas's sureness, he mourned more his own powerlessness to grasp it. He had tried, as passionately in his own way as the old man in his, and it was no use. But he would keep on.

"Remember me," and "Remember who you are"—one or the other Thomas had started to say. Surely, too, Nicholas believed, he would have added, "But don't look back," or "Remember that." Was that it? "You don't have to do anything for me. You already have." Yes.

His mother grasped his arm and, gently applying pressure, led him toward the door. "Let's go home. It's all over," she said.

He let her lead him.

"You must be exhausted, dear," his mother said as soon as they arrived home. "Why don't you try to get some rest? Father O'Mara and I will make the arrangements. Uncle Bob will stop by later, when he's finished at the hospital."

Nodding somberly, Nicholas wandered into the library, still wearing his father's overcoat. He noticed he was sweating heavily. He slipped out of the coat and folded it carefully over the wingback chair.

Ash spilled from the fireplace. The desk was cluttered with papers. He flipped through them—policies, business letters, appeals from charities, mail-order brochures. Skimming abstractedly, he suddenly found himself reading his own letter from the seminary. It seemed so long ago . . . "It may not be what I expected, but overall it's just what I wanted," he had concluded, just a few weeks ago. What a pawky, fledgling, chimerical thing that confidence seemed to him now! Full of self-contempt, he tossed the letter aside.

He fished in his pants pocket for his rosary and began to pray. The repetition soothed him. He beseeched God for strength, for the resilience to survive this ordeal. His father's death and his mounting doubts about his vocation felt some-how connected, part of the same unfolding trial. He couldn't identify the link—it was nothing he could pinpoint or analyze—but all the same, he felt it. It was there, mysterious. Later he would probe, and try to grasp it.

The hypnotic prayers made him drowsy. He crossed to the sofa and stretched out, covering himself with the camel's-hair coat. Swiftly he found blessed sleep.

Nicholas bolted awake in a cold sweat. He heard the sound of voices coming from the living room, in strange, disorienting fragments:

". . . go to probate . . ."

". . . Nick has to . . ."

". . . a credit to the Church . . ."

". . . the community . . ."

Nicholas rubbed his eyes and shook the fearsome images from his mind. He felt like a child again, awakening in the middle of the night, frightened by puzzling sounds he couldn't identify, hoping Thomas would come to him.

He squinted at his watch; it was almost nine o'clock. On a bookcase, he noticed, stood the picture of him in his cas-sock, carefully fixed into a silver frame.

As he was about to go into the hall, Tina appeared in the doorway.

"Nicolai," she said, her strong brown arms reaching to enclose him. "My poor boy," she whispered, as he moved to return her embrace and placed his lips on top of her bun of hair. She smelled of cinnamon.

"How's my girl?" Nicholas said, moving her back, his hands on her shoulders. She scowled.

"You must not say that no more, Nicolai. A priest now . . ." she murmured, bowing her head slightly.

"Well, almost, anyway." He smiled. In her mind he was already ordained.

"You want dinner?" she asked, reasserting her domain.

"No, thanks."

"I bake cookies," she said with a knowing lilt.

"Maybe later. I should put in an appearance, don't you think?" he asked, motioning toward the voices.

She nodded.

He bent down and kissed her cheek. Her hand flew to cover it.

"I'll see you later, O.K.?"

"O.K.," she replied, laughing.

He found them in the living room, his mother serving coffee. Father O'Mara, as irritatingly natty as ever, bounded over to him. The priest used their home as his "cave," his secular retreat. Well, all priests had them, places where they could shuck their collars, let off steam, and hoist a few.

"Feeling better now, my son?"

Nicholas flinched at the facile, paternal presumption.

"I guess so."

"'Tis a terrible shock, but mercifully he didn't suffer long." His mother handed the old pastor a demitasse. He gazed at it in mock wonder, then grimaced comically in distaste. "It was God's will," he said, consigning it to a side table.

"Right," Nicholas said listlessly, the bromides of condolence infuriating him.

"And how are things at the seminary?" O'Mara asked breezily.

"*Optime, pater.*" Things were just fine. There was no point in opening *that* can of worms, Nicholas observed to himself with grim humor.

"Excellent. We're all very proud of you. Himself especially, may he rest in peace."

"Thank you, yes, I know." Wouldn't he ever shut up?

Father O'Mara moved to the sideboard and poured himself a tall whiskey. Nicholas turned to greet Dr. Toppings.

"We did everything we could," he said in a small, beaten voice.

"I know, Uncle Bob." Nicholas lacked the strength to comfort him.

"Some things are just beyond our power."

"I understand," he replied weakly. "Thank you." Nicholas hated this, hated to feel the pleading in his voice.

"Sit down, dear," his mother said softly. "Can I get you something?"

"I'll have a brandy. Please."

She rose gracefully and poured him a tumblerful. She handed it to him and then caressed his forehead, pushing back his tousled hair. He inched away, gulping the liquor, feeling its fire surge through him. She returned to her chair.

"The funeral will be Friday morning—a Solemn High Mass at the parish," she told him.

"The archbishop himself will be the celebrant," Father O'Mara announced proudly, as though such rare respect to one of his parishioners ultimately complimented him, like appearing on a papal honors list, like being elected a Knight of Malta. . .

"When do you have to go back?" Uncle Bob asked Nicholas.

"Right after, I'm afraid." Nicholas could see his mother was distressed by this.

"I'd like you to give the eulogy," she said.

It was too much. He couldn't. He'd break down.

"Mother, please, no, let Father O'Mara or Uncle Bob—"

"No," Dr. Toppings insisted, "it should be you."

"Your father would have wanted it, I'm sure," Diana declared pointedly, confidently, as though the mere invocation of Thomas's authority would stifle protests. Even now his word was law.

"All right," he acquiesced. "I'll try."

"It'll be a major funeral, Nick," the pastor interjected. "Everyone will be there." His enthusiasm was repugnant. He sounded like a salesman, as though funerals came in sizes, like steaks. Did he count the house? Did attendance define the solemnity of the service? "But no one expects a full-scale panegyric." He chuckled condescendingly. He seemed irked that Nicholas had capitulated so easily, failing to woo him. "Just a few heartfelt words, Nick, short and sweet."

"O.K."

"You must be famished, dear. Do you want me to get you something?" his mother asked.

"No, that's O.K."

"You should eat something. You're terribly thin. Are you sure they're feeding you properly?"

"I'm all right," he answered fiercely. "Just leave me alone." Surprised at his vehemence, he was embarrassed. "Really, I couldn't eat, not now. But thank you." She regarded him stoically, her eagerness to please him thwarted, retreating behind that familiar, arctic smile.

"As you wish."

"I think I'll just go to bed." With that, he rose and made his abrupt good nights.

"Sleep well, dear." She grasped his arm awkwardly and kissed his cheek. Uncle Bob, tears welling in his eyes, shook his hand emphatically. From his debonair perch against the mantel, Father O'Mara twirled his highball glass against the chandelier's golden light.

"See you at Mass tomorrow morning?" Was it a question or a command, Nicholas wondered.

"Of course. Good night." At this point, feeling ready to drop on the spot, Nicholas didn't really care. He climbed the stairs slowly and entered his bedroom, dropping fully clothed onto his bed and pressing his face deep into the pillow.

The next morning during Mass, Nicholas rededicated himself to his vocation in his father's memory, and vowed to give his life at the seminary a fresh chance. He would try to expunge his doubts and chasten his pride. He owed it to himself, and to his father, to apply himself with renewed fervor. He needed to be patient, to trust in God. Becoming a Jesuit wasn't some wild-goose chase. Give it time. If things didn't work out after a decent period, he'd deal with it then. When the time came. *If* it came.

Now the familiar church refreshed his zeal and reminded him of his old discovery, the goal his gaze was fixed on. The rich, ancient silence reassured him, the timeless rituals and comforting smells reminded him who he was. He hoped the Vatican Council would leave that intact. It was an eloquent silence, resounding down the centuries, "Dear Lord," he addressed it, "forgive me for my fears and my weakness. Help me to be steadfast. If I've been wrong, made a mistake, show me, give me a sign. If I really do have a vocation, *show me*, so the doubts that torment me will cease. Amen."

He gazed across the empty pews and saw the altar boy sniffing out the tall, stately candles, as he himself had done a thousand times. He felt in control of himself once more, at a semblance of peace. His mind was made up.

Two telegrams were waiting for him on the hall table when he returned home. Fetching coffee from the kitchen, he sat down in the library and tore the first open. It read:

> THE FATHERS AND BROTHERS OF ST. IGNATIUS SEMI-
> NARY EXTEND THEIR DEEP SYMPATHY ON YOUR
> UNTIMELY LOSS STOP OUR PRAYERS ARE WITH YOU
> STOP ETERNAL REST GRANT UNTO HIM O LORD AND
> LET PERPETUAL LIGHT SHINE UPON HIM FR E C KANE SJ

Nicholas tossed it aside and opened the second. It read:

> AESCHYLUS WROTE IN OUR SLEEP PAIN WHICH CAN-
> NOT FORGET FALLS DROP BY DROP UPON THE HEART
> UNTIL IN OUR OWN DESPAIR AGAINST OUR WILL

COMES WISDOM THROUGH THE AWFUL GRACE OF GOD
STOP I AM THINKING OF YOU SCOTT.

It was gracious of Father Kane to wire, but he'd half expected that. It was the decorous thing to do. But Scott! How had he managed it? Nicholas was profoundly moved. And, oddly, comforted.

23

More than eight hundred people came to pay final homage to Thomas Manion. As the organ swelled sumptuously, the pallbearers bore the bier toward the catafalque. The archbishop, flanked by a deacon and subdeacon and acolytes soldiering candles, waited with hands solemnly pressed together, upraised as though to Heaven, just behind the communion rail, its golden brass twinkling. Sunlight poured through the stained-glass windows. Legions of friends came to mark the passing, proud men kneeling in commiseration and honor. In the sanctuary, Lyon attended in a side pew on the gospel side, by the baptistry. The altar held two huge vases teeming with red tea roses.

Beside his mother in the front, Nicholas felt proud. The mayor, the editor of the *Courant*, colleagues and competitors, Catholics, Protestants, and Jews—they were all here. Even a few of Nicholas's old schoolmates had come, eyeing him with curiosity. Tina knelt a few rows back. Despite his irritation with Father O'Mara, Nicholas had to admit it was an *event*. His father would have been pleased.

The archbishop, magisterial in his black vestments, his confident chant collecting the mourners in its austere embrace, moved authoritatively across the altar, celebrating the Solemn High Requiem. Nicholas immersed himself in the ancient, consoling service. The choir commenced the *Dies Irae*, beautiful voices joining in urgent plea. Translating effortlessly, Nicholas echoed them inwardly, tolling the terrible, thrilling words:

> *"Lo, the Day of Wrath, that day*
> *Shall the world in ashes lay . . .*
> *Then shall written book be brought,*
> *Showing every deed and thought*
> *From which Judgment will be sought . . .*
> *How then shall my life appear?*
> *Who the saint my prayer to hear,*
> *When the just himself shall fear?"*

It worked. Somehow, against all odds, it worked—easing despair, recovering meaning from the abyss, asserting an eternal connection.

> *"Who just judge of vengeance art,*
> *Thy forgiveness now impart . . .*
> *Whilst with shame Thy throne I near,*
> *Thou, O God, my crying hear!"*

Only thus, Nicholas believed with every sinew of his soul, was the fiend ground down, time's tawdry charade thwarted, and a perpetual present proclaimed. The living and the dead were indissolubly linked, fellow participants in the same triumphant mystery.

The archbishop towered in the pulpit, his miter glistening, his crosier clutched in his left hand. He read from the Bible, his cadence momentous:

"Happy are they who die in the Lord.
In those days I heard a voice from Heaven,
saying to me: Write: blessed are the dead,
who die in the Lord. Henceforth now, saith
the spirit, that they may rest from their labors;
for their works follow them."

He beckoned. Holding his notes, Nicholas rose, genuflected before the Communion rail, and walked toward the pulpit. He watched the aged prince of the church descend; then he climbed the stairs.

It was his first moment in a pulpit. As he surveyed the congregation, it seemed a melancholy serendipity. Would that he could have forgone the honor. Drawing a deep breath, he began:

"My father was a proud man. He would have exulted to see you all here today, not because of your respect, though he cherished it as well earned, and not because of your affection, though he embraced it as generously given. He would have exulted, rather, because this community, comprising such restless diversity, together asserts a connection between past and future, proclaims continuity and coherence within the pitifully brief span of human life.

"Here, in this Catholic Church he loved so passionately, in the presence of his wife and son and pastor and friends, he bids farewell in the bosom of the community he valued above all else and spent his life striving adamantly to preserve.

"My father was a self-made man, self-driven. Faithful husband, loving father, civic leader, successful entrepreneur, he was *par excellence* a believing, practicing Catholic. His faith never wavered. His devotion never weakened. He faced death with a scornful eye and a confident heart. He was a tenacious Pauline; the Romans and the Roman Church were his masters. He possessed—in spades—what they call *virtus*, that manly strength, that patient commitment to the truth that in secular terms signifies a religious spirit. As the Jesuit poet Gerard Manley Hopkins wrote, 'the just man justices . . . makes all his goings graces.'

"We do not come here today to mourn Thomas Manion, but to bear witness to his lifelong grace. As we grieve our loss, we rejoice in his triumph. Tomorrow and tomorrow and tomorrow we shall miss him. But his loving memory and example we will carry with us all our days.

"Several years ago my father spoke his own best epitaph: 'I never doubted for a second that a man, if he could cut the mustard, could jump clean and straight from this vale of tears to the beatific vision.'

"Godspeed."

The cortege paused at the nave, the choir singing, as the archbishop, having exchanged chasuble for cope, circled the coffin, blessing with incense and holy water. "And with Lazarus who once was poor," Nicholas prayed with him, "may you have everlasting rest."

"I am the Resurrection and the Life," the archbishop began, having completed the aspersion. "He that believeth in Me, although he be dead, shall live; and everyone that liveth, and believeth in Me, shall not die for ever."

Father O'Mara was blessing the grave. First with holy water and then with incense he conducted the ancient ecclesiastical *vale*.

In the sharp sunlight they stood in a horseshoe formation with the gaping grave at the mouth, the trilling of birds nature's only recognition.

"*Oremus*," O'Mara led them. "*Deus, cujus miseratione animae fidelium requiescunt, hunc tumulum benedicere dignare . . .*" O God, by Your mercy rest is given to the souls of the faithful; be pleased to bless this grave . . .

Imploring the angels to guard this grave and set free

Thomas's soul from the chains of sin, O'Mara handed Diana a trowel. She hitched the skirt of her black suit like a genuflecting nun, scooped the earth, and scattered it on the coffin as pallbearers slowly let the ropes inch through their fingers.

"*Kyrie eleison.*"

"*Christe eleison.*"

"*Kyrie eleison.*"

"Have mercy on us all," Nicholas echoed.

"*Pater Noster,*" O'Mara began, racing through it.

"Thy will be done," clamored in Nicholas's ears, every wound's balm and every torment's surcease. In that sovereign faith was all doubt dispelled, and all tragedy but the pivot for the annealing mystery of grace. Through the glass which we now darkly see, the unfathomable sows its brute seed; but immanent everywhere is the hand of God, and one day, returned to light, we will see it plain: insuperable, numinous.

I know it, I believe it, Nicholas told himself, so why, dear Lord, *why* can't I feel it?

If this was only Thomas's joyful *introit* into eternity, why did Nicholas want to flee?

He took the trowel and repeated his mother's submissive *ave.*

"*Requiescat in pace,*" O'Mara said.

"Amen," the assemblage prayed.

Nicholas glanced around furtively. Father Lyon was there beside Diana, his eyes fixed on his shoes. Directly across stood Hal Patter, the insurance man who'd been one of the judges at the Optimists' oratory contest. Catching Nicholas's glance, he flashed his febrile grin.

His hand raised in blessing, O'Mara intoned, "*Requiem aeternam dona ei, Domine.*" Eternal rest grant unto him, O Lord.

"*Et lux perpetua luceat ei,*" they replied. And let perpetual light shine upon him.

Thomas's light, which had blazed like a comet across Nicholas's life, was quenched. But his memory would be a star, and never extinguished.

It was over. Turning toward the waiting car, Nicholas saw Lyon take Diana's arm and cradle her against his shoulder. He whispered something in her ear, and she nodded. The pallbearers brushed dirt from their trousers and walked away. Uncle Bob stared briefly at Nicholas, and smiled gamely before trudging off.

Nicholas lingered by the grave, as though his stubborn refusal to leave could stave off the finality of the farewell. He knelt to pray. Above the chatter by the cars, its very existence an assault on his possessive heart, he heard a trumpet. Its strong, mournful tolling carved the air. Dum-da-dum. Taps.

Turning swiftly, Nicholas spotted a soldier about a hundred feet beyond the grave.

Karl. In full Marine Corps dress.

Nicholas clambered to his feet and raised his right hand in greeting. Karl continued playing, his eyebrows jammed together in furious concentration.

Plangent, soothing, commensurate. Taps.

A soldier willy-nilly of life, how his father would have loved this martial sendoff!

Finished, Karl lowered his bugle smartly to his left side, and saluted.

Nicholas heard the quizzical buzz from the parking lot, and saw Lyon gesture toward their car.

Tears welling in his eyes, he rushed toward Karl.

Karl's lips were parted in his old sprite's smile. He shook Nicholas's hand gruffly, then reached to hug him. Clasped to him, Nicholas noticed his hair had been shorn, the carroty curls brushcut away.

A little embarrassed, Nicholas returned the embrace for a moment, then pulled back. *Tactus. Noli me tangere.* It didn't matter with whom.

"How're they hanging, hotshot?" Karl asked.

"Karl, I—"

"I'm sorry about your dad."

"Karl, what in tarnation are you doing here? Mother said you were in North Carolina."

"Yeah, Quantico. They finally got me"—he grinned—"as you can see. But I had some leave coming, so when I got the news . . ."

"Unbelievable," Nicholas said.

"I figured I owed him."

Nicholas stepped back and examined Karl's uniform. "Very spiffy."

"So where's yours?" Karl demanded, never a preener. "Don't tell me the old iron-knees I hung around with musters in *that* getup—it looks brand new."

"We don't get our clerics—our dress clothes, if you will—till we take vows."

"Doesn't seem like fun unless you can wear the uniform," Karl said quickly. Then, as though to prove he'd meant no criticism, he added, "But what do *I* know?"

They started walking toward the parking lot.

"Nick, it was him that gave me that scholarship, right?" Nicholas just stared, nodding.

"Yeah, I figured it was. Too much of a coincidence. Nobody but you knew enough about my business."

"He didn't want you to know."

Karl clapped him on the shoulder. "No sweat."

"He would have been honored that you're here. *Is* honored. He knew how you felt about playing for people."

"He was different."

So he was.

"So, how're your folks?"

"Same as ever. Mom slaves away, and Dad's got a new project." He paused and looked at Nicholas sardonically. "Frozen Chinese food."

They laughed together.

"Well . . ." Nicholas began.

"I know, I know. Don't say it. God, I'd give anything if just once one of his schemes would hit the jackpot."

"Maybe this time," Nicholas suggested unconvincingly.

How awful and unnatural for a son to be unable to help his father.

"Yeah, and maybe the Corps will go coed. Fat fucking chance." Suddenly he thrust his hand to his mouth and looked sheepish. "Oops, sorry!"

" 'S all right," Nicholas said. "I haven't been completely purified yet." He wanted to tell him he was still much the same; no need for deference.

Mischief danced in Karl's eyes. "Better not open *that* can of worms."

Nicholas laughed, remembering. "You're right."

"So, when do you go back?"

"This afternoon."

"Is it what you expected?"

"Pretty much." God, he wanted to talk, but there wasn't time, and besides, Karl could never understand. Even as kids, they'd been in different worlds, hadn't they?

"No regrets?" Karl bulldogged.

"Not to speak of."

Karl stopped, at the edge of Thomas's grave. Nicholas turned back to face him.

"Nick, I'm glad. I really am." He seemed uneasy, but determined. "I think of you."

Nicholas's heart was in his throat.

"Same here," he mumbled. "Do you know where they'll send you?"

"Europe, I guess. Looked like Cuba two months ago. Now, who knows? It was a pretty close call."

"Nicholas!" he heard his mother call.

"Well, pal, take care," Karl said.

"You too."

"Oh, don't worry about me. It's sure funny, though."

"What?"

"All the time we were growing up—everything was ahead of us, nothing was impossible, especially for you."

"And?"

"We just didn't have a clue. It's a whole new ball game out there."

"Scary?" Nicholas asked.

"*Crazy*." He twirled his finger about his ear.

Nicholas heard Lyon summoning him. Time to go.

"Take it easy," Karl said.

"I—what I mean is—Karl, I . . ."

Karl stared straight into his eyes, his eyes shimmering. "You don't have to say it."

The tears finally escaped, cascading down Nicholas's cheeks, a torrent, for his father, for what he had been, for himself, for what could never be.

"I've got eyes, Nick. I always could read you like a book."

Nicholas wiped his eyes, and grinned.

"A *comic* book," Karl added.

To hell with *tactus*! Nicholas reached to hug his friend.

"Thank you, thank you so much, Karl." Then he turned and started off. "See you," he called back.

"You bet. I'll be around."

Nicholas neared the car. Diana was waiting.

"Hey, hotshot!" Karl called. "Just one thing—"

"What?"

"Who the hell was Kilroy, anyway?"

Nicholas laughed, pressed his finger briefly to his lips, then tossed off a salute.

He was here, but now he's gone, Nicholas thought. Let Kilroy stay with my father.

After the burial, as Gerald drove them to the station, his mother spoke. "I'll write you, once the will is probated. Whatever specific bequests he made, you'll be the main beneficiary. You're a rich young man now."

"Mother, don't . . ." It couldn't matter less. "As a novice, I have no . . ." She had no sense of timing, having been silent for so long.

"Of course, dear," she interrupted. "However, if things should change . . ."

"I'd really rather not discuss it." This was the last thing he wanted to hear.

"Nicholas, you're deeply upset. I simply want you to remember your home is here. I am here. If it doesn't work out, you can always come back."

"Mother, please—" He couldn't take any more.

"Don't say anything," she snapped. "I love you, Nicholas."

He was ashamed. "I know I haven't been much comfort to you, much of a son, really."

"No!" she said. "Stop. I love you. That's *my* business."

The car pulled in at the terminal, and he grabbed his bag.

"Thank you," he said.

"Pray for me," she whispered as she waved goodbye.

He pulled the coat tightly around him, and hurried off.

Part Three

ACT OF FAITH

24

When Nicholas arrived outdoors the following Monday, he was late for the communal rosary. The other novices had already formed bands and ambled off. Uncertain of what to do, Nicholas suddenly spotted Scott in the nearby grounds, pacing aimlessly in the light snow, and called to him.

Scott looked up, waved, and sizing up the situation, he strode over and offered to say rosary with Nicholas. They circled the grounds slowly, praying aloud, never for a moment deviating from decorum. When they had finished, Scott whispered, "I'm so sorry about your dad."

"Thank you. I loved your telegram." Nicholas looked at him and felt his eyes begin to tear. He turned away and kept going toward the main building. Once there, he saw Simpson huddling with two of his clique. By the cold glint of victory in his eye, Nicholas knew what Simpson intended to do.

TUESDAY, DECEMBER 18, 1962

The desks in the ascetory were pushed back. The novices stood in a horseshoe, with the Master at its mouth. Particular

Chapter was another *exercitium modestiae*, occurring once every month or so, whenever Father Kane decided. Designed to nourish charity, or "supernatural affection," as it was also called, it was an opportunity for public admonition by one's peers.

Today, Nicholas knelt in the center of the horseshoe, his hands clasped and his head bowed, as one by one the other *primi* volunteered their spiritual critique.

Nicholas welcomed any break in the routine, but being under the gun oneself, he now realized, was no picnic. Still, since everyone sooner or later would be kneeling where he was, the sessions rarely strayed beyond bland generalities.

"Brothers, let us begin," Father Kane intoned.

Bartlett was first. "Well—um—Brother Manion sometimes shows unwonted haste in the hallway."

"And he sometimes forgets to fasten his cassock," the next one put in.

"Next?" the Master pressed.

"Occasionally, Brother wolfs his food and makes slurping sounds," Brother Bennett offered. "Especially dessert," he added, stimulating a few nervous giggles.

"During *recreatio*, Brother rarely joins in," another said. It was true, Nicholas had no defense, abandoning flag football because it didn't meet *his* standards, preferring a pickup handball match with one of the *secundi*.

It was Simpson's turn now.

"Reverend Father and loving Brothers," he began with ominous formality, "by authority of holy obedience and in the spirit of Christian charity, I accuse Brother Manion of violating the rule of threes during the rosary." Here he paused, and curiosity quickened. "And I further accuse Brother Manion of indulging in a particular friendship with Brother Turner."

The room was now rapt; Simpson had waved the red flag. It was a serious charge, shocking less in its concrete details than in its suggestive vagueness, its dark and potent innuendoes. Several novices glanced nervously at Nicholas and hurriedly turned away in embarrassment. Others stared, avidly scrutinizing his reaction.

Nicholas was indignant. True, he had technically violated the rule of threes. But there were mitigating factors, and only an ax-grinder like Simpson would have upped the ante this way. A cautious tactician, he had obviously concluded that the skein of minor infractions Nicholas had committed would support, in the Master's juridical account book, the public uttering of this incendiary catch-all. Two seminarians, of different years, were having a particular friendship. Nicholas could not fathom the basis of Simpson's enmity, but he was sure it was real, for he now stood branded before his fellows and before Father Kane by that stigmatizing code word: PF.

Nicholas stared at Simpson for a moment, then turned away. In a firm, even voice, he spoke: "Reverend Father and dear Brothers, I humbly thank Brother Simpson for his criticism and accept it in the spirit in which it was given. It is true that I violated the rule of threes, and while there were reasons for it, it was a fault and I do repent it. *But*," he continued, his voice rising, "I cannot, in conscience, acquiesce to his calumny."

Gasps of surprise swept the room; this was unprecedented, absolutely not done, quintessential bad form. "There is no truth whatsoever to the charge of particular friendship, and I deny it absolutely." He knelt, shaking, every eye on him. Several shook their heads as though impressed by his reckless bravery, but certain of its imminent quashing. Averting their eyes, they inched backwards as though subconsciously separating themselves from this firebrand. Simpson could barely suppress his glee; this was more, much more, than he had ever dared contemplate. Resistance, let alone denial, instantly legitimized his action. Father Kane stared sternly, seemingly undecided as to whether it was wiser to quell this rebellion immediately, in public, or to defer dealing with it until later, in the privacy of his office. After several moments the Master rose, cast a final, enigmatic glance at Nicholas, and left the room. Kane had seemed wary, but also intrigued, like a commander so used to unquestioning obedience that a threat to his authority is almost a welcome surprise, an unexpected opportunity to reassert it. Resistance, even when foredoomed to defeat, was the only flint against which power could strike sparks.

After breakfast the next morning, the Beadle pointedly told Nicholas: *"Pater magister vult te videre."*

"Me?" Nicholas stalled.

Mantello was unamused. *"Te. Nunc."* Kane had evidently decided to act swiftly, there being no more flagrant affront to obedience than publicly rebuking the forms, fixed and hieratic, of religious authority. Even if the charge was arbitrary or false, meek submission was the insignia of a good novice.

As he approached the Master's door, Nicholas understood that he had ripped the fundamental fabric of seminary life. While he knew the Master could—and would—exact repentance, he was glad he had done what he had done. He could not win the point, but he had succeeded in making it. It might serve to forestall future mischief. And it signaled to the Master that Nicholas was not someone who casually stifled his sense of justice. It introduced an alien note of democratic fair play into these ancient authoritarian walls; Nicholas would not be cowed by time-honored forms or fazed by traditional rubrics of behavior that had no intrinsic connection with the spirit of religious life. If he believed he was right, he would follow his father's example—he would stick to his guns.

Nicholas knocked on the Master's door, and was called in.

He found Father Kane kneeling at his prie-dieu, head pressed to the wood in prayer. Elaborately crossing himself, the Master rose and motioned for Nicholas to be seated. He sat down behind his desk and began.

"Well, Brother Manion, how are you?"

"Very well, thank you, Father." He paused. "Still afloat, at any rate."

"Are you finding it any easier to sleep lately?" asked Kane.

"I think I'll always be an incurable night owl. But I slept like a log last night."

"I see." Kane ignored the implication. He took off his dark glasses, plucked a handkerchief from his sleeve, and began to polish the lenses.

"Of course, at the beginning there are, for some of the novices, problems of adjustment. Some, who've always shied from the limelight, find the transition so smooth as to be nonexistent; they transplant effortlessly. Others, who are—like yourself—more, shall we say, mercurial, find the change in tempo unsettling. All that energy which found several suitable channels in the world seems here to have no outlet."

"Exactly," Nicholas replied. "You get the impression at times you've been developing your talents only to find them ignored here, or—"

"But of course, Brother," Kane interrupted drily, "we realize this period of absorption in menial tasks is only temporary, a brief imitation of Our Lord's hidden life. What is individual in us, our talents, as you put it, will blossom forth again, but, one hopes and prays, transformed and ennobled and galvanized by the guiding insight that they serve God and not ourselves."

"I understand the theory, Father," Nicholas replied irritatedly. "Don't you think I've told myself a hundred times that my ego is just balking at sacrifice? But trust can carry you only so far. How can you serve God with any distinction if you can't *be* yourself? Honestly, there's no way I can order a new personality. Why pretend you can make a drone out of someone who is—mercurial?"

Father Kane looked squarely at Nicholas and replaced his eyeglasses. His lips parted in an indulgent smile, but his gaze was steady and cool.

"No, no, you're exaggerating just a little, aren't you? Although you seem to think so, we are hardly exhorting you to perform 'internal surgery' on yourself. All we ask is that you have a little patience. Your zeal, your curiosity, your restlessness are all to your credit. But they can't have free rein just yet. As you'll appreciate, no sculptor can deal with a subject that persists in jumping about. No. He must keep still and allow the artist to work. Creation takes time. You are, in a sense, the subject of divine artistry, and the infusion of God's grace requires a certain amount of prudent, trustful passivity. Doesn't that make sense?"

"Yes, it does, Father," Nicholas answered. The Master had a point. But, pursuing his analogy, how long was the subject supposed to sit there? "Of course it makes sense. It's just that I'm starved for a little stimulation. I'm tired and I'm bored and I'm worried. My mind is restless. We have no newspapers, no magazines, no 'worldly' books. What's happening in Cuba—or Berlin? I'm famished for news, and I just don't see how getting some would endanger my spiritual life. Sometimes I think there's a streak of anti-intellectualism around here, as though knowledge were a weapon needed to battle the enemy, but better forgone if the enemy doesn't exist. It's like Saint Thomas à Kempis saying he'd rather feel compunction than know its definition. As though they were mutually exclusive!"

"Now, now," the Master replied, "it's all a matter of priorities, isn't it? The Society of Jesus has a pretty impressive record of intellectual achievement, I'm sure you'll agree. We can boast some of the world's finest scholars, scientists, even artists. Murray and Lonergan and many others. But they are priests first. And they all went through two years of novitiate. Two years identical to your own. At the beginning of training, we concentrate, rather reasonably, I suggest, on creating the proper context for those subsequent achievements. *Ad maiorem dei gloriam.* To the greater glory of God. *God*, not man. Not ourselves. That is our motto and that is our proper motivation. All that we do, from Alphonsus tending his door for forty years to Rahner combing the mysteries of salvation, is equal, equally worthy, in God's eyes. We are His servants, and all we do is to His glory, not our own. So we devote two years to building a rocklike foundation of faith and spiritual solidity on which each novice can erect a life that will, according to his talents, serve God and man. In your enthusiasm to get on with things, to be doing, you may be overlooking how painstaking the construction of that foundation must be. It takes a great deal of time to be sure that ours really is a vocation. It's not uncommon for someone to be attracted to us by the glamour of our active life—teaching, preaching, intellectual pursuits of every type. But we must know why we are here, why we do these things. It is finally the *why* and not the *what* that matters in religious life, the spirit rather than the letter. Our concern is souls. Unlike politics, for example, in the service of God motives are more important than results. In government, we may concede that an evil man, with selfish motives, can accomplish social good. And we can judge him and applaud him on the basis of those results, for his motives are for God alone to judge. Because we seek only the results, they are all we have a right to reckon. But God, seeing all, cares less for the quantity of success in the world's eyes than for the quality of attempt in His own. The world lusts after prizes. But it is purity God loves."

"Do I detect in your choice of words, Father," Nicholas asked, "the reason of this visit?"

Father Kane stiffened in his chair. His mouth twisted briefly into a grimace, as though he found what he was about to say very distasteful.

"As usual, Brother Manion, you come to the point, and spare me the indelicacy of raising, arbitrarily, what I find a most painful subject. It is indeed of purity that I wish to speak with you. Purity. And obedience."

"And not, I presume, as abstract virtues," Nicholas said.

"Again correct," the priest replied. "No, it is of, of . . . of concrete, if inadvertent, scandal that I must speak. It has been reported that you have been displaying singular interest in one person, almost to the exclusion of others." Nicholas struggled to stay calm. As boldly as he dared, he answered the tacit charge.

"I really am amazed that some people's favorite pastime is indulging in nasty imaginings about my friendship with Scott."

"Brother Manion, I'll overlook your tone because you are naturally jealous of the rightness of your affection. I am implying nothing, merely relating an observation that has been brought to my attention. On more than one occasion, I might add. I have been told you have visited Brother Turner's cell, and that you both repeatedly violate the rule of threes. Do you deny this?"

"No, Father, I don't, but—"

"Then we can consider it confirmed."

"But, Father, we're friends. We like to spend time together. What can possibly be wrong with that?"

"Don't be *faux-naif*. You have a special rapport with Brother Turner. Well and good. We applaud your affection for one another. As long as it does not become . . . unreasonable."

"Now, really, Father, if you're suggesting—"

"I am suggesting nothing, Brother Manion. I am merely reminding you that the rule of threes, the rule of privacy in the cells, and so forth, all exist for a purpose: so that no interest, no attachment, however laudable in itself, interferes with our purpose in being here. You are, I think, rather intemperate in your friendship. Brother Turner, naturally, is flattered by your attention. Even though he is older, and seemingly more experienced . . ." he added cryptically,

"Brother Turner undoubtedly is gratified by your care and finds your company congenial. But such friendship demands great energy and emotional investment. And I'm not at all persuaded such an investment is prudent in view of our purpose here."

"I don't understand, Father. What do you mean exactly?"

"Let's assume for the moment that, as far as your spiritual life is concerned, this relationship is not a distraction, but an asset. Well, does it end there? What about your friend? What about *his* vocation? Have you stopped to consider that your friendship might be a distraction, even a temptation, to him?"

"No, but—"

"No? Very well, then, I suggest you do so."

"But, Father—love of God and love of a person are the same thing, aren't they? What did Xavier say? This is a company of love, not *servile fear*?"

"Yes, yes, of course," Kane answered abruptly. "But this is all a question of degree. Moderation." He made it sound like four words: *mod-er-a-tion*. "You are, underneath your businesslike exterior, something of a romantic, Brother Manion. Your friendship has a romantic flavor, possessive, idealistic, defiant. This can lead to problems—"

"Father, I really don't—"

Kane's voice was steel. "Problems of interpretation for those around you. I don't for a moment believe you have done or have even contemplated doing anything . . . scandalous, but what you do, in all innocence, might be an occasion of scandal. Your stand yesterday merely draws more attention, not less. Won't you see that?"

Nicholas felt that this had gone far enough. "In other words, denying a false charge merely fuels suspicion. So accept injustice, and the speculation and suspicion are stifled. That's perverse. What I really see, if you want to know, is an inconsistency in what you've been saying. Only a few moments ago you claimed that in religious life it was the purity of motive that was paramount. All right, *my* motives *are* pure. If others have nothing better to do than weave gratuitous fantasies, why should I submit? It's a matter of principle!"

"But you have forgotten my simultaneous allusion to politics," the Master replied, sighing. "We are not dealing with God's attitude toward your friendship, but that of the community. Or rather, with the attitude of certain of its members. My responsibility is to watch over all of you. And the reaction of some, right now, is not an ethical problem, but a political one. Or, more accurately, one of public relations. Form protects us from mischief, and the tradition of public penitence transcends the legitimacy of any specific fault charged. My chief concern is maintaining a community that is harmonious and productive, and I cannot in conscience ignore anything that disrupts that. If you'd come to me privately to deny the charge of particular friendship, it would be different. I would have counseled greater discretion and allowed the matter to drop. But your public defiance has raised the stakes, don't you see?" Father Kane paused, then went on, appeal evident in his voice. "I'm not asking you to care for any friend less. I am telling you that it would be wise to be more prudent and restrained in your demonstration of care, and that you must publicly retract your obduracy."

"So . . ." Nicholas said carefully, "to avoid disturbing a few of my fellow novices, I should beat my breast in repentance and censor what is for me something fine and strong and good."

Father Kane eyed Nicholas intently. "Precisely. If the charge is false, offer the injustice up. As to your friendship, don't deny it. Let it grow. It's a blessing, and not so common it can be taken for granted. But don't wear it on your sleeve, don't flaunt it in such a way that it can be misunderstood. Enjoy it, but do so within the limits of our life here. Serve the institution and it will serve you," he said sententiously. "Is that so unreasonable?"

"I suppose not."

Nicholas heard the petulance in his voice, but Father Kane seemed satisfied. He seemed visibly to relent and relax. "Very well, then. That will be all for now, Brother. I will expect you to repent your disobedience publicly and to moderate your friendship with Brother Turner, more for his sake than your own, perhaps. You can have a wonderful future in the Society. Just go a little easier." He rose and extended his hand, awkwardly pulling it back before Nicholas could grasp it, and halfheartedly improvising a blessing. "I trust the subject is closed."

"Thank you, Father," Nicholas said, and walked out the door.

25

All that day, Nicholas's anger mounted. His first impulse was to rush to find Scott. But he didn't want to get him any deeper in dutch than he already might be. About that much, at least, Father Kane was correct; he had no right to drag Scott into his problems.

He needed time to breathe; he had to get away for a while. The more he nursed the idea, the more appealing it became. No one need know. Nicholas sensed that by leaving the seminary grounds for a while, after lights-out, he might finally be able to achieve the perspective he needed to clear his head. If only he could talk to his father . . .

At ten o'clock he pulled on warm wool pants, his bulky fisherman's sweater, and a sturdy pair of rubber-soled walking boots. Grabbing his gloves and the camel's-hair coat, he tiptoed down the stairs and slipped out the back door. The skeletal trees glinted against the low, black sky.

He walked through the orchard and past the brook into the woods. The cold air seized his lungs. His icy path lit by a few pale stars and a bone-sliver moon, he pushed branches aside as he pressed forward. Last week's snowfall had already vanished.

He was on the edge of the seminary property, in front of the winding road that led to the village of Cornwall. Scaling the iron fence and dropping onto the other side, he noticed that his coat was filthy: he had fallen during his trek. In the distance, lights flickered. He could hear music, faintly: "O Come All Ye Faithful." It was almost Christmas. He clutched the coat tightly to him as he tramped along the road, fumbling for clarity. To succeed in the seminary, you had to negate yourself. Your self. But if you did that—if you knuckled under on a matter of principle, went against your conscience, in fact—then who *were* you, really? To efface yourself meant you were nothing but a passive receptacle. A slave. Could a free man choose that? Such *self*-sacrifice seemed like a suicide. Now, that was truly a mortal sin.

There was a gas station just ahead. He could see the attendant in his greasy overalls, filling up a battered maroon Rambler. I'm probably lost, Nicholas realized, but no matter. He moved forward.

Emerging from behind the station, a man appeared, dressed in a shiny brown suit. As Nicholas passed by, he heard mumbled conversation. A door opened, then closed; the motor revved. Hearing the hum of the car, Nicholas shivered, envying the driver's warmth. It was time to turn around and head back; if he retraced his steps carefully, he'd be all right.

"Can I give you a lift?"

The car was beside him, the man leaning across the passenger seat, its window open a crack. "No, thank you. I go the other way. I was just about to turn around."

"No problem," the man said. "I've got time. Come on."

"O.K.," Nicholas said, opening the door and climbing in. "This is really nice of you." The heater was going full blast.

"Where to?"

"Just a few miles," Nicholas answered, as the man made a U-turn. "I'll show you where."

Nearly bald, the man's few tufts of lank hair were slicked down to give the illusion of density. He was sweating.

"Live around here?"

"Yes."

"A student?"

"Uh-huh." Nicholas clasped his hands tightly and leaned toward the heater.

"You look like you could use some coffee." The man looked over and smiled. "Or cocoa. How old are you, anyway?"

"Eighteen."

"There's a thermos and some paper cups in the glove compartment. Help yourself. Unless you'd rather stop at a diner?"

"No, this'll be fine." Nicholas opened the compartment and reached in. "Can I give you some?"

"Lay it on me."

He poured two-thirds of a cup and handed it to the man, then gave himself some. He took a sip. "Wow! It's scalding!" He had burned his tongue.

"Careful. I should have warned you." He reached inside his jacket and pulled out a pint bottle. "This'll take the edge off it," he said, hoisting it. Four Roses.

"No, this is perfect." Nicholas cradled the cup in his hands, blowing on the coffee to cool it.

"Suit yourself." Placing his cup on the dashboard, the man dextrously uncapped the whiskey and took a hearty swig.

"Thanks all the same."

"What're you thanking me for?" he said brusquely. "What's your name anyway?"

Nicholas paused for a moment. "Manion. Nick Manion."

"Don't lie to me!" It was a snarl. Nicholas didn't know what to say. This guy was *something*. "It's really my name. Why would I lie?" This was ludicrous.

"Don't try to kid me," the man growled, pulling the car to a sudden stop alongside the road. He began to bounce on his seat, slamming his fists at the steering wheel like a punch-drunk fighter showing the neighborhood gang how much punishment he could dish out, and take.

"What's the matter?" Nicholas asked, a little afraid.

"What?" The man flashed a strychnic grin. "No, it's O.K. My mistake." He turned the ignition key, then lowered his head. "Shit, what am I gonna do?"

Nicholas couldn't just sit there. "Sir, what's wrong?"

"Don't call me 'sir'!" he snapped. "What am I—your old man?" He giggled horribly. He must be on the verge of a breakdown. I've got to get away, Nicholas thought. I've got my own problems to worry about. But this guy might come after me; I should try to mollify him, if I can, calm him down. And in a way, Nicholas was morbidly fascinated by what might happen next.

Holding his coffee cup between his thighs, the man poured more whiskey. "I can't handle this stuff, I really can't. I do what I have to, but . . . it's such a joke." He patted his jacket pocket. "I've got Miltowns in this pocket and goofballs in the other one. I'm fucked up. Look . . ." He reached into his pants pocket and extracted a cracked brown wallet. He flicked it open. Nicholas saw that his name was Dennis-something. "Traveler's checks! I'm no dope." He eyed Nicholas shrewdly. "I wasn't born yesterday. Dangerous to ride around with too much money." He chuckled eerily. " 'Specially if sometimes you like to give a youngster a hand. Get rolled if you're not careful. But I guess I don't have to tell you that." He grinned, putting his hand on Nicholas's knee. He lowered his head to the steering wheel. "I just can't find the handle." Nicholas shifted his leg. "But I'm tough!" His fist felt like hickory as he hit Nicholas on the arm.

I should jump out right now and start running, Nicholas told himself. Even if he follows me, I could lose him in the woods. Despite his strength, he had to be at least forty, and couldn't have Nicholas's stamina.

Like a mind-reader, at that moment Dennis stepped on the gas and leapt back onto the road.

"Sure you won't have a snort?" He held the bottle under Nicholas's nose. "No? Don't know what you're missing." He took another swig. The car veered back and forth on the road. Luckily there were no other cars around.

Nicholas almost laughed. Somehow, this out-of-the-blue encounter fit right in with the collapse of his lifelong trust in the fixed order of the universe. He had lost control. His world wouldn't behave, didn't make sense. He was the victim of his own moral hubris. He should have run while he had the chance. But he had stayed. It was so interesting. More than from mere concern, which was patronizing, the priest-in-training doling out succor, he had stayed selfishly, frozen with curiosity.

Nicholas believed his inner chaos only reflected the world's. Out here the seminary's rules didn't apply. Even the Church's teachings, so tidily rational, made no allowance; this man's pain was savage, but real.

"We're almost there." He spotted the iron fence. "You can let me off now." He put the half-drunk cup of coffee on the floor.

"I don't see a house," the man said suspiciously. He brought the car to a stop.

"Just past the woods. I take a shortcut."

"For your moonlight ramblings."

Nicholas looked at his watch: 12:10. "Thanks for the ride."

"Stay a minute." There was a plea in his voice. "You know, you turn me on."

"I'm sorry, but . . ." He looked toward the woods.

"Look at me!" Nicholas obeyed. "You're beautiful." He ran his hand across Nicholas's hair. "All those curls, like fleece." He pulled his hand back. "I want . . . oh, shit, help me. I don't know what to do."

"Don't you have a family to go to—I mean, if you're sick?"

"*Sick*! Don't you call me that, you little sis. We'll see who's sick." He drained the last of the whiskey. Lowering his window, he tossed the bottle out onto the road. "And don't keep looking away all the time. I know I'm no prize." His face gleamed like sirloin.

"I don't know what to say, how to help you." The motor's sound grated.

"I—I—I . . . Oh, Christ, I don't know. That's the whole thing." He took a deep breath. His head was hanging down onto his tie as he muttered, "Let me blow you."

"I have to go now. I'm sorry."

"Listen, Norm—"

"It's Nick—"

"Whatever. Come with me. We'll get a room." He stared into Nicholas's eyes, his lips spread in a smile, a smile that seemed sulphurous at the edges. "Please." Nicholas shook his head. "My cock is iron. Feel it." He gripped Nicholas's arm, trying to twist it downward.

"No. Impossible. Leave me alone."

"I'm good."

Nicholas opened the door, his arm still held in the powerful grip.

"Never mind!" the man yelled. Nicholas saw his lips curl in defiance. "Keep your lily-white body. Probably a dud anyway." He seized Nicholas's chest with his right hand. Nicholas heard his coat rip. "Christ, when I saw you I thought you had tits!" With a vicious pinch, he let go. Nicholas jumped out, his heart racing. He could smell the whiskey. He turned and began to scale the fence.

"Still waiting for your balls to drop?" Dennis yelled after him as he ran.

His arms felt heavy, as though he were moving underwater. It was pitch dark. Brittle branches snapped in his face as he rushed through the woods. His throat was raw, his tongue cottony. He thought he was going to throw up. Gulping the cold air, he felt the nausea back down his throat and settle like a lump in his stomach.

It was his own fault. His "No. Impossible . . ." rang bitterly in his ears. A fat lot of help he'd been. Who was he kidding? His smug arrogance, his vehement disgust. He was hardly a complete innocent. Instead of finding some way to help him, he had pushed the man over the edge.

The truth: it threatened him. Not the *man*—Dennis, he had a name!—but the grotesque reflection he presented. In his thwarted, belligerent, self-denying way, Dennis had sensed a kindred spirit. And Nicholas, as though forced to stand before a funhouse mirror, saw . . .

I'm not like that! he cried in his heart. I'm not!

Recognition hit him like an icepick.

He was sitting on a boulder, just past the orchard, staring at the slumbering seminary.

How could it be true?

He thought suddenly of Karl, lying against the grass in the backyard. How many times had they wrestled there, straining to pin each other, lathered with sweat, pouncing fiercely? And how often, and with thrilled expectancy, had Nicholas, hard, lengthening along his thigh, maneuvered himself so that he rubbed against Karl, hard himself?

He could see it so clearly, pushing, accelerating, his feet digging into the grass until he flipped off, all effort spent, his groin pulsing. Chagrined but trembling, he felt the sticky warmth. He would sit up then, and brushing the grass stains on his jeans, nonchalantly stuff his T-shirt half inside his belt, so that it hung in camouflage across his crotch like a pennant.

And there they squatted in his room, the magazine spread before them. "Just letting off steam," Karl called it. Maybe for him.

That day at the villa, in the woods with Scott, twisting and turning in the mud—he had to face it all now—had he not felt himself yielding to the old, familiar rhythm, the same deceptively playful, proudly muscular, utterly carnal dance? Prone beneath the trees threaded with lightning, had he not been on the verge of coming when, with herculean will-power, he pulled away?

Nicholas stood and headed toward the seminary. He was beyond doubt now.

26

He climbed the back stairs all the way to the fourth floor. Scott's room was the far end, opposite the *secundi lavatorium*.

He turned the doorknob quietly and slipped in. Easing down onto the edge of the bed, he shook Scott awake.

"What—?"

Nicholas closed off his exclamation with the palm of his hand.

"Scott, just listen," he whispered. "Please. I don't want to be alone tonight. Let me stay here. Please? For a while. I need to be with you."

Scott's eyes showed his confusion. Nicholas could tell his instinct was to say no, but because he could hear Nicholas's urgency . . .

"O.K., Bro," he said softly, motioning Nicholas to lie beside him, on top of the covers.

Nicholas doffed his coat and rested his head on Scott's shoulder. He could feel the pajamas against his tingling cheek. He was shaking. Scott reached his arm around, cradling him against his chest, his finger grazing Nicholas's face.

"You're freezing." Nicholas sighed deeply. "It's O.K.," Scott murmured. Nicholas felt torn by the shock of belated vision; anger and relief, fear and consolation warred within him. He was crying. "Hush, now. There." Scott stroked his cheek, brushing away the tears. Nicholas buried his face in his friend's breast. "Just relax, Nick. It's O.K."

After several minutes, Scott asked, "Feel better?"

"Yes, yes." Nicholas clung to him. He could feel Scott tense. Nicholas looked up into the gray eyes, now full of amazed warmth, and felt him relax. Nicholas stared, running his fingers through Scott's black hair, browsing in wonder over his skin, tracing with trembling fingers his sharp cheekbones. He leaned toward him, searching for but finding no surprise. Scott moved forward to join their kiss. Tenderly at first, then fiercely, Nicholas pressed himself to Scott, who did not flinch. He caressed him as he lifted the covers back. It was apocalyptic. Nicholas felt, as never before, the presence of God.

Afterwards, Nicholas lay quietly beside his friend. At last he was in tune with himself. Whatever detours his twitching conscience had hounded him into, now at last he had arrived at the place he had always been destined for, meant for, where the ragged center of his heart could emerge from the shadows and claim the light.

He felt himself apart, as before, but now with elation. There was, strangely, no guilt. He had simply begun to listen to an inner music he had ignored or refused to recognize or heard only in furtive, discordant fragments. Now, listening intently, he found that despite proscriptions to the contrary, it possessed both beauty and integrity. Different, of course, but fine. *His.* And more, it was this theme that, having started, must not stop, would not be stopped; it was the bold passage of his being.

Whom did he have to placate, twisting himself, chipping

away, applying camouflage? Who could demand that he distort himself with "internal surgery"?

No one.

He thought of Father O'Mara. It was "always concupiscence in the confessional," he said, always *De Sexto*, so aptly named: the Sixth Commandment. That's what they called it in the Baltimore Catechism, the book with all the answers neatly numbered, to be learned by rote.

But concupiscence was just the word the O'Maras of this world used to reason away the cramp of every benighted soul upon this planet. It was always purity, the desert of the heart: not the mercy of old age; not the innocence of youth; not riches and not deprivation; not the pomp and power of new Croesus, not the blight and despair of old Lazarus, not the succor of family and not the scourge of being alone—nothing exempted man. In God's image he knelt, in a host of places, with a babel of voices, all different and all the same, huddled, shivering in the dark, crying for the light, frightened, hopeful, flawed, courageous—a multitudinous community.

Nicholas felt his whole stunted, emotional history at last requited. Only love. The reach of love was a miracle of variety, but love itself was constant, a mystery confounding and ridiculing the limits of mere biology. The lover, charged with the imagination of God, wore a catholic face.

But this christening signified exile, Nicholas knew that. He had been stung by a logic so vehement he had no choice except surrender. But the Church did not see it that way.

Had "mortal sin" lost its terror? Perhaps that horrific null was itself nullified by its own meaning. What was it, really? A failure of self, a perversion of spiritual potential. How could you sin if you were true to yourself?

Could God, having made him, now refuse to love him? Surely, if He meant anything at all, He had to be more than a supreme accountant, toting up "faults" on an infinite set of *culpa* beads. Surely He expected more of us than saving our souls mechanically. Even in this secular age, surely Divine Justice could not wear so utter a blindfold.

He could take his time. If he must now go against the trinity of home, school, and church, he must do so with a calm head and a sense of his own history. For every creature casts a shadow; only the blind need no light.

He thought of how schooled forgiveness sometimes only deepens guilt. Let an Achilles' heel grow weak enough, and you could get used to limping. You could even, Nicholas supposed, get used to a penitential chain.

But self-forgiveness was entirely different, a new order of atonement. At-*one*-ment, he said silently, separating the syllables. That took the accumulated momentum of a lifetime; it did not spring from the blue.

Nicholas was certain. If the human vocation—to discover who we are and why we are here—was a mystery, its imperative was clear: to seek God as best we could in all things, in the depth and amplitude of the heart, through good and evil and love and hatred; to find His hand, walk in His light, see Him face to face. In ourselves and in each other.

Being Christlike meant grappling with fate, armed with your own truth. To starve your soul by plagiarizing pleasing selves so that others would love you was a suicide so subtle you discovered one day that, in a sense, you never truly existed as a person at all.

The Church could tell you what to do, but not how to do it without losing, if not your soul, your self. Could there be such a distinction? Nicholas had no alternative; to find Christ he had to find himself. That was impossible for him in the seminary, and perhaps in the Church.

After Nicholas told him what had happened—Simpson's charge, Father Kane's cool, remote analysis, and the surreal ride with Dennis—Scott said, "At least you won't be expelled. Kane will understand, you'll see."

What was he talking about? Expelled? They had to leave, of course. That was obvious. "What can *he* do?"

"I don't understand," Scott answered. He seemed genuinely puzzled.

"Today changes everything," Nicholas declared. "It would be wrong to stay."

"Are you nuts? This changes *nothing*."

"No."

Scott was plainly amazed. "What do you mean, 'No'?"

"It's dishonest," Nicholas replied calmly.

Scott shook his head in astonishment.

"I swear, sometimes I don't understand you. I mean, I hear the words, but they don't make any sense. Dishonest!" he repeated disgustedly. "This has nothing to do with our vocations, for God's sake!" He pulled his pajamas back on.

"For me it does." Nicholas had seen priests who clung to a bitter charade: impostors full of self-contempt, going through the motions; or the secret, solitary drinkers like Father O'Mara. They stank of bad faith.

Such hypocrisy was deadly. Trying to have it both ways was to live a coward's lie. The end never justifies the means. To pretend otherwise was a prison from which there was no exit.

Nicholas had no intention of becoming a pathetic buffoon. He was free to be himself. No one and nothing held arbitrary authority over him. That was not a defeat; it was a revelation.

Things weren't completely clear yet in his mind. He felt like an infant, seeing the world upside down. He needed time to adjust, to acquaint his brain with fresh signals, to right the lenses.

"Well, I'm not leaving, you can bank on that," Scott whispered. "Leave? No way. The seminary's the only place for me, can't you see that? I stumble, I yield to temptation, I sin. I'm weak, I admit it." He looked plaintively at

Nicholas. "But if I ever left, I'd stop trying." He got up.

"I don't see it that way. I'd be a hypocrite if I stayed when I knew I couldn't—no, *wouldn't*—follow the rules."

"Why must you be such an extremist? Either-or. In or out. It's just not that simple. You're too hard on yourself."

"Maybe."

"You don't have to quit, for God's sake. You act as though you're the center of the universe—it's all a stage to you. The drama of Nicholas Manion and his need for perfection. We're *all* fallen, Nick. Just because you found out doesn't mean you have to quit."

"It's not quitting." Scott just didn't see.

As though suddenly remembering that he was older and presumably wiser, Scott shifted gears.

"Nick, God doesn't expect perfection. Do you think there are no sinners in the priesthood? They just hang in there. That's all He asks, that we *try* to do His will."

"And He demands nothing beyond our strength?"

"Of course not."

"He gives us no trial that we cannot win, no test we cannot meet?"

"Right."

"There you are, QED."

"I don't understand," Scott persisted.

"O.K. I'll spell it out. I sin because I'm human, right? But then I confess, and making a firm resolution *not to sin again*, I make a sincere Act of Contrition and receive absolution. That's how it works, correct?"

"Yes."

"I cannot—no, I *will* not—make that promise. Not when I know full well I have no intention of keeping it. Do you understand?"

"Bro, Bro, listen—it's all my fault. I should have stopped this. I had no idea—"

"Don't you dare!" Nicholas said.

"I'm trouble, I admit it. I've always known that, a bad bet, but sometimes my emotions get the better of me, that's all. I care for you so much—"

"No!"

"—It's all my fault . . ."

"No," Nicholas repeated. "I knew exactly what I was doing. I'd do it again."

Scott paused to think. Despite himself, he seemed pleased. "We'll just have to make up our minds not to do it again. Forget about leaving."

"Avoid the 'occasion of sin'?" Nicholas asked.

"Right."

"You're lying, Scott. What's worse, you're lying to yourself."

"I'm not," he said in a tiny, petulant voice.

Nicholas waited patiently. Scott stretched his arms, then yawned deeply. It was the middle of the night.

"You'll feel different after you get some sleep. You'll see," Scott said.

Nicholas said nothing.

Scott bent to kiss him. Nicholas stood up and offered his cheek. "I do love you," Scott whispered like a child. "I have from the first moment."

"I know," Nicholas said. "That's what's so sad." He walked out.

27

He awoke with a start at the sound of the bell. Bright sunshine poured through his narrow window. He felt refreshed,
though he couldn't have slept for more than a couple of
hours. Right after Mass, he would go to see Father Kane. He
would tell him about going AWOL, but not what happened
afterwards.

He would have left sooner or later. Yesterday simply
telescoped things. What had happened with Scott was only
part of the story, a fragment of the larger truth: he did not
have a vocation. Sexuality was just one of several signs that
he did not belong. Nicholas would think it over carefully, but
he saw no alternative; he was not made to worship God here
in this way.

He had been unfair, though. Scott had made peace with
himself here; it was not hypocrisy but love that had made him
open his arms. Nicholas had no right to try to draft Scott into
his decision. Each of them was free to steer his own course. It
was no one's fault. Nicholas grieved, but he was calm, reso-
lute. Perhaps such moments as they had shared cannot last,

perhaps their loveliness is lethal, like force roses expiring outside their perfectly controlled atmosphere, vanquished by the real world. Nicholas wasn't sure. But he was not afraid to find out.

Father Kane sat behind his desk, still as a rock.

"Brother Manion, how do you feel?"

"I'm all right, Father."

"Good. As you'll appreciate, there is no precedent for a situation such as this. Disobedience must be punished. But you've had a bad shock. Your father's death, and so on. I certainly have no desire to add to your pain. But willful irresponsibility cannot go unpunished. I cannot pretend nothing happened. I have the community to consider. After prayerful reflection, I have decided to put you on indefinite probation. You will be sent home—to recuperate. I've already spoken with your mother."

Father Kane rose and approached Nicholas.

"I urge you to think carefully about your vocation. Our life is not for everyone. It's no disgrace to recognize that it's not for you, if that is God's will."

"I know," Nicholas murmured, strangely touched. Leaving, at least, he could do Kane's way.

"It takes a great deal of courage to admit you've made a mistake, much more than stubbornly persisting in error. If the wrong choice has been made, all the diligence and good-will in the world won't smooth the path."

" 'Many are called, but few are chosen'?" Nicholas asked.

"Precisely. 'They come, they go,' as the novices say." Father Kane continued, "I don't presume to know what your decision will be, but I'm confident it will be the proper one. Let your conscience guide you. Divine will is mysterious, but God loves us all equally."

"I believe that," Nicholas said.

"If you find—as a matter of principle—that our life of

obedience is not for you, there is other, important, Christlike work to be done elsewhere."

"Matter of principle"—it was his father's phrase.

"Father, why is it so hard, finding our way—?"

"For priests too, Brother Manion," he interrupted. He removed his glasses and rubbed his eyes. "Things have changed since I was a seminarian. They *are* changing. We're imperfect, groping like everyone else. Twenty years ago, I wouldn't have dreamed of questioning authority. Now 'why?' is all I hear. It's fundamentally healthy, though I admit it was more peaceful in my day." He sighed and put his glasses back on. "Faith will provide. Otherwise, as Saint Augustine says, 'Love God and do what you will.' " His hands were clasped in that familiar, prim grip. It made him seem vulnerable now. He just didn't know where to put them, Nicholas realized. "Would you like me to hear your confession?"

Nicholas shook his head. He refused to bring Scott into this.

"Very well, then, Nicholas, have a safe trip home. And let me know your decision. It's up to you."

He extended his hand, and Father Kane shook it warmly.

"Thank you."

The priest raised his hand in blessing, his lips moving in murmured benediction. "Bless you, my son."

28

The school was deserted. No would-be Cousys were grinding away in the gym this Christmas vacation. The late-afternoon sun streamed through the windows, making the polished hardwood floor gleam. The air was thick with his past, the familiar sweaty odor hanging ripe in the air down the years.

Nicholas thought back to the championship game last April, when he had twisted his ankle viciously and Karl, a Leatherneck even then, had come galloping off the bench to replace him until the novocaine had done its work. He'd checked his man like a maniac, and even lucked in a couple of baskets. Now he was in Munich. Thomas had been there too, that day, cheering them on.

Only nine months ago . . .

Lyon was in his office when Nicholas knocked at the door.

"Come in," he boomed from inside.

As Nicholas peered in, Lyon sprang to his feet.

"Nick—I heard you were back. How are you?" He

bounded out from behind his desk and grasped Nicholas's hand in greeting.

"Depleted," Nicholas replied lamely, returning the greeting. He searched Lyon's face for some hint of suspicion or reprimand or disappointment, but he was as buoyant as ever.

"Sit down," he urged, pointing to the chair in front of his desk.

"Bad as all that, huh?" Lyon resumed his place. "Well, I hate to break it to you, but you look terrific."

"Quoth the medic to the amputee . . ."

"You want to discuss it? O.K., give." He sat back, eyes alert, eyebrows at attention.

"I don't know where to begin. I think I'm shell-shocked or something. Just no zip at all." He looked at Lyon in mute appeal.

"You're depressed, it's understandable. You've been through a lot. The thing to do is relax. Just like football—it's the guys who go rigid when they're tackled that bust something. It's easier to absorb the shocks if you go limp."

"Right now I'm about as limp as a can of Franco-American." Nicholas laughed despite himself.

"Good man."

"Father, it's just not working out. I can't hack it—obedience, the 'discipline,' the whole bit. The thing I keep turning over in my brain is, where did I screw up? I wanted so much to do well, to be 'solid,' but, almost from the beginning, my body and my mind seemed in revolt. No matter how much I analyze, I keep coming up with the same verdict: I just don't have a vocation. I wanted one, I *willed* one, but I don't have one."

"O.K., you may be right. But if you are, you're not entirely to blame for the . . . mistake. Before you left, there were several times I wanted to sit you down, right there, and get you really to examine whether God was calling you and not the other way around."

"You wouldn't have changed my mind."

"I know. That's why I didn't speak up. You were very sure of yourself. But I still feel somewhat responsible. Without meaning to, I'm afraid sometimes we nudge our best students a little—'direct their intentions' is the phrase—into believing they owe us the grateful compliment of a vocation. Seventeen, eighteen is awfully young to be renouncing the world. At that age, you've barely begun to experience it." Lyon laughed. "I'm not cut out to be a Pied Piper. Just look at my results. I suspected, unconsciously perhaps, that you looked on the seminary as a refuge as well as a challenge." He chuckled dolefully. "But in this vale of tears, as JFK has pointed out, there are no safe havens."

"No kidding," Nicholas replied nervously. "What I hate most is feeling like a quitter, that I let everybody—you—down."

"Mister!" Lyon snapped. "That's just pride, doom-eager pride. You haven't failed, you've just made a strategic retreat."

Lyon didn't understand; Nicholas didn't know how to make him do so. "You don't know the whole story. It's not just the priesthood, it's me. My coordination's all fouled up. It's like I'm a fastball hitter and all of a sudden I'm seeing nothing but screwballs, swinging at air like a spastic."

"Well, do what a good hitter does: adjust. Nick, look at this objectively; you made a miscalculation and you got hurt, but there's no permanent damage done. You're clear in your conscience about leaving?"

"I think so," he answered. "Yes."

"O.K. If a person, with all the goodwill in the world, repeatedly finds he can't adapt, isn't that a sign from God?" He scratched his forehead. "Let's see whether I can remember. In the Spiritual Exercises somewhere, isn't there a bit about this? 'A man who, time after time, is unable to obey with a good conscience, should take thought regarding some other path of life in which he can serve God with greater tranquility.' Doesn't that about cover it?" He seemed pleased.

"It also says, 'He who wills the end, wills the means.' "

"Fair enough—but only if the end is proper. Otherwise, technique would be its own reward."

"*You* managed it."

"Nick, to want to be what we admire may be seductive, but it's stupid. Number one, it may not be admirable at all, and, number two, it may not be what God has ordained for you. *Nemo dat quod no habet*, remember?"

"I remember."

"Unfortunately, we all think with our pasts. That makes for trouble, shocks—"

"But I gave myself totally, and God betrayed . . . no, not that, but . . . surprised me. I did the betraying myself, I guess."

"Let me finish. Shocks, *surprises* come our way, hound all of us. But without friction there's no progress. 'Know thyself'—that's the whole shebang. We can change the grain by going against it."

"At the price of truth, our own personal truth?"

"No, of course not."

I know he's trying to comfort me, Nicholas reflected, but he doesn't know the half of it.

"Father, the thing is, I don't know what I *believe* anymore. I've hoodwinked myself in so many ways I'm riddled with doubts."

"Serious doubts, really?" His brow was knit with concern.

"Yes."

There—I've said it! Nicholas was relieved.

"Are you saying you've lost your faith?"

Had he? The real question, Nicholas thought, is what "the faith" is. He believed in God; life was too glorious to be a bacterial accident. He loved much of the Church—the sacraments, the rituals, the prayer and the music and the community. And he knew in his bones that right and wrong were real. Man had to be accountable for his acts. Nicholas did not doubt the basic meaning of Christ's blood sacrifice, the good news of love and redemption. He still had his faith. But was there room for him in the Faith? That Faith, in all its suave legalism, had been ripped from him like his father's coat. Yes, it had been a warm and protective garment. And surely he might miss it. But once soiled and torn, there was no putting it on again.

Lyon was waiting for his answer.

"Lost or misplaced, I don't know . . ."

"Because you found out you're not who you thought you were."

"Exactly."

"Well—tough!" That shocked Nick bolt upright in his chair. "Nick, look—there's a bit of Savonarola in you. All or nothing. Action is fundamentally impure, it can't be helped. But you're harsher and more unforgiving toward yourself than is healthy. As demanding as you can be of others, you demand even more of yourself. No one's a superman. Inside you there's a great reservoir of goodness, but you keep it locked up like a strongbox."

"I don't understand."

The sun, spearing the window, was fixed like a spotlight on Lyon's head. He paused, and lit a cigarette. What's he getting at, Nicholas wondered.

"You're a bit of an emotional illiterate, you know. Relax. Feel. Let it out. Your heart needs a gift of tongues."

Why is he attacking me?

Lyon pressed on. "It's a great tragedy—you're a human being, with the usual weaknesses and maybe your own special cross thrown in for good measure."

Had he talked with Kane?

"Remember what Stevenson said: 'We all have thoughts that would shame Hell.' *Nota bene*: all." He bit his lower lip, then went on. "Your central problem is care. No one's good enough for you—especially *you*! Your standards are so extreme, who could live up to them? *Frater, noli scrupulare.*" He smiled.

"But, Father, you're a priest, you withdrew from the world . . ."

"There are no Edens, Nick. That's what Original Sin means."

"And if there were, something in us would foul them."

"Right. You're a very competent chameleon, but being 'all things to all men' isn't the same as twisting yourself into what others want you to be. You may satisfy them for a while and even con yourself, but in the end it can't work. You can't buy off the truth. *Know thyself.*"

"What if it means a one-hundred-eighty-degree shift, that you're a different person entirely?"

"You can handle it."

"Whew!" Nicholas sighed. "When I goof, it's sure a beaut!" He felt better. So why was his nose running?

"Here," Lyon said, tossing him a handkerchief. "That's two you owe me."

Of course—after the Optimists' contest.

He was weeping.

"I feel like such a sissy," he mumbled, his voice cracking, but choosing the word carefully.

"Mister, tears are just as manly as muscles. And I've known some pretty heroic sissies."

Does he know? Can he tell?

Nicholas looked into Lyon's eyes. He does know. And I'm still here.

"So what's next, what are your plans? You can't hide your light under a bushel, you know."

"I don't know. Probably Harvard." He hadn't really thought about it.

"That's eight or nine months away. We could use a hand . . . grade-nine History and English?" He made the proposal nonchalantly, but Nicholas intuitively knew it was a carefully considered offer, a lifeline.

"Would you really?" Nicholas was deeply touched. "Thank you."

"Think about it."

"I will, but don't count on me."

"Fair enough. You'll let Kane know?"

"Of course."

"Good man. Now try to cheer up." He smiled warmly. "You're *not* a totally different person, you know."

"Maybe not, but more than you can imagine."

"I can read between the lines."

"And yet you still believe in me?" It was amazing.

"You bet I do! Whatever happens, follow your conscience and you can't go far wrong."

"Even if it leads me out the door, away from the Church?"

"Even then. Not if it's just weakness, self-indulgence, an 'erroneous conscience.' But if you're sure, if your conscience is 'informed'? 'They come, they go.' Do they still say that at the sem?"

"They sure do."

"Well, same for the rest of us poor devils. We've all got to scramble to salvation as best we can. Finally, it's all a matter between us and God."

Nicholas took a deep breath. He was suddenly exhausted.

"They still reading à Kempis these days?"

"Yes. Every Saturday for fifteen minutes."

"Well, it's been years, but here goes: 'Be not angry that you cannot make others as you wish them to be, since you cannot make yourself as you wish to be.' "

Nicholas laughed. "Gotcha. That's some consolation, I guess. But you still have to try, right?"

"Try like a tiger. Always. If you don't strive for perfection, Heaven is just a fairy tale. But give yourself a break.

Perfection's the goal, all right, but the battle is lifelong and most of us never even approach it. You're on a new track, that's all. You'll adjust, and you can make it work."

"It's so scary."

"It's fear of the past that makes the future scary. You are a good and gifted man—accept it."

"What do you think I should be?"

"You'll know. If we've done our job at all well, you'll know. In the end we're all free. We don't have to obey anyone but ourselves. And, of course, accept the consequences. There's dignity in that."

"I'm still afraid."

"It takes great courage to stand alone. But you've got it."

"*Nemo dat?*"

"Exactly. *Nemo dat.*"

"I think I'll take my time before I settle on a career. God knows, I've got plenty of interests."

"It's up to you."

"But not a Jesuit."

"No," Lyon answered. "You served your time and gave it your best. You'll always be one of Ours, at least a little."

"Well, I'd better get a move on," Nicholas said, rising from a chair.

"Keep me posted, mister."

"I will. Thank you, Father."

Nicholas saw Lyon raise his right hand in blessing. He crossed himself and walked out.

It was dark already. If he was expecting censure, he'd come to the wrong place. Lyon still believed in him, still cared for him, he couldn't doubt it.

Some things lasted after all.

Who knows, he thought, perhaps there's still a place for me in the Church. But he doubted it. Change would come. It had to. But slowly, painstakingly, grudgingly, like a continent inching into a new age. Only an earthquake could make Nicholas welcome today. And such a seismic convulsion might topple the institution itself. The Church couldn't transform itself overnight. That was not the secret of its survival.

But change it must. And John XXIII was no Canute, barking at the sea to halt. His openness was genuine. The alternative to change was decay, slow disintegration, irrelevance, moribundity, until finally, played out, sclerotic, it became extinct, a brontosaurus to be gawked at uncomprehendingly.

It would not happen tomorrow, or soon. Maybe not even in Nicholas's lifetime. But he was certain; change would come.

29

CHRISTMAS EVE, 1962

He faced his mother across the sun room. It was time to give Father Kane his decision.

"Nicholas," she said, "we have some unfinished business. Now that you've relaxed a little." She was sitting on the sofa, sipping an amber liqueur. He crouched in a wicker chair, his legs resting on a stool.

"A showdown, Mother?" he asked wryly. Habits died hard. She was still a remarkably beautiful woman, her porcelain skin free of wrinkles, her lush hair empty of gray. A glacial smile crossed her lips. She had slipped from youth toward middle age like the afternoon sun blurring into dusk—grudgingly but gracefully.

"Not exactly. More like revelation." She could play his game.

"I'm listening."

"To begin with, your father made you his sole beneficiary. He made a trust. I'll receive the income until I die. Then it will revert to you. And the house is yours as well, upon my death. You're a very wealthy young man." She sipped her drink, then continued, "There is a second trust, which comes to you immediately. Under the current conditions, it should amount to five, perhaps ten thousand per year. But the funds are not to be released to you so long as you remain in the seminary. The will was most explicit. But on the day of your ordination, they would be released, in toto, to dispose of as you deem fit."

"I understand."

"While we're on the subject of money, I feel I must speak to you about that evening last summer. Just before you left. You remember?"

"Of course."

"And I would be right in assuming you examined the check I had intended to give you."

"Yes," he answered wearily. "Ten thousand dollars."

"It was absurdly maladroit of me, I admit, but I wanted to shock you, to make you think, to prevent you from rushing in recklessly, committing yourself prematurely. Like *I* did."

What had she said?

"I had hoped I could, by tempting you, make you defer your decision, delay till you were older, postpone it. Go to college, take even a year of travel. An opportunity I never had. Rightly or wrongly, I felt you were still so very young, and needed time to mature. But I saw the look of disdain on your face, and lost my nerve."

He had misunderstood her terribly. "It's all right. I wouldn't have been tempted," he said.

She eyed him frostily.

"It was a . . . gauche thing to do. But I meant well."

"I know you did. Now."

She seemed satisfied.

"Very well, then. When will you be returning to St. Ignatius?"

He paused, then smiled faintly.

"Do you think Harvard would let me enroll for the second semester?"

She was astonished. For once her aplomb vanished.

"It's highly irregular, but I imagine it could be arranged. We could contact the dean of admissions. You remember how impressed he was with you? He seemed genuinely sorry you decided against going there." She smiled, tremors of disbelief tugging her lips down, but her sheer delight overwhelming them.

"Fine. And I'd better call Father Kane."

"Nicholas, my dear, I don't wish to intrude . . . but are you at peace with this decision?"

"Completely," he answered.

"I wasn't going to say anything, but you've seemed different since you saw Father Lyon—calmer, less intense. You're truly sure?"

"As sure as I can be."

"It's more than your father's death, isn't it?"

"Much more."

"You've grown up."

"Mother . . ." he began, emboldened by their newfound intimacy, "I don't know quite how to say this, but, at the seminary . . . with Scott—"

"Your friend?"

"Yes, Scott Turner. I found out—"

"He's very dear to you, I can see that."

"More . . ."

"Well, you two can still be friends."

"You don't understand."

"I do." She said it simply, without a trace of judgment. Nicholas felt a vast relief.

"Still, I won't lie to you. It's hardly what I would have wished for you. But it *is* your life."

"Yes."

"It's a tremendous challenge—I won't say 'cross'—

perhaps the hardest you'll ever face. But you're strong enough."

"Am I?"

"You're my son, aren't you?"

"I am."

"Nicholas, there's something else I must say to you." Cold fire shone from her eyes. "I know that you believe your father and I had no real life to speak of, and from the time you were old enough to observe, there's been merit in that view."

"Don't," he pleaded.

"It's funny," she continued. "I wanted a child to bind him to me. I'm not sure I really looked forward to motherhood, but one had to try. In our day it was expected, virtually the purpose of marriage. Today, of course, it's different. Women can admit it now. Anyway, Thomas was like a force of nature, you couldn't resist him, not when he was in the grip of some dream. More than anything, more than me, it seemed, he yearned for a son."

"Mother, you don't have to—"

"Let me speak," she interrupted fiercely. "I have been silent too long, far too long. I must tell it, just once, and you're the only one here." Her voice was full of emotion.

"Go on." It was painful, but he was fascinated.

"I think I sensed intuitively that you—a child—would steal him from me. I wonder how many miscarriages are willed by that anxiety? Anyway, childlessness, a barren woman, was looked on as the great tragedy.

"Instead, for me, *you* were. From the moment you were born, he pulled away, lost in you. He moved into his own bedroom. He locked himself in his library, night after night." Nicholas could not look at her. "I was confused, miserable. What had I done? I ransacked my memory for some unforgivable offense, some terrible betrayal. Slowly I realized it was nothing I had done. He put me aside like a broken appliance. What was I to do? Become one of those shriveled women whose sensuality is poured into cooking? Spend my life shopping?" she asked scornfully.

"In time I stopped dwelling on it. The constant re-creation of pain can turn you into Lot's wife—did she ever have a name?—petrified, looking backward. I used to watch him staring at you, willing himself into you, more demonic than a mesmerist. How could I compete? All choice excludes, but his was total. I couldn't demand, and he needed an equal challenge. He was so mercurial. I can't love like that. It seems excessive. I don't have the equipment for it, the stomach. Love—for me—was just not in his repertoire."

"You couldn't fight back?"

"Everything had already happened. For a time I resented you, blamed you, but that only made things worse. After all, I told myself, you were only a child. I don't think I'll ever forgive myself for pushing you away."

"Mother, please don't," he begged.

"No, let me finish . . ." She sat staring at her glass. "He tried, but he couldn't give to me anymore. Something had crippled him—at least where I was concerned. Which is ironic, since I'm sure that's how you thought of me."

"No, that's not true."

"In time I realized his door was shut permanently. I lost myself in routine. I know I must have seemed cold to you, but sometimes sensitivity is just too terrifying."

"I understand. But couldn't you have left—?"

"Nicholas, your generation behaves as though words have no meaning. A vow may not be broken."

"But Mother, even the Church is becoming aware of the cost, the suffering. It must change, adapt . . . especially when it comes to marriage, human sexuality."

"And what is your idea of sexuality?" she asked acerbically.

"A metaphor, I suppose. A way of expressing pleasure and pain—at best, love or the hope of love—"

"Of course the body is a metaphor, but it is God's! In His image we are created. We defile that image by reducing it to banal gratification. Your father, you must know, shared my belief in that respect, if not my bed . . ."

"But surely, if you were so unhappy—?"

"I was Mrs. Thomas Manion. Whatever came, that is who I was. My-*self*. Don't you comprehend?" She glared at him. "I said the words solemnly. There was no escape clause, no time period. You intended to take vows. Would you have done so with reservations?"

"No, of course not," he admitted. That was crucial.

"Well, then . . ."

"But what about separation?"

"Not even that. Your father would never have countenanced a separation, nor would I."

"But wouldn't both of you have been happier apart?"

"Nicholas, for all your brilliance, you know so little. Whoever said we have a guarantee? Whoever promised us we'd have what we wanted, simply because we needed it so much?"

"Mother, what can I say? I'm so sorry."

"I don't want your pity. Or even your sympathy. I'm telling you all this for a reason. We're all so sure of ourselves when we're young. Everything seems possible. So we rush in carelessly, and before we know it, we're trapped."

"You're saying it nearly happened to me." He understood now.

"Exactly."

"And could still happen?"

"Unless you're careful. Try not to be so definitive, so extreme. That's one aspect of your father you could happily forgo."

It was true.

"Don't be so quick to judge your future. You may have more surprises in store for you. Do what you must—but not to please or displease your father, or me, or anyone. Do it for yourself."

"Yes, I see."

"Dear, I know this is not pleasant for you, but having had you taken from me once, or having pushed you aside, I couldn't keep still now."

"You didn't stay because of me?" Nicholas asked, aghast.

"No, dear." She laughed easily. "I was never taken in by *that* cheap deception. I stayed because of the vow. There was nothing I could do, nothing. 'For better or for worse.' We survived. He loved you and not me. That was all."

Nicholas was overcome with compassion. She had suffered so, and he had never noticed. He remembered that afternoon in the car, coming from the graveside. "I love you," she had said. "That's *my* business." Wouldn't it be ironic if *her* strength was *his* saving inheritance?

He stood and walked across the room, sat next to her. He took her arms and felt her tremble, then stiffen infinitesimally. They had not embraced in so very long. He cradled her proud head in his arms, bending down to kiss her neck. He felt her relax into his arms.

"We're together now," he said.

She pulled back and patted her hair.

"It's sad, isn't it?" She smiled. "Our hopes are so incompetent." She smoothed her skirt and took a deep breath. "Would you like me to play for you?"

Nicholas could only nod.

She walked over to the piano and opened the music that rested against the stand. She sat down, placed it securely before her, then, each hand in its turn, limbered her fingers. Then she extended them straight over the keys.

"Sonata Number Twelve. Mozart," she said. "The adagio."

The room was as silent as a sacristy. Its daily ascension

accomplished, the early-afternoon sun cascaded through the windows, transfiguring the yellow room in a golden effulgence. She began . . .

The music was elegiac, processional, insistently tolling. But somehow, underneath the tender, unblinking sorrow, there was joy as well. And triumph.

30

Late that afternoon the doorbell rang. Two workmen lugged in the trunk from the seminary. He led them up to his bedroom, then tipped them and escorted them out.

He walked back upstairs, full of curiosity. He unlocked the trunk and examined the contents. It was all there: his black clothes, his missal, even the "discipline" and the chain, his "light" book and toilet kit. He felt like an archaeologist sifting shards, relics of a lost civilization. They seemed now like talismans, foreign, puzzling, suggestive, but finally unknown, unknowable.

Later on he would carry it all down to the basement, except for the missal and the toilet kit, and throw it in the furnace. His father's overcoat too: there was no use for it anymore. But he would keep Scott's nugget, like the hermit's penny.

He pictured the seminary. They should be just about ready to start in for dinner. He remembered the day during the Long Retreat when McMurtrey had seemed to vanish into thin air, as now Nicholas had done. Time, back then, had frozen for a moment, McMurtrey in his absence still claiming his place, in the pew and at table, until they closed ranks, their solidarity purifying the contaminated space.

Did he, Nicholas wondered, similarly linger on briefly after his departure? On some of them, at least, he believed his mark would last. For most of them he would dull into a vague blur, but he hoped Bartlett would remember, and Bennett. Certainly, Simpson would not permit himself to forget, and Scott would not be able to forget.

And Kane? Nicholas hoped his leaving would not for the Master constitute a defeat, a reason for self-rebuke. He was, after all, a decent man doing his best in a precarious job. Nicholas wished him some of Father Moriarity's blessed forgetfulness.

Nicholas felt apart, as he always had, but now without sadness. Back then, when the logic of his faith seemed impregnable, he had fought to fit himself in. Back then, everything had seemed possible. Confidence so blithe now seemed hopelessly naive. A fool's paradise. Willy-nilly, he was on his own and must make his own mapless way, lighting out for that inner territory whose limits only the cloistered heart need fix.

Well, not entirely. He was in many ways the same as he had always been. He still had values and, he hoped, the same fundamental goodwill.

If I am to be what I must be, he reflected, I am also all that I have been. There were many places he could put his talents to use, new ways he could serve the message of Christ, humbler roads to walk toward a kind of sanctity. The *what* and the *why* did not matter—only the *how*.

What point was there to religious education, to its sweeping heuristic drive, if you could not face the truth? He had made his vigil steadfastly. If he had discovered that the

Faith was friable, he knew in his bones that he could never be content with unbelief. But no one else could be one's salvation, that much he knew. And he was only human.

That night had been inevitable. Not in its specifics—the details were merely the occasion of shaking the scales from his eyes. But, sooner or later, his whole emotional and intellectual history insisted, he would have sprung free, like a runner knifing through the line into broken field, hurtling to daylight.

He was no Esau, selling his birthright. If ethics had any meaning at all, it was not the act but the doer that determined moral judgment. Real love was a matter not of form but of content.

What was it they said? "Once a Catholic, always a Catholic"?

Time would tell. Even the Prodigal Son did not return all the way. Hadn't his father run to meet him?

In three days, Nicholas would leave for Harvard.

"You'll go far," his father had prophesied so many years ago. But he could never have guessed this unsuspected Nicholas bracing for a new twist in the road.

Would his father have understood? It violated all his training, his stern code. Would he have flinched, condemned, cast his son aside in bitter spite?

His mother hadn't. Lyon hadn't.

No, of course Thomas wouldn't have. For all his flaws, even to think that sadly underestimated his love. "You're my son," he had said as he lay dying. "That's everything."

And God? Surely He was more than His institutions; He could not be as intractable as His Church.

Nicholas remembered his meditation, when the specific, singular, personal love of God had seized him with numinous force. It had to be true. Nothing else made any sense. What was it Father Kane had said? "He loves us all equally."

He did not demand that anyone turn against himself. That was the most vital matter of principle of all. *Self*-denial was the ultimate perversion.

His father, with his passionate assurance, never swerved one inch from his chosen path. His mother, her hope cruelly rebuked, kept her vow. Lyon and Kane, each in his own way, the tidal *why*s clanging in their ears, steered their unruly flocks into the future. Scott and Karl, on separate paths, managed to keep going. Now Nicholas, surprised by himself, faced his future, chastened but unafraid.

So do we all construct our lives, stung by the cramp of salvation, our destination hidden, seeking sovereign light.